I0575072

Red Rock Canyon
The Missing Years- Part IV
A Tyrell Sloan western adventure

Written by Brian T. Seifrit

Email: **briantseifrit@gmail.com**

Web site: www.booksbybriant.ca

Cover art by: Getty Creations, Burnaby, British Columbia

i

The Missing Years- Part IV
A Tyrell Sloan western adventure

Published by

Edition 2

ISBN: 978-1-7773280-2-3 Paperback
ISBN: 978-1-990215-11-7 Hardcover
ISBN: 978-1-7773280-3-0 eBook

Dedication:

To all readers of my western series Red Rock Canyon- this is the fourth book.

Acknowledgements:

To my wife, my children, and Bill Jenkins for his editorial suggestions, *thank you.*

"Let me take you to a place you have never been."

BTS 2000.

Chapter 1

Friday, September 18, 1891.

It was 8:00 a.m., when Ed McCoy and Riley Scott opened the McCoy's office.

"Today is the day Colby is released. Think he learned anything, Riley?" Ed questioned as the two of them sat down.

"Only Colby can answer that question. After all, he did get two more days added to his twenty for getting saucy with Cannon," Riley snickered. "Will he ever run with the Rebel Rangers again? Chances are that he will. In hindsight, I ain't so sure he's learned a damn thing. I hope he has. He ain't all that bad, Ed. Pretty straightforward I'd say. Only he knows what he's going to do for the rest of his time on earth. I hope for his sake that he walks the line."

"Running with that cousin of his, Alex, though, makes me wonder if he'll even see his twenty-fifth birthday."

"A kid like Colby has a lot of potential whether he has a cousin such as Alex or not. It doesn't mean anything," Riley pointed out.

"I suppose you are right," Ed nodded in agreement. "One thing we can't ignore though is that it is possible that the two of them, Alex and Colby, are going to try and bring in Matt Crawford if Brady and Travis ain't rounded him up yet. That concerns me some."

"The two of them are free to do that though, Ed, if that is what they intend. They ain't breaking any laws in doing so."

"Nope, you are right there too, Riley." Ed paused as he looked at his dirty fingernails and began cleaning them with a small penknife he kept in his vest pocket. "I guess we'll have to see what comes of it if anything," he continued cleaning his fingernails.

Riley looked on and shook his head, "What? Have you all of a sudden become a woman?"

"Huh," Ed responded as he looked up.

"That there that you're doing that there is woman stuff."

"Don't you clean your nails, Riley? They were dirt ridden."

"I do but I don't use a woman knife. That little stubby thing you got there ain't much more than a thread cutter," Riley chuckled.

At this time, Brady was getting ready to head over to Frank Diamond's ranch to pick up a new horse, so that he and Matt Crawford could head back to the Fort.

"I hate having to tie you up like this, Matt. But, I really ain't got a choice," Brady smiled as he finished securing Matt to one of the barn beams. Kneeling next to him, he continued. "Besides, Buffalo Chips, and that damn pig, Chops, will keep you company whilst I'm gone. I don't reckon it'll take me too long to get back."

"Ah, it's all right, Brady. I get it," Matt made himself comfortable. "You walking over to that ranch?" he asked.

"I reckon that be best. A man looking for a horse; claiming he ain't got one, might turn some heads if he's riding one, don't you think?" Brady stood, stuck a piece of straw between his teeth, and inhaled deeply. "I best get. I should be back in an hour or so."

He looked again toward Matt, nodded, smiled, and exited into the morning. It took him almost thirty minutes to walk the distance to Frank's ranch. When he knocked on the door, a tired and hung-over Frank Diamond greeted him. He looked at Brady quizzically for a moment.

"You're Brady right? You're here to pick up a horse."

Frank leaned against the doorframe to keep himself from falling over.

"That's right. Today is Friday. Last we spoke you said you'd have horses today," Brady looked toward the barn and back to Frank.

"I do as a matter of fact. They came in early this morning. I ain't had time to sort them out. Feel free to head over to the corral. I'll meet up with you shortly."

"Will do; thank you, Frank. I'll see you over there."

Brady turned and made his way over to the corral. A dozen horses neighed and farted as he approached. He leaned on the top rail and looked them over, trying to figure out which one he wanted. He decided on a painted stallion. Of all the ones tramping around, the painted stallion seemed to be the only one that caught his eye. There was something about the stallion that, he liked. He couldn't put his finger on it but that was indeed the one, he wanted.

Finally, Frank showed up.

"There they are, a dozen untrained horses," Frank said as he too leaned against the corral.

Brady looked over to him somewhat distraught. "Untrained? You mean they aren't trained to take riders?"

Frank began to chuckle.

"I was only kidding with you. They are broke."

"Damn it, Frank, you had me all disgruntled," Brady shook his head. "I like that painted stallion. What will you sell him to me for?" Brady asked as he pointed the horse out.

"I ain't so sure you want that fella. He ain't that cordial."

"What do you mean?" Brady asked with curiosity.

"He was ridden here by one of the horse sellers. He swapped him out for one of the others. Said he was fed up with the damn horse's antics. That is all he said to me. I ain't sure what might be wrong with him. He does look like a fine animal though, doesn't he?"

"Damn right he does. He's the one I want, no matter what any horse seller might have said. What's he going to cost, Frank?"

"Two hundred cash dollars and you join me for a shot of whiskey," Frank smiled. "How does that sound?"

"The cash ain't a problem, but whiskey this early in the morning, I don't know, Frank." Brady wasn't really in the mood for whiskey. Hell, he hadn't even had a first cup of coffee yet.

"What is a matter with whiskey in the morning?"

"I really ain't got the time. I need to make tracks easterly, back to the Fort."

"I guess I can't convince you. I'll gather the horse for you." Frank opened the gate and slipped a lead over the horse's neck then led him back to Brady.

"You got a bridle, reins, and saddle, ain't ya?"

"I do back at the outpost. I wasn't going to carry them with me," Brady looked the horse over. "He's a fine looking animal; well worth the two hundred dollars you're asking for him," he reached into his pocket and handed Frank the money.

"You have a bridle and reins I can borrow, Frank? I'll leave them at the outpost and you can pick them up later."

"Sure do," Frank grabbed a set from the post on which a few old bridles and reins dangled. He handed the best set over to Brady who slipped the gear on the painted stallion and swung up onto its back.

"You want a receipt for that animal, Brady?"

"I reckon it is best. Wouldn't want someone claiming I stole his horse later on down the line."

"All right, follow me over to the house and I'll write one up."

Brady turned his horse and walked alongside Frank as the two made their way back to the house. It took Frank a few minutes to write up the receipt. He reached up and handed it to Brady, who was still mounted on the horse.

"There you go, Brady. You are the proud owner of a pinto stallion, sold by me to you for two hundred dollars."

"Thank you, Frank," he looked the receipt over. "It looks good. Thank you for the horse and maybe if I meet up with you again, sometime, I'll take you up on that offer of a whiskey."

"I'll look forward to that day," Frank said with a smile.

Brady nodded his thanks. "Nice talking with you, Frank and thanks for the horse. I'll be seeing you." Turning the horse, he headed back to the west trail outpost to gather up Matt Crawford and head for home. It took only a few minutes to make the distance now that he was riding a horse. Tying the horse to the horse rail, he entered the outpost through the backdoor. Harvey was stoking the fire and putting together a pot of coffee.

"I'm going to have coffee ready in a few minutes, Brady. I take it you got your horse?" Harvey set the pot down on top of the stove.

"A pinto stallion; he's a nice looking animal too." Brady sat down at the little table.

Harvey pulled up a chair opposite of him. "You forget something, Brady?"

"Huh? Oh, right Matt. I guess I should go gather him now."

Matt was sitting on a bale of hay as he opened the barn door and entered.

"Harv's got coffee brewing, Matt. I figure we'll have a cup or two and set off," Brady said as he untied him.

"Sounds good to me I'm ready for a four-day excursion back to the Fort and what lies ahead," Matt said as he smiled. "It can't be any worse than being tied up in a barn with a man-eating hog and a mule so full of hot air it hasn't done nothing except pass gas since you've been gone."

The two men made their way back to the outpost and sat down. The coffee was brewed by now and Harvey poured them each a cup.

"Thanks, Harv," Brady said as he took his cup and brought it up to his lips. "Mmmm, you make damn fine coffee, you know that, Harvey?"

Matt followed suit and agreed with Brady. "Yep, I'm sure going to miss your coffee, Harvey."

"Hell, once you get things all squared away, Ron," Harvey shook his head, "I mean Matt, you can stop by anytime. The coffee is always free." Harvey smiled as he took a sip of his own. "How many days do you figure, Brady, that'll it take for the two of you to make the Fort?" he questioned.

"It ain't going to be quick. The law states that I have to lead Matt's horse and have to be in control of it at all times. I'll be leading him. That'll slow us down some. I figure by the end of the week we ought to be close if not already there," Brady answered.

He knew things could often change, and fast too. He knew in the back of his mind that there was a real possibility that he and Matt could run into Colby Christian and Alex Brubaker. Colby, he knew was scheduled to be released that day, and if what he and Travis had assumed, chances were that both Alex and Colby were heading west to the town of Willow Gate in hopes of picking up Matt on their own. If he and Matt happened to come across the two of them, things could go awry. For now, though, he wasn't going to concern himself with all the possibilities. His job now was to get Matt Crawford back alive and that was it. That was all he was going to concern himself with... for the time being.

Chapter 2

Colby Christian stood at the front counter of the Mounted Police station at the Fort, waiting to receive his belongings and whatnot. The twenty day, plus two more, sentencing of community service, he had been sentenced to by Judge Larsen was now complete. Constable Rick Bash opened up one of the prisoner' storage compartments as he dug for his things. In a way he was going to miss the kid, but that was life, Colby had done his time, worked his ass off for the most part. Not once did he flinch at anything the law threw at him.

"Tell me, Colby," Bash began as he approached with Colby's things, "are you going to miss this place?" he half teased.

"Not likely, only thing I might miss, Bash, were our tiffs," Colby smiled. "Just hand me my stuff, Bash, so I can step out of here. It's been a while since I walked any place without you tagging along."

"I don't suppose I can blame you for feeling that way." Bash laid the bag down on the counter and opened it. "As per Canadian law, you are entitled to a new clean pair of pants, undershorts, socks, and shirt upon release." Bash handed the new duds over. "Boots and hat is up to you. Here is your rifle, the box of shells that came with it and another box provided to you by the Government. Those are also something you are entitled to."

"You're giving a fellow like me all this new stuff? What the hell for?" Colby was somewhat appreciative and at the same time, a bit perplexed. He had pants, socks, and shirt. *Why would he be entitled to these?*

"Like I said, it is law these be provided for you. If you don't want them, Colby, you don't have to take them," Bash looked at him and shrugged. "It is up to you."

"I ain't so stupid, Bash, that I'd turn down new clothes." Colby stripped down right there at the front counter and tossed his dirty clothes on the floor behind him. Bash didn't bother making any argument. He simply shook his head as Colby dressed in his new things.

"How'd you manage to get my sizes right Bash?" Colby asked as he buttoned up his shirt and tucked it into his pants.

"We don't pick the sizes. The law provides them in three sizes, small, medium, and large. If they fit, that is good; if they don't, too bad."

"I guess I got lucky then 'cause these fit fine." As he reached for his rifle, the front door to the station opened and in walked Alex Brubaker, Colby's cousin. Colby turned to face him, as he looked his rifle over.

"Morning, Alex." Colby pointed the rifle in Alex's direction and smiled. "No worries, Alex. She ain't loaded, just making sure the sights are true."

Alex didn't smile back. "Are they?" he simply asked.

"As best as I can tell they are, yep," Colby leaned the rifle against the counter as Alex made the distance.

"Finally, free to walk, eh? It looks like they dressed you for a funeral. Nice new duds," Alex said as he approached.

"Damn right. They fit like a rawhide glove too," Colby, said referring to Alex's right hand.

"I don't see no humour in that at all, Colby," Alex made clear.

Colby turned and faced Bash, "Ah, no use being sore, Alex. Anyway, Bash, I reckon I had a few dollars when I came in. You ain't handed that to me yet."

"Your cash is right here, Colby. There is a few dollars more in there too, the coins you found fixing up the Snakebite's boardwalk and a few donations from McCoy's men."

Bash handed the leather satchel over. Colby didn't bother counting any of it and instead only shook the money satchel.

"Sounds like it is all there thank you, Bash. You can keep the dirty clothes. I ain't got a need for them no more. I guess I can gather my own horse from the stable or does the law need to hand him over to me as well?"

"We'll get to that. You need to sign here, though. It states you got all your personals, clothes, guns and such."

"It seems to be more of a formality to leave than when I came here," Colby shook his head. Taking the quill pen from Bash and signed his name. "There. I'll meet you at the stable, Bash," Colby said as he and Alex began to exit.

"Give me a couple of minutes, Colby."

"That's fine, I think I want to take a walk anyway, get some of that mountain air. It's been a long while since I walked in freedom and not as a puppet for the law." Colby pushed the door open and stepped out for the first time in twenty-two days without any lawman tethered to his side. He inhaled deeply. "Freedom, no more nights tucked away behind a cell. I'll tell ya, it has been the longest twenty-two days of my life. I'm damn glad it is over."

"Shit, it was twenty days, Colby, not twenty years."

"But that bastard Cannon added another two, claiming I bad-mouthed him on too many occasions. It might as well have been years though, Alex. It sure felt like it," Colby chuckled, "feels damn good to finally be done with it."

The two of them walked in silence for a few minutes. "Now that you can walk free, Colby, once you gather that horse of yours we should head west. The sooner we get moving toward Willow Gate the better."

"I ain't leaving here yet, Alex. I'm going to grab a room at the Snakebite, buy you and me a steak dinner and a bottle of whiskey. Before we head west, I need to stop in on old Riley and take him up on that offer of a drink he made some time ago. I owe him at least that."

"What do you mean you owe him? Jesus Christ, Colby! We got a job pending; ten thousand dollars, remember."

"I remember fine, Alex. One day ain't going to make a difference." Colby carried on walking toward the stables. Alex grabbed him by the arm and spun him around so the two of them were facing each other.

"If you remember, why the *Hell* are we having this conversation?"

Colby yanked his arm from Alex's grip and stared at him. "Alex, you ought to know better than to grab me like that. Don't do it again."

"Whatever. What the hell is a matter with you?"

"That ol' bounty hunter helped me pass my time and gave me respect while doing so and never judged me once. I ain't leaving here until I see him and take him up on his offer of a shot of whiskey. If you don't like that, Alex, go on ahead without me. I'll catch up to you long before you make Willow Gate," Colby made clear.

"I think I wasted my time even coming here. I thought we had agreed on tracking down Matt Crawford once the law set you free. I don't see any reason not to get and get now."

"Like I said, Alex, one day; that is it or hop up on your horse and I'll follow behind."

Alex shook his head. "That one day, Colby, could be the difference between ten thousand dollars cash or no cash at all. How can an old washed-up bounty hunter be worth more than that?"

"Washed-up or not, I'd bet that ten thousand dollars that he can still take a round out of you. Now, I ain't going to argue in this regard no more. Either stick with me 'til tomorrow, enjoy a good meal, a hot bath and maybe a can-

can girl or two come night, or don't, simple as that." Colby turned and continued to walk toward the stables.

"Goddamn it, Colby," Alex responded in derision, "I want my can-can girl to be blonde."

Stopping, Colby turned, looked at him, and smiled. "So, we leave tomorrow."

"I reckon. I always hate arguing with you, you're such a pain in the backside. Besides, I could use a hot bath. Ain't had the time in the last while," Alex responded as he sniffed at his armpits and crinkled his nose. "Yep, need a bath."

Finally making the distance to the stables, Colby leaned on the top rail while Constable Bash gathered his horse, led him to the gate, and handed him over.

"Here he is, Colby, in as good shape as when he got here."

"Thank you, Bash. Can't wait to get on that red dun's back and ride out of here." Colby cinched up his saddle, swung up and tilted his hat, "I'll be seeing you, Bash. Thanks for the hospitality," he commented.

"Are you fellows going to be leaving the Fort today?" Bash asked curiously before Colby scooted off.

"Apparently not," Alex interjected. "Colby here seems to think he owes that ol' bounty hunter Riley a visit."

"It ain't anything that I owe him. Only want to show the man some respect," Colby shook his head as he turned his steed and headed toward the Snakebite Hotel. "I'll meet you at the Snakebite, Alex."

"Right behind you, Colby, once I gather my horse. Grab us two separate rooms," Alex hollered as he started to walk back to where his horse was tethered. He was glad in a sense that they were sticking around. He had sent a wire a few days earlier to their cousins down south near the border, and invited them to give him a hand in tracking down Crawford. He told them in the telegram to come to the Fort and if by chance, he and Colby weren't there to head west. He hadn't told Colby yet, and as he made his way to his horse, he wasn't sure he was even going to. He'd surprise him with the entire charade. Staying an extra day or two wasn't a bad idea after all. It assured that when they left the Fort, their cousins would be with them, even if Colby didn't like the idea.

Bash watched as the two of them headed toward the Snakebite. Free as Colby was to do whatever, he wanted as long as it was within the law, there was nothing, he could say or do to make sure that the two cousins left, the Fort. He could only hope they would hold the peace.

Deciding to let Ed and Riley know that Colby and Alex were going to be visiting Riley later, Bash made his way over the McCoy's office. Ed and Riley were sitting in the backroom drinking coffee and bullshitting as he opened the front door and stepped in. Hearing the door open and the little bell that rang when it did, both Ed and Riley stood up to meet whoever had entered.

"Morning, Bash," Ed said as he approached the counter. "What brings you?"

"Morning, Ed, Riley. I just set Colby loose. He and Alex plan on spending the night at the Snakebite. Colby wants to pay a visit to you, Riley. I thought I best let you know."

"That is all right. I ain't concerned about that. It'll be a different visit without the law being tied to his belt loops," Riley smiled. "I don't reckon he means me no harm. Or do you know something I don't?"

"Nope, not at all, in fact I'm pretty certain from the conversation between him and Alex that he only wants to take you up on that shot of whiskey you offered up while he was in the custody of the Mounted Police. He's free now to do whatever he wants," Bash made clear.

"I do appreciate your concern, Rick, but you really didn't need to come all the way over here to inform me of such."

"I know. I was only doing what I thought to be in the interest of all. Better you know than to be surprised."

Riley nodded, "I suppose. Since you are here, Rick, you want a coffee?"

"I could likely use one; haven't had one yet. Sure, I'll join you fellows."

"Then, let's go have a sit down and coffee," Ed said as Constable Bash and Riley followed him to the backroom. The three men sat down and Riley poured them a coffee.

"What's the law going to do now that they ain't got no hoodwink buckled down in their holding cells?" Riley asked with a chuckle.

"Same as always I suppose, keep peace and order, uphold the right, and keep the folks of the Fort safe from harm and wrongdoings. It'll actually be nice to get back to the norm. I might even get myself a little R&R. I've had a lot of restless nights and cumbersome days over the last while," Bash took a drink from the tin cup in his hand.

"Restless? Cumbersome? Jesus, Rick, you weren't looking after Billy the Kid," Ed responded.

"I certainly wasn't, but any man who runs with the Rebel Rangers is no different than a *'Billy the Kid'*. The Rangers don't choose everyday folk to run with them. I reckon there was something special about Colby that the Rangers liked. It makes him as dangerous as any outlaw."

"We know the kid can shoot. That's likely what the Rangers saw in him. Dangerous though, well, I ain't so sure he is. The time I spent with him while he helped dig my well was pleasant. Not once did he come across to me as dangerous. Misguided is what I'd say."

"We all have our opinions, Riley. You have yours and I have mine. From the law side of things, Colby Christian is a felon and ex-Rebel Ranger. He's an outlaw, simple as that."

"I ain't arguing that point at all, Bash, no sir. I know he is an outlaw an ex-Rebel Ranger and a Brubaker. That doesn't make him dangerous, makes him unlucky is all," Riley shrugged his shoulders. "Like I said, the time I spent with Colby and the things we talked about I never once thought of the man as dangerous. What I did learn about him is that he's a damn hard worker, learns quickly and ain't afraid to take charge of any situation. You saw that when you helped those few times. He outworked each of us and when we weren't sure how to proceed with one thing or the other, he took control. Pointed out what it was we were doing wrong."

There was a short pause while the three men contemplated. It was true. Colby did put all he had into helping Riley dig his well while he was doing his Community Service sentence. In fact, if it wasn't for Colby, Riley would still be hauling water to his homestead, a pain in the ass at the best of times. The bottom line was, Riley Scott, bounty hunter extraordinaire, had nothing bad to say about Colby Christian other than the obvious.

"All I'm saying is that I have as much respect for Colby as I have for any man."

"You might say that now, Riley," Ed began, "but you've been in this business long enough to see how a man can change from what we believe him to be to what he truly is. Things change from one moment to the next all the time."

"Character don't change though, Ed, and I saw in that kid a lot of good. I'd bet it outweighs the bad we all know he might have inside. Colby's only problem from what I've seen is influence. He's been influenced by the Rangers and his cousins. I've said it once and I'll say it again. He's been misguided," Riley was firm about that.

"Only time will tell what might come of Colby Christian. To keep this conversation from going in circles, I thank you for the coffee, Ed, Riley, but I should head back, fill out some paperwork and finally put the last twenty-two days behind," Constable Rick Bash said as he slid his chair out from the table and stood up.

"I suppose we should try and get some work done today as well." Ed and Riley stood up from the table and followed Bash to the front entrance.

"Thanks again, Rick, for stopping by and filling me in on Colby's intent to visit me later. Although we might have different opinions, I do appreciate you letting me know."

"No problem, Riley."

Riley nodded his respect. "We'll be seeing you, Rick."

"Have a good day, gentleman," Bash said as he exited and headed back to the station.

"With that out of the way, what do you suppose we should do today to keep ourselves busy?"

"I ain't so sure I know, Ed. It's Friday or as I like to say, five day. How far along do you figure Brady and Travis have got?"

"Until I get a telegram from one or the other, it's a hard guess. I reckon though, if they ain't come across Matt Crawford by now, they'd be getting close to Willow Gate if they managed twenty miles a day give or take and didn't run into problems. Hell, they left on the ninth."

Chapter 3

It was 10:00 a.m. when Brady and Matt finally said their goodbyes to Harv and headed east toward home. For the first few miles, they rarely spoke much, as neither had much to say. Matt knew what was coming and Brady was somewhat disenchanted at the possibility that Colby and Alex may very well cross their path. The morning sun was warm and a gentle breeze blew, making Brady's hair frolic as the gusts came and went.

"Wish that damn hog never ruined my hat. Feels a might strange not wearing one all this time," Brady thought back to his first encounter with the hog known as Chops. The hog took his hat on their first introduction and had kept it ever since. Brady shook his head as he recalled how it all happened. *Damn hog anyway,* he thought to himself as they continued east.

By midday, they were perched on top of a ridge on a nicely sun-lit, grassy knoll. They had travelled near five miles give or take. Brady took a swig from his canteen and handed it over to Matt.

"There is a small stream down yonder some," Brady pointed. "We'll let the horses drink there and might even consider setting up for the evening. We get a good early start in the morning and I reckon we can put behind us at least fifteen miles."

"How far along do you figure that Colby fella and his cousin will be by then?" Matt questioned.

It was a good question, but Brady didn't have an answer. "Hard to say, Matt, I'm not even sure they'd be heading this way yet. Only today was Colby set free, a man and horse can only travel twenty, maybe twenty-five miles on a good day. The Fort is a good four-day's ride under normal circumstances, but when a man has to lead a prisoner, the circumstances ain't so normal. I don't suppose we'll have to concern ourselves for a couple more days on how far along they may be."

"I know a way to the Fort that not many know about. We could avoid them completely." Matt looked at Brady. "I know a lil' bit about Colby Christian, he ain't what you might think he is."

"What's that you know?" Brady took another swallow from his canteen.

"His family is from down south, Montana way. Long before Colby started running with the Rebel Rangers, he was a young shoe shiner. He made a few coins a day that he handed over to charity, whilst he lived on crumbs and slept under the stars. Somewhere between childhood and manhood, he took up a rifle and killed four men before he was sixteen."

"Four before he was sixteen?"

"Yes sir, they each deserved it, too. I was a Ranger during that time. The law was going to hang him for murder. Turned out, though, that the men he buried were also the men that killed his family. The law let him be once they learned that. My point being, he ain't any different than me. He has a killer instinct and, as you know, don't miss when he shoots.

That is why, Barclay Atalmore, and the Rebel Rangers took him under their wings 'cause, he could shoot an ear off a coyote at three hundred yards, he's a better shot than most. If we run across him and that cousin of his, we may be setting ourselves up to take lead," Matt, looked easterly toward the Fort. "We head north on that ol' horse trail down by that stream you're talking about and we could avoid the two of them, in case they is coming this way."

"Horse trail?" Brady questioned.

"Like I said not many know it is even there, but it is. It is the way, I travelled when I headed this way before Travis caught up to me. The trail is a bit overgrown, but it is safe."

"Hmmm, well I'll need to think on that some, Matt. I ain't so sure heading off the beaten path leading a horse with a bounty is the way to go. It ain't that I don't trust you none, 'cause I do, a bit leastwise, but maybe you're feeding me a line of horse hooey. You get my point?" Brady was candid as possible. Whether, he trusted Matt or not he needed to be cautious.

"I do. If you had a Bible in those saddlebags strapped to your horse, I'd swear on it that *that* ain't my intent at all. I know what is in store for me and I've accepted that not even knowing what the outcome might be."

"Like I said, Matt, I need to think on that some," Brady said as he swung back onto his horse. "C'mon, let's get to that stream."

It didn't take long to make the distance.

"Here it is." Brady dismounted and led both horses over to the stream to drink. Then he helped Matt get down. Handcuffed and all he wasn't as mobile as one might assume. Kneeling, he splashed water on his face.

"The horse trail ain't but a hop, skip, and a jump from here," Matt mentioned as he stood up and looked over to Brady.

"I ain't decided yet, Matt," Brady said as he removed the saddle from his horse. "I figure we'll set up here for the night, have some food and a good night's sleep. Come morning I'll let you know what I decided. Until then let's get some wood collected and get a fire going. We'll cook up some salt pork and beans."

"Let's get to it then," Matt tethered his horse next to Brady's and the two set about the tasks.

As darkness came and their meal finished, the two men sat near the flames. The stars in the sky looked like a million kerosene lanterns and a warm evening breeze gently caressed the trees and their branches.

"Sure peaceful, ain't it?" Matt poured another coffee and took up his place with his head on the saddle and his legs outstretched.

"Indeed it is," Brady responded as he looked up to the sky. "It is a clear evening, too, which will make for a good day of travelling come morn," he inhaled deeply as he averted his eyes back to the flickering flames of their evening fire. "You ever consider going back to law enforcement, Matt?"

"A time or three perhaps, but it is too late for me to do that now." Matt took a swig from his coffee as he contemplated. "I figure all that I have left is a noose waiting for me."

Brady nodded. "True as that may or may not be, Matt, if given the opportunity would you consider it?"

"Depends, I suppose. Why are you asking me that anyway, Brady?"

"Trying to make conversation, I suppose. You're not at all what I expected you to be."

"You expected me to be a cold-blooded killer without an ounce of integrity, huh?"

"I did. I won't lie to you, Matt. That is exactly what I thought of you. After spending some time with you though, I ain't so sure my judgement of you is justified."

"Ah, don't kid yourself, Brady. I am what all have said about me. I'm a killer. I have some regrets, but none that would stop me from killing the rest of those that cheated me, lied to me or attempted to kill my sister and the like. They were all bad men. I suppose, I ain't any better than they are. Hell, even the Pinkertons ain't all abiding lawmen. Some are as dirty as the outlaws they've apprehended, shot or hung.

The world is corrupt Brady, and I set out to wash all that away. I put some men to rest and spit on their graves, but I still have integrity, I knew what I was doing," Matt paused as he tried to make sense of it all. *What exactly had he accomplished?*

He was now heading to a fate unknown and there were still men on his *'Dead by Lead'* list that he hadn't had a chance to send to hell. So, what had he accomplished? That, was the underlying question that had been bouncing around in his head since he'd being outwitted by, Travis.

He thought about the conversations he and Travis had during that first night of his apprehension, the night the wolves and Black Dog pounced on him, making his arrest an easy one for Travis Sweet. He had every intention to kill Travis and to continue with his one-man slaughter of all those that he knew deserved nothing less. There were still a half a dozen men on his list, none of whom he'd be able to touch now.

Matt stirred uncomfortably. "Anyway, it don't matter none now. The corrupt will always live amongst the righteous, God fearing, and law abiding. That is life. Ain't a damn thing anyone can do about it," Spitting to the ground, he stood up. "One thing is for certain Brady, we have company. Don't look now, but there seems to be six Indians jus' beyond that stand of trees. They've been watching us for the past while. I reckon they rode in from the north along that horse trail. That likely makes them Blackfoot or Blood Indians. 'Less, of course, they ain't from the plains in which case it makes them trouble."

Brady turned his head slowly as to not cause suspicion. Sure enough, he too could see them. "I thought you said that horse trail was safe," Brady mentioned in a low voice.

"Under most circumstances I reckon it is. Right now ain't one of them circumstances. What do you think we ought to do?"

"I'm the only one armed. I'd say that ain't very good odds, Matt. 'Specially, since we can't be sure there ain't more. They don't seem too interested in starting a ruckus. We best sit them out I think."

"They'll wait 'til we're asleep and likely scalp us if they ain't from the plains. You do know that, don't ya?" Matt responded.

"It has crossed my mind, yep. I also wonder though, if that is the case why ain't they already done that?" Brady slowly cocked his rifle to be on the safe side of things.

"I ain't sure about that myself, Brady. It does seem odd."

Brady sighed. "What if they are only hungry looking for a handout? Think we should let them know we know they are there?"

Matt looked away from the fire and in the direction of where the six unknown Indians stood. It was then he noticed something different about the way they were dressed. They weren't Indians after all, but *longhairs*. "Could be Brady they ain't Indians. They are longhairs which even seems odder."

"Longhairs, hmmm, that does seem odd. What do you suppose they'd be doing way down here?" Brady questioned in silent surprise.

"Looking for something or somebody, I can tell you this: if it were you and I they is looking for they'd have found us by now, if you know what I mean. I reckon since we're still standing, we ain't what or who."

Brady nodded. "I say we wave them over, introduce ourselves. Let them know we ain't dangerous."

"You might want to think on that some, Brady. Apparently they don't need any invite."

Brady darted his eyes in the direction the men had been standing. He could see only one now; the others had simply vanished from his field of vision and the one he could see was making his way toward their fire. Brady stood up his rifle at the ready.

"Hello there. Is there something we can help you with, mister?" Brady asked as the man drew close.

The man stopped in the shadows before he replied. "That depends."

"It depends upon what?" Matt asked as Brady stepped forward and out of the fires light.

"We're looking for a man and two mules. On his back, he wears a bearskin vest. There is something we owe him."

Brady's gut tugged with apprehension. It sounded like to him that the man was describing Whiskey Tooth George who, in fact, he and Travis had run across, as they made their way west to track down Matt. Was it coincidence or something more sinister? That was the thought that came to Brady's mind.

"Nope, we ain't saw nobody looks like that," Brady said with conviction, in hopes to convince the man.

"It wouldn't have been today or yesterday that you would have seen him, if at all you had. Nope, he's long gone by now. I did see you though, Mister Brady McCoy. A while back, you and that Travis fella along with another man came upon a few of my dead kin. Killed by Indians, who were then chased off by the man I speak of." The man in the shadows stepped into view, "I have with me a small token of appreciation for said man. If it weren't for him more of my kin might be dead." The man held out a small satchel, "this here is five hundred dollars in gold. It is for that man."

"I ain't got any idea on who that man may be. Why are you telling me this and what do I care?" Brady asked with curiosity.

"You and your father are trusted men in the Fort. I think for another five hundred dollars in gold," the man held out another satchel in his left hand, "that I could hire you to find this man and give him my token."

"Hold up a second," Brady started as he tried to make sense of it all. "Are you saying you want to hire McCoy's to track down this man and give to him that satchel of gold on your behalf?"

"It is a completely sane proposition, Mr. McCoy. My people's lack of horses makes it a tenuous task to do, almost impossible as a matter-of-fact. So yes, I want to hire McCoy's to undertake the handing over of this gold. I heard tale the man goes by the name of Whiskey Tooth George, a mountain man. No different from myself and my people, except by belief and worldly possessions."

"I have to tell ya, Mister...," Brady began, hoping the man would give up his name so, he knew who, he was talking to.

"It is Vanfell," the man offered.

"Mr. Vanfell, I have to tell ya, this here is quite an uncommon way to hire McCoy's. Most folks pop into the office or do their hiring through telegrams and such. I ain't saying no by any means. Only I'm a bit confused on how this has all come about."

"Quite simple, actually, I knew it was only a matter of time that my people and I would come across you or that Travis fellow. Believe it or not, Mr. McCoy, I have scouts all through these mountains. They keep our people informed on events and such, people coming and going. I heard that, you and, Travis had been spotted, heading west. Because I know your business, I knew you'd be coming back this way," the man paused. And here you are."

"This talking from a distance don't make me feel too safe." Brady waved the man over, his rifle still in his hand.

"You have nothing to fear, Mr. McCoy. We seek your help; that is all."

As he approached the fire now, Brady could see that the man was in his early, or perhaps mid-forties, or early fifties. His hair was blonde with streaks of white, but all in all, he didn't look much different than any civilised man. He was clean and dressed in well-maintained buckskins. His eyes were blue and forbidding, and his persona was somewhat wild, overall though was a gentleman's gentleman, he was someone that neither Brady, nor Matt Crawford, would have expected to be one of the longhairs.

"Can I offer you a coffee, Mr. Vanfell?" Brady asked as the man sat down cross-legged on the ground near the fire.

"Thank you, Mr. McCoy. I will take a coffee," the man nodded his appreciation.

"My name as you already seem to know is Brady. You don't need to call me Mr. McCoy. This here is Matt." Matt nodded as Brady handed off a cup of coffee to the man.

"In that case, you can call me Leif," the man brought the cup to his lips and took a swallow.

Brady nodded and smiled. "Leif it is. You want to hire McCoy's to track down a man who goes by the name of Whiskey Tooth George and to hand over to him five hundred dollars in gold nuggets, for scaring off a bunch of Indians that killed some of your kin. Is that right, Leif?"

"It is."

"I do know of this man. He's got a bounty on his head for selling moonshine to those that don't need it, Indians mainly. We did track him this past summer and I do recall seeing your dead. I always wondered what had transpired. If what you are telling me is truth, then I guess he ain't the one that killed your kin, like I had assumed."

"He didn't kill any of those men. If it wasn't for him, there may have been more bloodshed and likely my people's numbers would be less." Leif took another swallow from the tin cup in his hand. Not often did his people talk with those that lived in the valleys. Sometimes though, it was necessary. This was one of those times. "Will McCoy's help us in this undertaking?" Leif asked as he looked into the coals of the fire.

"What I can tell you, Leif, is that ol' codger, Whiskey Tooth ain't an easy man to find, let alone track down. Some of the best in our business have been fooled by him. That don't mean 'no'; it don't quite mean 'yes' either. If we were to take this on, how would you ever know we managed to give him those nuggets?"

It was a fair question and one Leif was hoping Brady would ask. It showed honesty.

"I know a bit about you and the men that work for you. I haven't any reason to think you folk wouldn't do what you were hired for."

It was a fair answer. It showed trust.

"True as that might be, Leif, I can't make any promises that we'd ever see ol' Whiskey Tooth again. He ain't young. He could be dead long before we might get those nuggets to him."

"A man like that doesn't die easily. I know a bit about him too," Leif responded.

Brady looked across the flames and to Leif. "McCoy's will do what we can," Brady replied with sincerity. It wasn't going to be an easy task, but nothing in life really was.

"It is settled then? You'll accept this payment of five hundred dollars in gold?" Leif handed the one satchel over. "And this one is for Whiskey Tooth?"

Brady took both satchels and smiled. "I can write you up a receipt on a piece of paper if you care?"

"I see no reason for that." Leif stood up and dumped out the remainder of his coffee. "I have men waiting over yon. Take care, sirs," he said to both men as he turned and disappeared in the shadows.

"I never once thought them folk to be as civilized as that," Matt pointed out as he looked over to Brady.

"I guess we both learned something tonight."

Chapter 4

Meanwhile, back at Riley Scott's homestead, Riley, Colby Christian, and his cousin Alex Brubaker were sitting at Riley's fire pit conversing back and forth, as they were passing a bottle of whiskey around and were tying a bit of a drunk on.

"Tell me, Colby, where abouts you headin' now that you ain't got no lawman tethered to your belt loop?" Riley asked with a drunken slur.

"Ah, Alex here has some notion on tracking down a bounty to get me started off on a new foot. To be honest though, I ain't sure I'm even up to it," he looked over to Alex who had his head between his legs and was puking from all the whiskey they had consumed that day.

"Look at 'em, Riley, he can't even hold his own whiskey." Colby shook his head. "Shows he's weak, I ain't sure I want to be ridin' 'round with a man can't hold his whiskey. Shit, I might be steppin' into somethin' I ain't got a care about."

"Never mind him right now, Colby. You need to concern yourself with who it is yous are goin' after. I have to tell ya, both Travis Sweet, and Brady McCoy, are after the same man. It is Matt Crawford the two of you hope to apprehend, ain't it?" Riley took another swig from the whiskey bottle in his hand.

"I know that, Riley. I also know that you know I know about that lil' book Tanner McBride found in the McCoy's stable. Hell, I know you know I put it there," Colby responded as best he could with all the whiskey coursing through his veins.

Riley was laughing some when he looked over to Colby with his own reply. "You know," he started, "you said a lot of

I knows and you knows." Riley began laughing hysterically holding onto his guts as he did.

Colby was looking at him somewhat puzzled, his drunken body swaying this way and that as he sat there. He pointed at Riley and shook his finger. "Shit... you know what, Riley. I know I said all that." The two men now burst out into a raucous laughter pointing at one another and laughing even harder. Alex for one reason or another abruptly began to fire his pistol into the air as though he were shooting the stars. Colby tackled him and knocked him to the ground, fearing Alex was going to shoot one of them.

Falling to the ground, Alex's pistol slipped out of his hand, and he and Colby rolled around in the muck and puke, only to start laughing. Riley sat there confused and bewildered as he looked on and then he simply fell over and passed out. The evening at Riley's had ended, and the only one left standing and able to walk was Colby Christian. On the ground, passed out and drunk, were Alex and Riley.

"Huh, ain't that typical of women. Flower sniffing pansies," Colby muttered as he looked at the two men lying on the ground. Fetching what was left of the whiskey he sat back down and carried on finishing off the bottle. He tossed a few more pieces of wood onto the fire, gathered his horse, and headed back to the Fort and the Snakebite Hotel. In the morning, when Alex finally made his way back, the two would leave behind the Fort and seek the ten thousand dollar reward offered for the capture of Matt Crawford.

Chapter 5

Early Saturday morning, Riley woke to the sound of a pistol being cocked, blocking the sun with his hand, looked up and squinted.

"Where the hell is he, Riley, where is Colby?"

Riley still groggy and a bit drunk, snatched the pistol out of Alex's hand and stood up. "Jesus Christ, Alex that is one hell of a way to wake a man. I have no idea on where Colby is. Last I remember is the two of you rolling around in the mud. Maybe I should ask you the same question," Riley, pointed the pistol at Alex. "Where the hell is Colby?"

"I don't know." Alex responded now that Riley had the upper hand.

Riley looked over to where their horses were tethered the night before. "Did you note his horse is gone?"

Alex turned and looked. "Damn. Shit, I'm sorry, Riley. I didn't get quite that far yet."

Letting the hammer back on Alex's pistol, he tossed it back to him. He was surprised at how quickly Alex grabbed it out of the air and in a blink of an eye, had the pistol cocked once more and pointing at his head now. Riley stood still, never taking his eye off of Alex.

"I'm only going to tell you this one time, Riley. Don't come between my cousin and me," Alex snarled.

"I ain't got any intentions on doing that, Alex, none whatsoever," Riley assured.

Alex nodded. "Good 'cause if'n you ever do, it won't end pretty. Got that, old man?"

Riley knew one thing and that was that Alex's pistol was unloaded. Alex himself had fired all six rounds into the evening sky the night before. He really wasn't in the mood to make more out of the situation and would rather have had

Alex simply get off his property. That is, of course, until Alex called him an old man.

Slapping the pistol out of his hand, Riley punched him square in the mouth. Falling backwards from the impact, Alex stumbled and brought up his fists in retaliation to only be smashed a second time by Riley's southpaw. Blood spewed from Alex's split open lips as he fell to the ground. He kicked at Riley as he approached, but Riley avoided hiss kicking feet and picked him up by the scruff of the neck, and slapped him across the face with a stinging force that made Alex's face turn raspberry red.

Again and again, Riley slapped him until finally Alex fell to the ground. Exasperated, Riley inhaled deeply and sat down on the bench. He looked at Alex who was slowly getting up. "You ever call me an old man again we'll do the same dance. You understand?" Riley commented with authority.

"You are one crazy son-of-a-bitch, you know that, Riley? I could've put a bullet in your head," Alex said as he finally rose completely and looked at Riley, his eyes watering, and face and lips swollen.

"Not with an empty gun, you stupid bastard," Riley responded.

"Empty? What the hell are you talking about?" Alex asked as he retrieved it and pointed it at the empty whiskey bottle near Riley's feet. "I always reload my pistol when she's empty," he squeezed the trigger and shot the whiskey bottle, sending shards of glass hither and hence. He pointed it now at Riley. "Even when I'm drunk, Riley, my gun is my protector. I never neglect it," Alex's eyes were cold.

Riley swallowed deeply. "You mean to tell me, she was loaded the entire time?"

"Riddle me this. Did you see me put any rounds in it when I just now picked her up?"

Riley shook his head feeling like a greenhorn himself. "No, no I didn't," he was sweating a bit now. His pistols weren't even around his waist. On any given day, he knew he could put lead into Alex long before Alex could put lead into him, if ever confronted in the way that he was now. Today though it seemed wasn't his day.

Alex slapped his pistol back into its holster. "You and I had a good go here, and I'll dance with you anytime, Riley. You got lucky with your southpaw this time. Rest assured it won't happen again," Alex made clear. Turning he walked over to his horse and swung up on the saddle then looked back. "Heed what I said, Riley. Don't come between me and my cousin," Alex turned his horse and galloped in the direction of the Fort.

Riley looked on as the dust rose and shook his head. *Damn, I must be gettin' dull,* he thought as he stood up and stretched the muscle strain out of his back. "You ain't as sharp as you once were, old man," he said to himself as he picked up his hat and donned it.

Ed was on his way to the office when he heard the galloping horse approaching from the direction of Riley's place. He slowed his horse down and looked back. It was Alex Brubaker, Ed could see his swollen red face, and he stopped him. "What the hell happened to you, Alex?" he asked as Alex pulled up.

"I had a go around with that man of yours, Riley."

"You better not have hurt him, Alex, or I'll come down on you harder than a mule skinner."

Alex smiled and chuckled. "No worries, Riley is fine, it is me that took the brunt of it. He got lucky with that southpaw of his, is all. It won't happen like that ever again, I assure you." Alex kicked his horse's flank and continued onward to the Fort.

Ed turned his ride and headed over to Riley's place. Riley was sitting on the bench near the fire pit when Ed made the distance. "What the hell went on here, Riley? I just came across Alex. He says you two had an altercation of some sort." Ed swung off his horse with a sigh of relief to see with his own eyes that Riley was fine.

Riley waved his hand through the air. "Ah, I slapped him around a bit, for calling me an old man."

"Jesus, Riley, you are old," Ed said with a chuckle as he sat down.

"I sure feel it. The damn kid exhausted me. I certainly ain't as spry as I once was. Makes me wonder why I'm still in this damn business."

"Shit, that's your hangover talking. Looks to me like the three of you tied one on."

"That we did, that we did," Riley responded as he took a swig from the coffee in his hand and then dumped out the rest. "I guess work is beckoning us, eh?" he stood up.

"You even sure you can work today?" Ed asked with mild concern.

"Hell, I can work most any day, even after a go with a punk-ass kid."

"All right, well let's get then." The two men walked over to their horses. Ed swung up on to his, while Riley stumbled saddling up his own.

"You going to be okay, strapping up that saddle, Riley?"

"Shut up, Ed. I'll be fine once we get riding." After a few unsuccessful attempts, Riley was able to swing up onto his horse and the two men headed to the Fort and McCoy's office. "Its six day today, ain't it?" Riley questioned with a bit of a slur.

"When are you going to start calling the days of the week by their damn names... 'S*ix day*'. Why the hell have you lately been calling the days of the week, one-day, two-day, and so on?"

"Ain't sure, something I heard somewhere. Hell, why do we call the days Monday, Tuesday, and so on, and what were they called before then?"

Ed looked over to Riley and simply shook his head. Finally making the distance to the office, the two men corralled their horses and made their way inside. Ed added a few pieces of kindling to the low glowing coals. Coffee was next and he made it good and strong. "Once the coffee is brewed, Riley, it'll knock that hangover right out of you," Ed chuckled as he sat down at the table across from him. "Tell me, Riley what started that ruckus between you and Alex?"

"I already told you. He called me an old man. Plus, well shit... he pulled his pistol on me, which I thought was empty. The damn thing weren't though. He could have blown my head clean off." Riley shook his head as he thought about that.

"What made you think it was empty?" Ed was curious to know.

"He was shooting at the stars last night, fired off all six rounds. I know, 'cause I counted. Then this morning he had the damn thing pointing at me, asking where Colby was as though I had done something to the kid. I grabbed it out of his grip and asked him the same damn thing. I had no idea where Colby was or is.

Once we realised that Colby's horse was gone, I tossed the damn thing back to him, and I'll be Goddamned, that he didn't catch it in mid-air and have it pointing right back at me, telling me not to come between he and Colby. Drunk as I was, I figured the damn thing was empty so, I slapped it out of his hand and laid a whopping on him, to only learn after all that, the gun was loaded," Riley shook his head again. "See what I mean Ed. I ain't as sharp as I once were."

"I reckon you are. If you weren't as sharp as you once were, how the hell do you suppose you could've knocked that pistol out of Alex's hand, before he could pull the trigger?"

"I never quite looked at it like that. Shit, that does make me feel better. Thank you, Ed."

Ed stood up and poured them each a coffee. "This here will make you feel even better, old man," Ed said with sarcasm as he handed Riley his coffee and smiled.

"Going to be one of those days, is it?" Riley took a swallow from the tin cup of black coffee he held in his hand.

"Nah, I was teasing you, Riley. No worries."

It was then all hell broke loose outside in the street. There was a rapport of gunfire and the big front office window at McCoy's shattered as a stray bullet smashed through it and embedded into the front counter. Both Ed and Riley fell to the ground and pulled out their pistols.

"Jesus Christ, what the hell do you suppose is going on out there?" Riley asked as he peeked around the doorframe and looked on.

"I ain't sure. What do you see?" Ed asked as he looked on with trepidation.

"Not a damn thing." Riley stood up and made his way to the front entrance followed closely by Ed. Folks were running this way and that and in the middle of it, all stood Alex Brubaker and Colby Christian. Smoke from Alex's pistol and Colby's rifle still lingering in the morning breeze.

Nearest the Fort Bank lay two dead men. A lady ran by, saying that there was a robbery, taking place and that the two men across the street had shot the robbers. It was enough information for them to know what had taken place. They made their way over to where Colby and Alex stood.

"We heard it was you that knocked down them would-be robbers."

"Yep," Alex responded. "I made a deposit to that bank yesterday and I'll be damned if anyone but me is going to take it."

It didn't take long before constable Bash was looking over the men that lay in the street. Ed, Riley, Colby, and Alex looked on. "Is they dead Bash?" Colby asked from a distance.

Bash stood up and walked over. "Did you do this, Colby?"

"They was robbing the bank, Bash. Alex here has money in there. What was we supposed to do?"

Bash shook his head, "you might have considered getting their description and then reporting it to us."

"Here is something for you to consider. They'd have been miles away by then, Bash. C'mon... they was dealt the hand they deserved," Colby responded with little remorse.

"You were released from the clink only yesterday, Colby. Is this how you start your first day of freedom?"

"If'n someone is robbing the bank it is. You going to toss me in jail again, Bash?"

"Not sure what is going to happen. I will have to take both yours and Alex's pieces. Rifle and pistol, hand them over."

"Forget that. I ain't handing my pistol over, Bash. Why would there be a need to do that. No sir, I ain't complying with that," Alex made clear.

"Nor am I," Colby added.

"It's the law," Bash said with authority. "Until we can make sense of what went on here, I need both your weapons. Now don't make this any harder on yourselves than need be."

"No way, I ain't handing over my rifle. Forget it, Bash."

"Then you'll both be arrested. Is that what you want, Colby?"

"Arrested for what exactly?" Ed interrupted.

Bash looked over to Ed. "You stay out of this, Ed. It has nothing to do with you."

"I ain't going to stay out of it Rick. Alex and Colby killed two men who were trying to rob the bank, so what! It don't make any sense to me why you'd want their weapons. They did this town a favor."

"Favor or not, the law is the law." Bash looked again over to Colby and Alex. "I'll give you both thirty seconds to hand over them weapons. After that, I'll arrest you both and throw you in jail until we can get a circuit judge here, which could and will likely take days."

"Jesus Christ, Bash, that there is the stupidest thing I ever heard," Colby shook his head, he didn't want to be tossed back into jail. He had already spent enough time there. "I want my damn rifle back as soon as you make sense out of this," Colby said as he handed his rifle over.

Alex looked over to Colby and shook his head. "You're holding us up, you know that, Bash. Colby and I got business," Alex said as he looked back to Bash and handed over his gun belt and pistol.

Bash took the weapons. "I suggest neither one of you leave town. You'll get these back when we have looked into what all happened here, but until then you are both advised now to keep the peace and I'll say again, don't leave town."

"Shit, jus' yesterday you were asking if we was leaving town or sticking 'round, and today your telling us we can't leave; and to top it all off, you got our damn weapons too. The damn laws in this country are frigging messed up, I'll tell ya that," Colby shook his head.

"Look at it however you want. I really don't care. Now, go on, get out of here the both of you. Go back to the Snakebite and stay there."

Bash, Ed and Riley watched as the two men turned heel and headed back to the Snakebite. Riley inhaled deeply and looked into Bash's eyes. "Was that even necessary, Bash, taking their weapons and such?"

"Probably not, but the smell of whiskey on their breaths makes me wonder if they're not drunk. In which case, you are damn right it was necessary. I don't need two hoodwinks running around town feeling like heroes and sporting rifles and handguns. That could make for a messy day," Bash pointed out.

"So, you really couldn't have arrested them either, eh?"

"Not at all, Ed, like you said, they did this town a favor. I only wanted them to be unarmed for the time being. Until they sober up, leastwise. I'll get their statements later. What can you tell me about what happened?"

"It is quite obvious, don't you think, Bash?" Riley interjected.

"You fellows didn't see anything then?" Bash asked to be sure.

"We only heard the gunfire a couple three maybe four shots in all. I know one bullet smashed the office window."

Bash looked toward the McCoy's office. "Yep, I see that, well, I guess that is it. Can I ask you to take these guns? I have to see what the bank manager has to say."

"Sure, we'll take them. Want us to drop them off at the Mounted Police station?"

"That, or hold onto them until I come and get them."

"Good enough. I'll keep them at our office," Ed said as he took the weapons and watched Bash head across the street to the only bank in town. "C'mon, Riley, let's see what we can do about that window." Making their way back to the office, the two men stood on the boardwalk and looked on at the shards of glass and missing window. "Brady is going to have to come up with another motto," Ed mentioned.

"Or maybe you ought to simplify."

"Simplify? What do you mean, Riley?"

"We ain't McCoy's Bounty Hunting Services anymore. Three words Ed, that's all you need."

"You mean like *McCoy's Private Investigations*?"

"That is how I'd have it painted on, once you get the glass replaced."

Ed nodded. "I reckon so. Not sure how long it's going to take to replace a window that size. We best board it up for now. I'll have a talk with Innis later on to see when he can have the glass here and replace it."

"All right, in the meantime, you go ahead and get them guns put away and I'll grab a broom to clean up the glass." Riley opened the office door and both men stepped in. Ed locked up the guns and Riley went ahead cleaning up the broken glass. It took a few minutes and with the task done, they gathered a few planks and boards and sealed the gaping hole where the window once was.

"I guess that'll have to do for now," Ed replied, as he put his hammer and handful of nails he held in his hand, into the bucket that was used for such tools.

"Better than a hole I reckon. Just going to havta get used to not looking out a window for the time being," Riley added as they stepped back inside. "Actually you might want to consider putting a smaller window in place, Ed. Might be a little more work framing in, but makes for a smaller target," Riley chuckled.

Ed looked at the boarded-off opening. "You might be right in that regard, Riley. Maybe a smaller window is a better idea. I'll see what Innis has to say, once I get around to seeing him." Making their way to the backroom, they sat down at the table.

"Quite the thing that went on here today, ain't it?" Riley mentioned.

"It could've been worse. Could be those robbers got away with their kitty, leaving the Fort and bank penniless. I say it was good thing Colby and Alex put a stop to them," Ed took a swig from his coffee.

Riley nodded. "I would agree. I can't believe Bash took away their guns for killing them."

"Ah, he only did that to keep the two of them safe. They'll get their weapons back and might even get a reward if those folks they knocked down are wanted by the law."

"True enough, I kind of hope they is wanted. ' Cause I think Colby and Alex do deserve some kind of acknowledgement for protecting folks' money. I figure they should be given a reward regardless."

"Most of the town-folk would probably agree with you, Riley. But, the law don't care unless those they killed are wanted felons. The only reward the two will get, is they won't be arrested for murder, likely won't even get a thank you from the Mounties either."

Riley inhaled deeply. "I know. It is a shame too, 'cause if it weren't for the two of them," he began, referring to Colby and Alex, "there'd be two gunmen running around robbing banks and such. The good thing is there are now two less bad guys here on earth. Whether the law thanks them or not, I'm pretty sure once folks hear about what transpired here today and that Colby and Alex are the ones who put a stop to it, they'll get thanked by many."

"On another note though, Riley, if those two they killed belong to one gang or another, they may have also stirred up a hornet's nest. There'll be men gunning for them in that case."

"I never quite thought about that. Good point you make there, Ed."

Sometime later, minutes before they were going to close shop and head for home, Bash showed up. He managed to get statements from a few witnesses as well as from Henry Purdy, the bank's manager. As far as the law was concerned both Colby and Alex were free and clear on any wrongdoing, and Bash was there to get their weapons. Ed unlocked his gun cabinet and handed them over.

"I've talked to both Alex and Colby before coming here. They've sobered up enough that I think it is safe for them to get these back. Thanks again, for keeping them Ed."

"No problem. I was happy to do so. Also glad to hear they are both in the clear of any wrongdoing. Were those they shot down wanted for anything, by the way?"

"Hard to say offhand, we'll need to identify them firstly. I didn't recognize them from any of the wanted by law bulletins. That, of course, doesn't mean they aren't wanted. Trust me, Ed, if there is a reward for the two of them, dead or alive, Colby and Alex will receive it. If that is what you are getting at."

"I suppose in a roundabout way, it is what I'm getting at. The two of them ought to receive some kind of recognition, don't you think? After all they did save this town from robbers."

"They were also drunk and killed two unidentified men."

"Two unidentified bank robbers you mean," Riley pointed out with disgust at Bash's comment.

"Yes they were. There is no denying that. Like I said, they are in the clear and if there is a reward for those two they killed, they'll get it. Now, I got to get this rifle and six-shooter back into the hands of their rightful owners and a bunch of paperwork to fill out. Thanks again," Bash said as he nodded his appreciation then turned heel and exited.

Ed and Riley watched as he stepped out into the street and closed the door behind him. "You feel as though there is something up his ass, Ed?" Riley questioned as he leaned on the front counter.

"Bash is Bash. He's always got something up his ash...," Ed chuckled.

Riley smirked. "That's a good one, Ed."

"Sometimes I can come up with them. Nothing quite like Brady can though."

Riley could tell by the tone of Ed's voice that he was missing Brady or had some concerns about him. "Is there something you wanna talk about, Ed?"

"What do you mean?"

"I dunno. It sounded like you was concerning over Brady's well-being or something."

"Maybe a little bit. It's been a while since he and Travis headed west. Starting to wonder why I ain't got no telegram on what has been going on. Haven't even got one from Tanner yet and hell, he's been gone a while too. I don't know, Riley. Sometimes things like this pick at you. I know I shouldn't worry too much, leastwise not so much about Tanner. He's been doing this type of work for years. Brady on the other hand, well, I think sometimes he's still a bit green behind the ears."

"I can tell you, when I rode with Brady when we first started to track down Crawford, he's a lot sharper and prepared then you might know. He ain't stupid, he's got a lot of you in him."

Ed looked at Riley and smiled. "And that is supposed to make me feel better? I have bullet wounds riddling my body, almost died a couple of times. That type of thing isn't something you want your kids to go through."

"I can understand that, Ed. I wouldn't want any of that for my kids either if I had any. The thing is, this is what we do. We uphold the law in our own capacities. Brady ain't a kid anymore. He's a young version of his ol' man. Come on, let's close shop and I'll buy you draft at the Snakebite. It sounds to me like you need one."

"I probably could use a cold one. It's been a hard day at the office," he joked with a smile. Closing up shop, the two men headed over to the Snakebite and a cold draft. Sitting in a corner at a table all alone was Colby. Ed waved him over and he sat down with them.

"Where is Alex?" Ed asked out of curiosity.

"That is the thing. I ain't saw him since Bash gave back our guns. His horse is gone too," Colby shrugged. "Could be he headed west. I don't know."

"You think he left you here without saying where he's going?" Riley interjected.

"If he did, he can keep right on going. He might be my cousin, but he is a bit of an ass most times. His nose is always in the air, you know, as though he don't care about nothing 'cept his own self."

"Can we buy you a draft, Colby?"

"Sure could. Thanks, Ed," he said with a sigh. The three of them sat in awkward silence while they waited for their drafts and whiskey. The saloon door swung opened and they looked casually as to who came in.

"Awe, shit," Colby started as Alex and three more men stepped in. He turned his head and looked across the table at Ed and Riley.

Ed gestured with his chin. "What's a matter, Colby? You know those folks?"

"Sure do, one is Alex...," he began before Riley interrupted him.

"No kidding? Who are the others? I ain't seen them around before."

"If you'd have let me finish, you'd know. That's Alex's crew from years ago. All Brubaker blood each and every one of 'em. It might be trouble, it might not be. Could be he rounded 'em up to help us find Crawford. I won't know 'til I talk to him." Colby grabbed his draft from the table and made his way over to where Alex and his crew sat down. Pulling up a chair from another table, he slid it in next to Alex.

"Where the hell didja you come up with these bastards?" Colby asked with a smirk.

"Hey, Colby, it's been years. How the hell have ya been?" Brett Brubaker the oldest of the three brothers asked.

"Brett, Cape, Martin," Colby said as he acknowledged the three of them. "It has sure been a long while. How are the folks?" Colby took a long swallow from his draft and wiped his mouth with the sleeve of his shirt.

"They still living. They got that big ranch now, down east some," Cape Brubaker spoke up.

Martin, the youngest of the three brothers, rarely spoke when Colby had known them and he still didn't. He just nodded and smiled.

"So your folk's is well, you three are still living and young Martin still don't speak much," Colby continued as he looked over to Martin and smiled.

"If'n there is a need, I might say a word or two," Martin smiled back.

"Uhuh, sure, what's going on?" Colby shrugged his shoulders, as he looked directly at Alex a bit confused.

"Brett, Cape and Martin is here to help us round up that Crawford fella, is all. Ten thousand split five ways is still two thousand cash bucks. I wasn't sure you was up to the task. I sent 'em a wire a few days back whilst you were still behind bars. You got a problem with them helping us out?"

"You ought to know better than that, Alex. Ain't blood supposed to be thicker than water? Hell, the five us together again, I say cheers to that," Colby finished his draft and nodded. "I say we grab us another couple rounds, kiss this town good bye and head west. Crawford is a waiting."

All five men in agreement ordered a couple more rounds of draft, then left the Fort behind. Colby looked back at Ed and Riley briefly as the five of them left the Snakebite, tilted his hat and nodded.

"There he goes. What do you make of that, Ed?"

"He did say they were all Brubakers. I don't know what to think, Riley. I reckon that'll be the last we see of him."

Riley took a swallow from the draft in his hands. "I don't know about that, Ed. I think we'll come across him again one time or another. I only hope when we do, he's still living."

"Like I said one time before, men like Colby and Alex always seem to draw in trouble. Could be I'm wrong and in a roundabout way, I hope I am," Ed looked at his empty glass. "Figure we should get drunk, Riley?"

"Hell, I'm still trying to sober up from last night. A couple more draft, and you'll likely be hauling my ass around. I'm good to go, I think," Riley began to stand up.

"Hold up a second, Riley, I'll head out with you now too I guess, and before I forget, I won't be in tomorrow."

"What kind of thing you have going on tomorrow that'd stop you from coming to the office?" Riley questioned with surprise.

"Promised the misses that'd I take her on a picnic, weather permitting of course," Ed smiled.

"That is fine by me. I probably could use a bit of cleanup. I'll go over to the widow Donale's then sometime in the morning, take a shave and bath, maybe get some clothes cleaned."

"There you have it. We each got something to do come 'morrow. Let's get," Ed responded, as the two of them headed home.

Chapter 6

The Brubakers and Colby had made it about a mile or so west when in the distance they could see dust rising as though a hundred galloping horses were coming their way.

"What the hell you make of that, Alex?" Colby asked as the five riders slowed their horses and waited for what was coming.

Alex shook his head. "I ain't got a clue what that might be about."

Brett Brubaker reached into his saddlebag and pulled out a pocket scope. Peering through the scope, he could see a dozen riders approaching. They were a good distance away, but he could make the riders out. "Shit," he began, "what we have coming this way boys is the Montana Ridgeback gang. It looks like they are short two riders though. Cape, Martin, and I circled around these fellas a couple days ago. They weren't heading this way then. They are now, though."

"Short two riders you said?" Colby questioned as his mind raced with the possibility that the two missing riders were the two men he and Alex had killed earlier that day.

"They were fourteen strong when we passed them up. Don't know where the other two riders might be, they could jus' be lagging behind," Brett looked through the spyglass again. "I don't see any riders behind them."

Alex looked over to Colby. "Are you thinking what I'm thinking, Colby?"

"What might you be thinking, Alex?"

"Maybe them two bank robbers we put lead in was part of that gang."

"I'd say we are thinking the same thing then."

"Hey, Brett, ain't that gang wanted?" Alex spoke out.

"They are. Around five hundred bucks a piece, dead or alive, I think. Give or take a couple hundred."

For the first time Martin spoke up. "A quick calculation tells me they are worth six-thousand bucks. Are you fellas up for some fun?"

"What the hell do you mean 'fun', Martin?" Cape asked as he looked at his younger brother.

"They is short two riders, we are plus two. I know I can pick at least three off before they even know where the lead is coming from. And Colby, he can knock down that many or more."

Colby looked at Martin and smiled. "I like it! What do you say? Six thousand bucks is a lot of money. Like Martin pointed out, since they are wanted dead or alive, we could ambush them, kill the lot, and be six thousand bucks richer before the day ends."

"Jesus Christ, both of you is talking stupid. There is twelve of them and only five of us," Brett pointed out. It wasn't enough though to convince the others that their odds weren't good.

"First are you sure they is the Ridgeback gang?" Alex asked.

"Am so, as sure as I know we don't stand a chance, Alex, if you're thinking along the same lines as these other yahoos."

"I am, Brett, come on, we can kill them. If Colby here and Martin can knock down half of them, that'll leave only six. You, me, and Cape can handle two men a piece, think about it, Brett, six-thousand dollars, that is a thousand and some change for each of us."

Brett shook his head. "I think you're all crazy, but I ain't one to ever turn down a good gun fight. Let's get these horses under cover somewhere and set up an ambush."

"That is what I wanted to hear! Let's get!" Colby exclaimed as he and the others headed for cover among some trees.

Finding the perfect spot, Colby and Martin crawled onto a couple boulders that jetted out of the ground and waited. The others hid on the other side of the trail. Using hand signals the five of them waited until the approaching riders were within rifle distance. When they finally were, Colby and Martin started firing, gun smoke and the loud clap of echoing rifles erupted in the quiet of pre-evening.

For Colby it was as though everything was in slow motion. Every shot he fired hit its mark and Martin kept up the pace. The smell of gunpowder wafted in the air as the Ridgeback gang split up and darted for cover. True to their word, Colby and Martin had thinned out the gang by a half-dozen. Six men now darted this way and that, but Colby managed to knock down two more. It took only a few short minutes to end the reign of the Ridgeback gang. Not one member of the gang was left standing. The ground on which the dead lay was crimson like the western sky.

"That is the last one, Alex. Nice shooting!" Brett yelled from his position.

"Jesus, I can't believe we took out the Ridgeback gang."

"We sure did! Got 'em all too."

Martin and Colby now made themselves visible and they walked over to meet up with the others. "Told ya it'd be fun, it sure kicked the shit out of a boring Saturday, that is for certain," Martin said with a crooked smile. "Anyone bleeding?" he asked.

"Looks like we all managed. I can't believe we did that. I felt the adrenalin surge through my veins like the mighty Oldman River! Man, what a ride," Cape said as he holstered his pistol.

"I guess we got a dozen dead men to gather and horses too. C'mon let's get to work," Alex said as he swung up onto his horse and the five of them went about gathering their kills and the dead men's horses. It took longer to do that than it did to shoot the men down. With the bodies of twelve dead men draped over twelve living horses, the Brubakers and Colby headed back the way they had come.

"What do you reckon Bash is going to say about this, Alex?" Colby asked.

"It don't matter one damn bit. Someone owes us a nice bounty for these dead men. That is all that matters," Alex smiled.

"I suppose you is right." Before the sun set that evening, the Brubakers and Colby made their way back to the Fort. Onlookers were in awe as they lead the twelve horses carrying twelve dead men down the street.

"Who the hell you got there, folks?" one onlooker asked as the five men passed.

"The Montana Ridgeback gang, all dozen of 'em," Brett spoke out as the five of them continued on to the Mounted Police station. Finally making the distance to the station, Alex and Colby swung off their horses as a small crowd of people gathered to look on, and catch glimpses of those responsible.

"The five of them alone brought in those men?" a bystander asked, as the crowd began to grow.

"They say it is the Montana Ridgeback gang. Quite the thing, ain't it?" another man answered.

"It is indeed," the first man responded as he looked on.

Alex and Colby walked up the stairs to the front door of the station. The door was locked, so Colby pulled the bell rope. The bell rang and a few moments later Bash answered. Opening the door, he was surprised to see Colby and Alex.

Last he heard was they had ridden out of town. Now, here they were standing on the stations front stoop.

"Colby, Alex, what is going on?" he asked.

"Evening, Bash, got some dead men for you," Colby responded.

"What? Dead men, what are talking about?" Bash stepped out onto the stoop and looked on. There was a small crowd of people standing nearby, and twelve horses with men draped over them. "Jesus, what have you gone and done now, Colby?"

"It weren't jus' me; I had help. Those men on them horses, they're the Montana Ridgeback gang from down south. The five of us," he began as he gestured toward Alex and their three cousins, "the five of us got the opportunity to take 'em down, so we did. We speculate them other two men that tried to rob the bank is the missing two men from the gang."

Bash made his way down the stairs and over to the first body. He grabbed the dead man by his hair and lifted his head so he could have a look. "Yep, that one is gang member, no doubt about that," he shook his head. "It's going to take some time to identify them all. I guess you'll be staying here in town for a day or two, until we can make head or tails out of this," he looked at the three riders sitting on their horses. "Who might these folks be?" he asked.

"That is Brett, Cape and Martin Brubaker, cousins of ours," Alex spoke up.

"Cousins huh?"

"I'm betting you didn't think there were many Brubakers around, eh, Bash?" Colby questioned with a smirk.

Bash looked at him. "It doesn't matter what I may or may not have thought, Colby. If you say they're your cousins then I guess they're your cousins. As for these dead. Like I said, it's going to be a day or two before we'll even be able to identify each of them. If it is the Ridgeback gang, you got some reward money coming your way. A nice fat sum, too." Bash looked on toward the single file of horses that lead up the street. "You folks can lead these horses over to the stable. We'll get the dead off their backs then. I'll meet you up there, Colby." Bash turned heel and headed back up the stairs and front door. He watched briefly as Alex and Colby, and the others headed toward the stable. The small crowd that had gathered followed close behind. They always did when such a spectacle came to town.

"All you folks can turn around and go about your business. There is nothing for you to see here. Now, go on!" he yelled from the station's stoop. The crowd hummed and hawed as it slowly dispersed. Those who did hang around did so discreetly. He waved his hand through the air in derision. *There is always going to be one or two, isn't there*, he thought as he entered the station. There really wasn't much, he could do about it. One or two gawking was always better than a baker's dozen.

Gathering up his Mounted Police formal wear, Bash quickly dressed into it. Suited and dressed appropriately now, he headed out the back door and made his way to the stable where Colby and the others waited. "Let's get these dead loaded on the wagon so I can get them to the undertakers," Bash said as he removed the first man and slung him over his shoulder.

Colby, Alex, and the brothers swung off their horses and followed suit. The dead men were stacked like a cord of wood. The wagon wasn't quite big enough for twelve dead men. With the task done, they turned the horses loose in the corral. Eventually they'd be auctioned off or bought outright.

"That takes care of that," Bash said as he wiped his brow and looked on at the twelve additional horses that were now the responsibility of the police. They darted this way and that circling around the corral until finally settling. They'd all have to be checked over for any kind of branding and returned to their rightful owners if any branding were found. That though, was for another day.

"I have some paperwork for you folks to fill out, but by the time I'm done sorting out these bodies it'll be too late for that. I'll expect the five of you to stay close and come by in the morning. That is all," Bash said as he retrieved two horses from the barn so that he could hook up the wagon.

"We'll be seeing you in the morning, Bash," Colby said as the five of them swung up onto their own horses and headed for the Snakebite Hotel.

"Guess we is stuck here in this shithole for a couple more days, eh, Colby," Alex stated as they made the distance to the Snakebite.

"I guess so and we might as well make the best of it. We'll be gone from here soon enough," Colby said as the five of them tethered their horses across the street from the hotel. "How much kitty we got left, Alex?"

"Twenty six dollars and a couple of coins how much money you three got on yous?" Alex asked Brett.

"I have a couple bucks, six, or seven. Ain't sure what Cape and Martin might have. How much you two got?" Brett looked over to Cape.

"I have five. Martin, what you got?"

"Fifteen or so," Martin replied.

Brett and Cape looked at him. "Where did you come up with fifteen dollars?" Brett asked.

"Was the last pay I got, before we got that wire from Alex to meet him here."

"So between us we have what?" Cape began to add the numbers, but Martin already had the answer.

"Jesus, you should have stayed in school longer than the four years you did spend there, Cape. We have forty-eight, maybe fifty bucks."

"That ain't a helluva a lot is it?" Alex questioned somewhat distraught. What were they going to do now? They had to wait at least a couple days before any reward money would be handed over, if any at all were to be handed over. With only fifty bucks to their names, it was going to be a long wait.

"Shit, quit your bellyaching, Alex. It is the same amount, we had when we left here earlier on. We'll make do," Colby replied.

"Earlier on, we were heading west. Now we're stuck here for a day or so. Need money to stay in town," Alex rebutted.

"Hell, we don't have to stay in town. We could camp out, sleep under the stars, same as we would if we were still heading west," Brett pointed out.

"See, Alex, there is always a solution. It is the cheapest and simplest one in my opinion."

Alex shrugged his shoulders with indifference. "We could grab one last hot meal, though. I'm a bit hungry."

"All right, it is settled. We'll camp-out, grab a meal tonight, and see what morning brings," Colby said. The five of them made their way across the street to the Snakebite. Grabbing an empty table, they sat down among the stares and whispers of those who were drinking whiskey and swilling beer.

"Sure feels awkward having all these folks staring at us, don't it?"

"Don't worry about it, Martin. Folks are curious that is all that is. They saw us toting in twelve dead men. If it were you or I sitting among those folk, we'd be staring too," Brett said as the barmaid came by to take their order.

"Evening, Colby, Alex, gentlemen," the young lady said as she acknowledged the five of them. "What can I get for you?"

"Five drafts and a round of steak," Colby replied.

"Will that be all?"

"For the time being I reckon it is enough to get us going."

"I'll bring you those drafts right away. The steak will take a couple minutes," she said as she pranced away. Returning a short time later with their drafts, she set them down. "These are on the house."

"Really?"

"That is right, Colby, these and the steak are on the house. You fellows did this town a favour earlier when you stopped those would-be bank robbers. Kitty and Jim agreed to letting you have whatever you want, free of charge."

"We weren't expecting anything like that. Tell them we said thanks."

"Will do, Colby, now enjoy your drafts. Your steaks will be ready soon."

Colby nodded. "We will. Thank you very much." By the time they were finished with their meal and a couple drafts each and because of what folks were slowly learning about the five of them, town folk began treating them like heroes, as Riley had predicted, offering up their own rewards of money, employment, and places to stay, all of which they declined. Instead, they headed out onto the plain and set up an evening camp.

With their bellies full and thirst quenched and still fifty dollars rich, things weren't so bad after all. There was a real possibility that in a day or two, they'd be six thousand dollars richer. If, by chance, they ever did bring in Crawford, they could add ten thousand to that.

Sitting around the fire that night conversing and reminiscing about the past, brought back good and bad memories for each of them. Although both Alex and Colby were from different backgrounds, it mattered little. They were family and sometimes family was all one had, rotten eggs and all.

The Brubaker brothers were raised on a farm by a hard-working father with an iron fist and a god-fearing mother. They were often referred to as the 'fearless three'. Together they had taken on cattle rustlers, Indian raiders and the like. In a sense, they brought law and order to otherwise lawless lands where they once lived.

They never bragged about their past triumphs. There was no need for that. The people they knew did that for them. They never had the reputation that Earl and Alex Brubaker had, nor did they have a reputation like that of Colby Christian. Earl, Alex, and Colby were the rotten eggs of the family or so they had always been told.

They knew different though. Neither Alex nor Colby was rotten. Earl on the other hand was. It wasn't any great loss to them when they received the news that Earl had been gunned down. Even now, as they sat around the fire, none spoke of that.

It played hard on Alex, as it rightly should, Earl being his late brother and all. Somehow, though, he was managing. He had long forgiven Travis Sweet for killing Earl, or so he claimed. Earl had slipped up and lost his life the same way as Alex lost his fingers. They drew on a man that proved to be quicker on the draw. It was that simple. There was no one to blame for that but themselves.

Deep down though in the pit of his gut, like rot, Alex believed that Travis owed him and one day he would be looking to collect. Until then he was content to be with his cousins, the Brubaker brothers, and Colby Christian. Together, he knew, they were quite the formidable adversaries to anyone wanting to cross their path. Undeniably, the five of them together were a force to be reckoned with.

Chapter 7

Rising before the sun, Martin Brubaker tossed a few sticks
onto their past evening fire. When the flames took, he
warmed his hands and looked out across the plain. He
admired the beauty, and serenity of its openness as the sun
began to shine and twilight turned into dawn. Giving the
others a few more minutes of sleep, he checked up on their
horses' and saddled his own. By 8:00 a.m., all five of them
were standing at the front doors of the Mounted Police
station, ready to sign whatever paperwork Bash needed them
to sign. They were surprised somewhat, when it wasn't Bash
who answered the door, but Lieutenant Bob Cannon.

"Colby, Alex, the brothers three," he said as he greeted
them. "We've been waiting for you." He held the door open
and gestured for them to come in.

"Where is Bash?" Colby asked straightforwardly.

"He's here. Come on. Let the Government buy you
fellows a coffee. We got things to go over," Cannon said with
authority.

"Yeah, we know, wasn't expecting you is all."

"When I hear about a recently released prisoner whether
they were sentenced to community service, or straight jail
time, has been involved in... well let's see, fourteen deaths in
less than seventy-two hours upon release, you can bet I'm
going to be here when he explains himself."

"We ain't broke no laws, Cannon, if that is what you is
speculating. Those two men Alex and I offed yesterday and
those twelve we brought into Bash last night are all members
of the Montana Ridgeback gang. And even if them other two
isn't they all got what they deserved."

"Is that what you think Colby?"

"Damn right it is, you going to tell me different, Cannon?"

The Missing Years- Part IV
A Tyrell Sloan western adventure

"At the moment, nope, not until I get your reports on what transpired and we identify the bodies with certainty, will I be condemning or condoning any one of you." Opening a door to an interviewing room, he led the five men in. He pointed to a coffee pot. "It's fresh and it's free so help yourselves, I'll be back shortly with Bash and paperwork. Get comfortable, gentlemen; this could turn out to be a long morning." Cannon closed the door, and made his way over to his sparse office and retrieved some documents and whatnot.

Colby poured himself and the others a coffee as they waited. "Like Cannon says, it's fresh, it's free."

The five of them conversed and speculated as they waited for Cannon and Bash.

"What do you suppose that law man Cannon as you refer to him as, means when he says *'could turn out to be a long morning'*?" Brett asked as he took another swallow from his cup of coffee.

"Who knows?" Colby shrugged his shoulders, "Cannon is an ass, more so than Bash. He's playing his part as the high and mighty law allows. We ain't got nothing to worry about, Brett, not a damn thing. We'll answer their questions be done with it, and wait for the bounty to be paid. We didn't break no laws whatsoever it is legal to bring in bounties.

Come next year, though, that might be different from what I've heard. Things might be changing, but as of now, we're protected by the current laws. Sure we ain't got no badges, and we don't belong to no Bounty Hunter club, but we did bring in twelve wanted felons and Alex and I stopped in their tracks two would-be bank robbers." Colby paused for a moment. "Hell, we had a good day, yesterday, I'd say."

"I don't reckon anyone of us could argue that point. We wiped some dirt from the earth and had fun doing it," Martin chuckled.

59

Somewhat taken back by Martin's remark, Colby looked over to Brett and Cape as though looking for answers on why Martin, 'the silent and peaceful', would say such a thing. The two brothers only shrugged and shook their heads. They didn't have the answer nor did it seem to bother them. Colby now looked over to Martin.

"It might have been fun, Martin, but it could've been deadly too. Don't let it go to your head."

"You are wrong, Colby. It was never going to be deadly, not for us leastwise. You know yourself how damn easy it is to knock a man off a galloping horse with a rifle."

"About that, I was going to ask you, when and where did you become so skillful with a rifle? Last thing I ever remember you shooting with was a sling that you made. From what I recall, you made it out of leather lace and piece of buckskin. You swung it around your head like David killing Goliath. You got damn good with that thing too," Colby snickered. "You remember that, Martin?"

"I remember that fine. Was good times back then, wasn't it?" There were a few seconds of awkward silence, as Martin waited for an answer. No one really knew how to answer, each had their own experiences, and each had their own memories. Some were shared and some weren't.

Finally, Alex spoke up. "I reckon they was good times, 'specially when we all got together every couple of years or so. In between those times though, things weren't always good. But, we're all here now, 'cept for Earl. That though ain't neither here nor there." Again, an awkward silence filled the room.

"If you are looking for some kind of remark regarding that, Alex, I reckon you're pounding your head against a wall," Colby responded somewhat sympathetic.

"Nah, I ain't expecting no kind of remark from either of you. I know how you all felt about Earl. Hell, I walk that path every day, and often feel about Earl the same as you four do. Nonetheless, he was my brother and no matter what, not one of us in this room can say otherwise."

"You got that right, Alex, and I don't think either one of us would ever deny that fact," Brett pointed out. Four or five years younger than Earl, Brett once knew a different Earl, not the cold-blooded killer he grew to become.

Whatever transpired in Earl's life that turned him into that man, died with him that day when he met up with Travis Sweet. No one knew years before his death on that fateful day, what it was or could have been that turned Earl into the man he eventually became. As time went by no one seemed to care. Earl Brubaker was dead now and for some that was reason to rejoice and for others it was time to forget.

The door to the interviewing room opened and Bash and Cannon stepped in. "Let's get to it," Cannon said as he and Bash pulled up chairs and sat down. "Which one of you wants to tell me about what happened last night? We aren't here to discuss the two thugs trying to rob our bank yesterday. That is a different item all together. So, who is it going to be that tells me the tale of the twelve dead men stinking up our town?"

"There ain't anything to tell, Cannon. Except that, the five of us was heading west. The sun hadn't even set yet, and as we was riding we were presented with an opportunity to take down a gang of hoodwinks, which we did. That is it. That is all there is to it, it ain't no more complicated than that."

"The five of you just happen to come across who you think to be the Montana Ridgeback gang."

"What do you mean 'think'? Bash already identified one of them to be part of that gang."

"He identified one of the riders to be a Ridgeback member. That doesn't mean a thing, Colby."

"Bullshit. It means everything and you know it. Next, are you going to tell us that the fella Bash identified, might have been riding with eleven other horsemen which were hell bent for leather and heading this way and had no association with the Ridgeback gang."

"Heading this way?" Cannon repeated, looking for affirmation.

"Damn right they was, and like I said they were hell-bent for leather too. Could be they was heading to 'your town'." Colby put emphasis on that part of the sentence. "Could be they was coming here to find out what might have happened to their friends who Alex and I laid to rest yesterday."

"Hold it right there, Colby. We aren't here to discuss that. As I said, that is a different situation all together and has no bearing here," Lieutenant Bob Cannon once more made clear.

"Anyone whosever heard of the Montana Ridgeback gang, knows they was fourteen strong, no more and no less. Those two men you don't seem to want to talk about are the thirteenth and fourteenth riders of that gang. You know it. Bash knows it. Hell, by now the whole town knows it. Why are you so eager to bury that fact, Cannon?"

It was then that Bash finally spoke up. "Hold your tongue, Colby. You are talking to a superior officer of the Mounted Police. If I were in that position and you spoke to me like that, I'd have you arrested."

"No worries, Constable Bash. I'll answer Colby's question. Those two men were seen robbing the bank, they were seen with guns drawn and were jeopardizing the town. You and Alex, or for that matter any other man or woman that would have interjected, are and always will be within the rights of the law as they are today to take such abrasive action. No questions asked. You see now how they don't have a place in what we are trying to establish here and now."

"Okay, so take them out of the equation. You know what that means right? It means there are two more Montana Ridgeback riders kicking. We'll leave them for the law," Colby remarked with a sneer. He was tired of the run-around already. It was always the same thing with Cannon: stupid questions, repeated questions, over and, over again, till one was practically blue in the face.

"If I can speak up here for a moment," Brett started.

"Go ahead, what is it that you have to say?" Cannon gestured for Brett to talk.

"When the three of us came this way a few days back, we came across fourteen riders. It was dark and so we headed in the opposite direction and circled around. We never saw them riders again, until last night. That is we saw twelve of them. I scoped in on them as they was a good distance away still, but like Colby mentioned, they were headed east and coming straight for us.

I finally was able to identify Davis Craigery as the front rider and a couple more of the Ridgeback gang. There was no doubt in my mind that they weren't heading this way for whatever reason. We quickly decided that the risk to take them down was well worth their bounty. As for them being two riders less, well, I guess not until they've all been identified can we be sure of anything."

Bob Cannon sat back in his chair and crossed his arms. He hadn't expected either one of the men to be so familiar with the Ridgeback gang, but clearly they were, right down to a name and the numbers of which made up the gang. There was nothing more, he or Constable Bash needed to know. Colby, Alex and the Brubaker brothers three had taken out the entire

Montana Ridgeback gang. They deserved the seven thousand dollar bounty as far as he was concerned.

That was of course if the two men Alex and Colby put to rest on their own were indeed Ridgeback riders. If not, they would certainly receive a large sum of the reward money, six thousand dollars to be exact. Cannon himself would make certain of that.

"There isn't anything else we need to know. We'll have all fourteen men identified in the next few days. If it all comes out in the wash, you folks will have a reward coming your way. I suggest you check back with us mid-week or thereabout," Lieutenant Bob Cannon confirmed.

"So then, you're done with your interrogation?" Colby questioned, as he and the others began to stand.

"There was no interrogation going on, Colby. As the law we are required to ask questions when fourteen dead men show up. It was a formality. That is all it was."

"Call it whatever you want, Cannon. Every time I talk with you, I go away with a bad taste in my mouth. We'll see you in a couple more days to collect what is owed us."

"You'll be welcomed to it, Colby." That was all Cannon said as he exited. Bash and the others followed behind.

"You know where the exit is," Bash said as he gestured toward the door.

"Do so, and we're headed out of it right now to look back only one more time, when we come to collect our rightful bounty. Good day, Bash, we'll be seeing you," Colby replied as the five of them exited into the early morning.

"Where do we go now, boys?" Cape questioned, as they swung back onto their horses.

"I ain't got much use of being here in town. I think I'll head back to where we camped last night. The four of you can do whatever it is you like, I guess."

"I don't think there is much of a point for any of us to stick around town. I say we pick up some supplies, food and such, maybe a bottle of whiskey, and like you say, Colby, head back to camp. In a couple more days we'll have some good hard cash in our hands I reckon."

"I reckon you are right, Cape. It will sure be nice to have some travelling money," Colby said as the men sped up their horses. Stopping off at the local food and grain market, Cape and Martin went inside and bought enough supplies to last the five of them. Alex, Brett, and Colby continued on to where they had camped the night before, making that place their home for the next couple of days. It was only by coincidence that later on in the day that Ed and his wife strode by.

Ed slowed the horse buggy down when he recognised Alex and Colby. Colby noted the buggy nearby and waved them over. "Hey Ed, and Misses Ed! What are you folks doing way out here?" he asked as Ed drew the buggy close.

"I might ask the same thing of you folks," Ed responded with a smile as they made the distance to where Colby and the others stood.

"This here is home for the time being. We got business to tend to in a couple days."

Right away, Ed felt a bit uneasy. What kind of business could the five of them possibly have? "Business?" he asked.

"Yes sir, the Fort law owes us some reward money." Colby smiled.

"For those two men you and Alex dusted yesterday?" Ed was curious.

"That and the twelve others we brought in last-night. I guess you ain't heard yet?"

"Heard what?"

"After the five of us left the Fort yesterday, we stumbled upon the Montana Ridgeback gang a mile or so west of the Fort."

"Hold on a second, the Montana Ridgeback gang you said?" Ed questioned with doubt.

"That's right. They were headed easterly, likely heading to the Fort. Alex and I speculate they were looking for their friends, which we assume were those two men we laid out. They were a dozen strong, so two men short. It ain't been proven yet, but in all likelihood, those two men were the missing riders. Anyway, to make a long story short, they rest in peace now."

"You killed them in other words?" Ed was surprised.

"Knocked them right off their horses," Alex responded with a snicker.

"Jesus! That is quite the thing. There is a decent bounty for that lot. Near eight, or nine thousand I reckon. Well done, fellas."

"Seven thousand, Ed, still a tidy sum, though."

"Damn right it is, Colby. I'd say the five of you deserve every damn penny of it too. It ain't easy taking on that many men in one swoop."

"There was nothing to it. Once we started firing they fell like shit-flies being sprayed down."

"You ambushed them then, eh?" Ed asked, he wasn't so impressed anymore.

"Nothing wrong with the way we took them down, Ed. Ambush or not, it don't matter none."

"It certainly doesn't. The fact remains that the five of you managed to do what many failed. That is all that really counts, isn't it?"

"I'd say so, yep."

"Uhuh, well, Colby, Alex, fellas," Ed began as he acknowledge all five men. "The Misses and I have a place to be, we'll be seeing you," Ed finished as he turned the horse buggy and he and his wife headed for home.

"Was that fella a friend of yours, Colby?" Martin asked.

"I ain't so sure. That was Ed McCoy from McCoy's Bounty Hunting Service there in the Fort."

"He's a Bounty Hunter then, eh?" Brett questioned.

"One of the best from what I know of him. Or at least was at one time or another. He's got a crew of four that works with him." Colby went ahead and named off the four men.

"Is Travis Sweet the same Travis Sweet, I might be thinking of?"

Alex looked over to Cape and took it upon himself to answer. "He is."

"That must burn you up some, eh?"

"He's just a man with a job is all I have more distaste for Riley Scott than I do for Travis Sweet."

"Yeah, why is that, Alex? You ain't told me your reasons for that."

Alex shrugged his shoulders. "I ain't sure, Colby. There is something about him, I don't like. Maybe it is his arrogance."

"Arrogance? Shit, Alex you're more arrogant then Riley Scott ever could be," Colby somewhat teased although it was mostly truth. "I think you are sore at the fact that we wasted one extra day in the Fort after they sprung me loose, so that I could show the man some respect for keeping me busy."

"He was frigging brainwashing you if that is what you mean. And no, I didn't give a care that we was sticking around. I knew Brett, Cape, and Martin were headed this way."

"Then, why'd you put up such fight when I said I wanted to stick around for a day or two so I could talk to Riley?"

"Like I said, Colby, he was brainwashing you."

"The hell he was, Alex. You ought to know better than that. You have some kind of a hard on for the man which not even your own damn self knows why." The two of them bantered back and forth a while longer and on more than one occasion got into each other's face. The brothers three sat in silent observation watching as Colby and Alex tossed words around.

Finally, Brett spoke out. "Jesus," he began, "before the two of you start swinging or putting lead into one another, I suggest you step away for a moment and take a breather. We don't need no family feuding being started before what it is we've set out to do is done. Now kiss and make up."

Alex waved his hand through the air. "Ah, you're probably right, Brett. I'm sorry, Colby; let's wash this under the bridge."

"Consider it washed under for the time being leastwise. When this is all said and done though, Alex, you and I will have some unfinished arguing to tend to."

"Fair enough, you son-of-a-bitch," Alex replied as the two of them began to chuckle.

"There, now that is a helluva a lot better than arguing over stupid shit stuff that don't mean a damn thing about nothing. Alex doesn't like Riley, Riley don't like Alex, Ed may or may not be a friend of Colby's, but Riley is. The whole thing is stupid," Brett, pointed out as he added another piece of wood to the fire. As day turned to dusk, and dusk turned to night, the day finally ended.

Chapter 8

Tyrell had been on the trail for five days since leaving Brady and Matt Crawford. Finally, after a hundred miles of trail, the town of Chase came into view. The first thing he did was send a wire to Ed letting him know that he was finally in Chase and that Brady was heading home with one Matt Crawford in tow. With that out of the way, he headed to the Chase Hotel. Pulling the horse to a stop, he tethered him to the horse rail, a young boy, and his mother walked by. Tyrell noted them and tilted his hat in a friendly gesture.

"That is quite a nice horse you have there, mister. What's his name?" the young boy asked as his mother tried to pull her son out of the reach of the stranger.

Tyrell understood the young woman's apprehension and he smiled. "No worries, ma'am, I might be dirty and unkempt, but your boy asked a fair question. Would you take offence if I answered?" Tyrell asked as he looked at the young lady.

"Well...," she began somewhat hesitantly. "I suppose not, but please keep your distance," she requested as cordially as possible.

Tyrell nodded with a smile. "The horse's name, son, is 'Horse' leastwise that is what I call him."

The young boy looked at him quizzically.

"Horse? That is a pretty silly name for a horse, why would you call him that?"

The boy was curious. Tyrell looked over his shoulder toward the horse. "He ain't mine. I borrowed him from a friend. I'm not sure what my friend ever called the horse, never paid much heed to that, so I call him 'Horse'."

"I guess that is okay then. He's still a nice looking horse." The young boy smiled as his mother, deciding that the boy had talked long enough to the new stranger in town, dragged him off in the opposite direction.

She looked back once and Tyrell removed his hat and nodded. "Have a nice day, ma'am, son," he said with a pleasant smile. He watched as the two turned down another street and carried on. Turning, he made his way inside. The smell of hot food and coffee permeated the hotel's lobby. Tired, hungry and in dire need of a hot bath, he walked over to the hotel lobby's counter. The man behind the glass greeted him with a smile.

"Good morning, sir, how can I help you?" the man asked as Tyrell leaned up against the counter.

"Are there any available rooms?"

"Always is here at the Chase Hotel."

Tyrell sighed in relief. The thought of a warm soft bed, food and a perhaps a hot bath was something he dreamed about over the last couple of days. "Good to know; wasn't sure there would be. What about baths, are they available?"

"Most certainly, a free bath comes with every two-day stay. It costs fifty cents otherwise. Rooms are eight dollars a night and that includes one meal a day."

Tyrell looked around. The Chase Hotel hadn't changed since he was last there only a few months earlier. To him, though, it seemed like years. A lot had taken place since then and it all had happened mighty quickly. "I stayed here not long ago and it cost me twelve dollars for a meal, room and a bath for one night. For sixteen dollars I can now stay two nights, get one meal a day and a bath?" he wanted to be clear.

"Yes sir, we can offer those prices now since we ain't that busy at this time of year."

"Uhuh, well book me in for two days. I ain't in no rush to get anywhere and one free meal a day plus a bath is a hard deal to come by."

The Missing Years- Part IV
A Tyrell Sloan western adventure

The man reached for the hotel registry and took down his name, and handed him a key to room number 4. "At the top of the stairs and to your right Mr. Sweet, you want your bath ready now or later?"

Tyrell sniffed his armpits and ran his fingers over his whiskered face. "Two or three days ago, would've been nice," he chuckled. "The sooner the better would be my guess."

"All right, it should be ready for you within the hour, ten o'clock or there about. How does that sound?" the man asked.

"Sounds like music to my ears. I'll see you then." Tyrell gathered his saddlebags and made his way to his room. Unlocking the door and stepping in, he tossed his gear on the bed and slumped into the sitting chair supplied. The room was small, but it had all he needed and he was satisfied with it. He sat in the chair not fully awake and not quite asleep, but somewhere between exhaustion and weariness. The bath, he knew, would revitalise him and some hot food and a good night sleep in a real bed was needed.

A thought came to him out of the blue and he tilted his head as he recalled in an early conversation with Ed regarding Matt Crawford that Matt had green eyes. From what he recalled, Matt's eyes were blue/grey. *Wonder what if anything, that might imply,* he thought about it for a moment. Perhaps in certain slants of light his eyes did look green. Shrugging, he waved his hand through the air as though he were swatting at a fly. For now, he'd forget about it. There was no need to think Matt wasn't Matt. Besides, he couldn't worry himself with such a small detail. Descriptions of folks were always mixed up for one reason or another. He had bigger picture in his mind that concerned him and that was

Gabe Roy. Willow Gate was some distance away, but in time, he'd get there.

Standing, he left his gear on the bed and exited his room. Stopping off at the hotel's front counter he asked if his bath was ready. It was. Making his way to the soap and steamy hot water that awaited him, Tyrell removed his clothes, and for the first time in weeks slipped into a hot bath. Cleaned and shaved, he now looked and felt like a new person. He dropped off his dirty laundry at the hotel's laundry and once more made his way to his room. Stretching out on the bed, he kicked off his boots and dozed.

Tanner McBride sat in the corner of the saloon, a deck of cards in his hand. He hadn't left Fairmount since his arrival a few days earlier. Instead, he was trying to build up his reputation as a gambler and so far had done well. He had doubled the eight hundred dollars he had when he arrived and was waiting on the next man to pull up to his table to try his luck against him. Shuffling the cards for the hundredth time, he looked around at the patrons in the saloon that day. None of the men he saw looked like gamblers.

Perhaps it was time to continue north to Hazelton. He had a job to do. Getting to the bottom on why a Pinkerton may or may not have killed Emery Nelson, one of McCoy's men, was a significant part of the job. What he had learned so far from the gamblers he had sent home penniless since arriving in Fairmount, didn't help him draw any conclusions. No one had even heard of a man named Miles Ranthorp, the accused Pinkerton who Matt Crawford claimed to be Emery's killer. Tanner hadn't mentioned Miles' real name, Thomas Lierpp, yet to anyone he had come across. For now, that was classified information and he had no intent on revealing it.

Shuffling the cards one last time, he put them back into their box and slid the box into his shirt pocket. Standing, he made his way to the front exit. As he was stepping out, a man was stepping in and they bumped into each other. The man was dressed in a three-piece suit and a leather patch was over his left eye. Around his waist were two shiny side arms. His greying hair told Tanner he was in his early to mid-fifties.

"Excuse me, sorry about that," Tanner said as he stepped to the side and let the man pass.

"Not to worry. By the way, I'm looking for a man goes by the name of Tanner. You know anyone goes by that name?" the man asked.

"Today is your lucky day, sir. I'm he," Tanner replied with a cocky smile. The man looked Tanner up and down.

"I heard tale you are looking for information on a fella goes by the name of Ranthorp. That man owes me money and not a small amount either, five thousand dollars to be exact."

Tanner shook his head. "You are going to be disappointed to know he's dead. I reckon you are out that money."

"Dead?" the man asked somewhat distraught.

"Yes sir. He took a bullet to the heart some time ago."

The man gestured toward an empty table. "Can I buy you a whiskey?"

"I wouldn't turn down a whisky." Tanner was interested to know where the conversation was going to lead. Any information he could get on Miles Ranthorp could go a long way in discovering how he fit into the circle of events that lead up to Emery's death. Making their way to the empty table, the two men sat down.

"Sorry I didn't introduce myself, Tanner. I'm Jack Calloway." The man reached out and the two shook hands for the first time.

"Nice to meet you, Jack," Tanner replied.

"Ranthorp is dead, eh?" Jack questioned as he waved the barmaid over. She took their order of a bottle of whiskey and two glasses. "I should have shot that bastard myself when I had the chance." The two men grew silent for a few minutes until their whiskey was brought to them. They nodded cordially to the young barmaid as she set the bottle and glasses down and then darted off. Jack pulled out the cork and poured a whiskey for each of them. "Are you a gambler, Tanner?" Jack asked as he shot back his whiskey and slammed his glass back down.

"I might be, Jack. Are you looking for a game?" Tanner brought his own glass to his lips and kicked back the whiskey.

Jack chuckled and waved his hand through the air. "I wouldn't say I'm a gambler per se, but I do loan money." He poured another whiskey and slid the bottle over to Tanner.

"I see," Tanner replied as he followed suit and poured another shot of whiskey for himself. "I guess that is where Ranthorp comes into the picture, huh?"

"Ranthorp came to me three or four months ago in desperate need of funding for a big poker game up in Hazelton. Said he'd double my money. He seemed genuine, offered up a land deal as a security pledge for the repayment of the loan. That is where I went wrong. Wasn't 'til I hadn't heard from him in a while, did I decide to look into the deed, only to learn it was bogus.

I saw him one more time from a distance after that. I should've shot him then and there. Once he noted me nearby, he skedaddled. I never laid eyes on him again. Was only recently did I hear that a fella, namely you, was looking for information on him. I headed this way a day later. Thought if you were looking for him, then maybe there was a chance I'd see him again." Jack poured another whiskey and slugged it back. "I guess I'm out that five-thousand and that pisses me off some."

"Damn shame to that," Tanner said as he rose his glass and finished his second shot of whiskey. There was a real possibility that Ranthorp owed money not only to Jack Calloway, but in all likelihood to a few others as well. It made sense now, just as Tanner had assumed that Ranthorp went after Matt Crawford for the reward of ten thousand dollars to clear up a debt.

Why he may have killed, Emery Nelson was another issue all together- *or was it?* There were a lot of unanswered questions and Tanner aimed on finding out exactly what it all meant. With nothing more being discussed about Ranthorp, Tanner stood up and slid his chair in under the table. "It was nice meeting you, Jack, but I need to get on with my day. Thanks for the whiskey. I'll be seeing you." Gathering up his gear, he headed north.

Earlier Monday morning, as usual the two men sat at the table and discussed the day's workload, which, at that time was next to nothing. Ed filled Riley in on what Colby had told him the night before as he and his wife headed home from their Sunday excursion.

"Jesus, that is quite the thing," Riley commented.

"I wouldn't go as far as to say that. They ambushed them." Ed took a swig from his coffee.

"That don't make no damn difference. How many bad guys have you and I ambushed? I'd say more than a dozen."

Ed nodded. "I suppose, I can't condemn them for doing it like that, I guess. Last night though, it seemed like they was bragging about it. And I've never taking kindly to folks who do that."

"That there might be out of line, the bragging and all. Still, five men knocking down that gang, is damn impressive, I think. No matter how they was knocked down, the Ridgeback gang had the five of them out numbered almost two to one." Riley stood up and poured another coffee. He was about to sit down, when the front office door opened. The two of them made their way to the front counter.

"Morning, Ed, Riley. I got a telegram here for yous."

"A telegram?" Ed was surprised.

"Yes sir, it came in this morning. It is from your man Travis."

Ed took it and read it over. There was a twinkle in his eye and a smile crossed his face as he read it. "Says, here that Travis is in Chase and Brady is heading home with Matt Crawford in tow. You made my week, Bud," Ed said as he looked over to him. "Thank you very much. And not a word to anyone about what you heard here."

"You never have to worry about that, I ain't never spilled the beans on what I hear or read in private telegrams. Glad it's good news, though. You want me to send a reply wire?"

"Sure do. Hang on I'll write something up." Ed reached for a pen and a piece of paper and jotted done a quick reply that simply read *'Received'*. He handed it over to Bud.

"That is it. That is all you want for me to send?"

"Is too," Ed, replied.

"One word telegrams ain't going to make me a rich man," Bud teased. "No worries though, I'll send it off right away," he added as he turned and headed back to the telegraph office.

Ed looked the telegram over for a second time. "This here is the best news I've read in a while, Riley."

"I could tell when you read it. It is good to know all is well."

"Damn right it is." Ed was definitely relieved. His boy was coming home! "Almost feel like I want to head west myself and meet up with Brady."

"Why don't you then?" Riley questioned.

"I guess I could, would you tag along with me, Riley, if I decide? Brady and Matt can't be too far away. They've had a couple days of travel already, which brings them a couple days closer to home."

"What about the work that is needed doing around here?"

"There really ain't much going on, Riley. A few days away from the office might do the both of us some good."

"What do you figure Beth is going to say about that, Ed?"

Ed scratched the top of his head. "I ain't really thought that far ahead yet."

"That's your first mistake, then, isn't it?" Riley winked at him and smiled.

"I'll run it past her tonight. How does that sound?"

"It ain't any of my business what the two of you might discuss. If she gives you the go ahead though, I'll ride along with you."

"That is good enough for me Riley. Thank you kindly."

"No point thanking me yet, Ed. You might end up hogtied to your front porch," Riley said as he began to laugh. He could actually visualize Ed being hogtied, which made him laugh even louder. "Jesus, I painted a damn picture in my head of you being hogtied and the little misses giving you a spanking." This made Riley laugh so hard that tears rolled down his cheeks.

Ed smiled and shook his head. "You go ahead and make all the jokes you want, Riley. Someday I hope to see you locked in with a woman that keeps you in line as well."

Riley wiped the tears away from his eyes as he tried to catch his breath. "You might not have to wait too long for that, Ed."

"Shit, Riley, are you telling me that an ugly SOB such as your damn self has a woman? When did that happen and who is the unlucky lady? Hold on let me guess. I recall a while back that you were trying to put moves on the widow Donale, is that the unlucky lady, Riley?" Ed smiled. He knew damn well that is who it was. It was common knowledge that the widow Malinda Donale and Ed's wife, Beth, were friends and friends shared things. Ed had known about Riley and the widow for a couple weeks already.

"I never once put moves on Malinda. I don't know what you're talking 'bout." Riley tried to hide the fact, but Ed wasn't a dummy.

"C'mon Riley, you now mentioned her by her first name. How many folks do you reckon call her by that name? I'll tell you. Good friends and family, that's who, everyone else calls her the widow Donale. You're either good friends with her, or you're family. Which is it, Riley?" Ed teased with a smile.

"Of course I'm good friends with her. She does my laundry, bakes me cookies, pies, and bread every now and again. I join her once, in a while for coffee. You know, all the stuff good friends do for one another."

Ed nodded his head. "Uhuh, you keep telling yourself that, Riley. She does all that for you as a good friend should, but what do you do for her?"

"Well... I, well, you know, keep her company and stuff."

"And stuff? What exactly do you stuff?"

"Jesus Christ, Ed you're making me feel uncomfortable, you bastard."

Ed laughed. "She has you wrapped, Riley, and you know it."

Riley shrugged his shoulders. He honestly didn't know where he stood with the widow. "Maybe she does, Ed. I don't know."

"What do you mean you don't know? C'mon, she talks about you with my Beth every chance she gets."

"I ain't sure where I stand with the woman. We have been spending time together as of late no doubt about that, but there ain't no stuffing, for the lack of a better term, going on. If you know what I mean?"

"Jesus, now you're making me feel uncomfortable, Riley."

At that point, the two of them broke out into a raucous laughter.

"Goddamn! Ain't it funny how two aged men could get embarrassed talking 'bout women? That's young men stuff."

The word *'stuff'* alone that Riley threw into that sentence made the two of them break out and laugh twice as hard. Poor Ed almost pissed himself.

"Okay, okay, that is enough of that shit," Ed said as he tried to catch his breath. It took a few minutes for them to regain their composure. "I'm glad that is over, I ain't laughed like that in a while," Ed added.

"It was damn funny and I don't know why. Something must be in the air." Riley took a swallow from his coffee. "Yuck, damn coffee's all cold now. What is on the agenda today? We've sat now for a couple hours and ain't accomplished a thing, 'cept splitting our guts."

"I don't know, Riley. Things have got slow, ain't they? Maybe I'll stroll over to Innis' today and get him to swing by and have a look at a window fix. The damn boards blocking the view look god-awful ugly."

"We ain't got any other work?" Riley, questioned, he was bored.

"Not as of yet, but who knows, maybe something will come about today. As of right now though, there ain't no bad guys running around that I know about."

"Hmmm, well damn it, I need something to do. Maybe I could head west myself and meet Brady and Matt. Do we even know where they're coming from? I go alone it might save your ass from being spanked."

Ed smiled and shook his head as he looked at the telegram again. "Travis didn't say where Brady and Matt are coming from. We can assume they'll be coming from the west."

Riley stood up and looked at the map that was tacked to the wall. It didn't help much. He knew the area well enough, though, that he knew he could find Brady. "We really got to update these maps, Ed. This one here is as old as the wall it's tacked to."

"They are outdated, but still give us the general locations of areas and whatnot," Ed responded.

"I suppose. What do you think, should I head west? I've been thinking some since that wire showed up that it is probably a good idea to meet up with Brady and Matt. If they've been headed this way for the past couple of days, they might be in and around the Crowfoot Pass. This time of year, it can get ugly up that way. Not to mention there'll be bands of Indians heading to their fall hunting grounds. I know most is cordial and all, but there is always that one, you know, that is going to be a prick."

"I guess it ain't such a bad idea that you go alone. Keeps me here running the place and saves my ass from being spanked," Ed chuckled. "If that is what you want to do, Riley, I ain't going to argue."

"Okay then, I'll gather some gear and extras, and head out as soon as I can. One-day today, so I reckon by four-day I'll have either already met up with them or we'll be on our way back."

"It's Monday, Riley."

"I know. You call it what you want, Ed. I call it one-day," Riley smiled.

By 11:00 a.m. he was saddled up and heading west. He packed extra bullets, a couple of extra rifles, food and such in case things went awry, as they sometimes and often did. Ed watched from the McCoy's corral as Riley's horse kicked up dust as he went. Turning heel he headed back to the office through the backdoor. Making sure it was locked he sat down at his desk and went over the business financials. That done with things adding up, he closed his financial ledger, stood, and headed over to Innis' place.

"Afternoon, Innis," Ed said as he found him in his shop.

"Hello, nice of you to stop by. I guess you're here about that boarded up window you have. I saw that last evening, and thought to myself *'yep Ed is going to need a window'*. I took the liberty to measure it. I have to tell you Ed, panes of glass that big are hard to come by. You ever think about making the window smaller. Maybe have it so it slides open?"

"You took the words right out of my mouth, Innis."

"You want a smaller window and one that opens, then?"

"I wasn't so concerned about it opening, but when I think about it, that might be nice too. How much smaller do you think is best, Innis?"

"The one that is there now is six foot long by six foot wide single pane. It is a big one. With some minor framing and adjustments, you might want to go four foot by four foot. It would entail doing some work to the outside and inside walls, to make sure everything is kosher. You get the thick double pane lead infused glass and that prevents it from being shattered, bullets will still go through it, but that glass might not shatter. It is good for safety. You'd have a bullet hole though."

"Lead infused glass? When the hell, did glass, like that come about? It sounds like it is almost bullet proof," Ed remarked with interest.

"Shatter proof is what they call it. It is new on the market and costs a bit more than regular glass. For the safety factors alone, I think it is worth it. Another thing I thought about, Ed, we could frame it to take four, two foot by two-foot panes. That way it is easier and in the long run cheaper to replace a piece if there is ever a need and someone shoots a bullet through it again," Innis smiled. "We could have one of the panes open still, if you'd like, for instance, one of the bottom panes."

"How much would something like that run me, Innis?"

"The two foot by two foot panes from what I've learned, are near three or four dollars each, so at least fifteen dollars since we'd need four panes. The sealer and stuff like lumber plus the hardware we'd need so that we could make one window open I estimated it to be between near the same give or take, of course this is only an estimate."

"I know that, Innis, and so far you have pretty much sold me on it," Ed smiled. He always liked doing business with Innis. All the fancy hand tools and stuff that he owned always made the work he did perfect. Plus, he always seemed to know right off the get-go what was needed for all the jobs that he ever hired him to do, right down to paining. Innis was a true professional woodworking craftsman and always a pleasure to work with. There was no doubt about that.

"My labor and shop time of course is the same as always, three dollars an hour. I figured my labor to be twelve hours in total. It might be less, but it certainly shouldn't be more."

"So around sixty or seventy dollars, that's not unreasonable at all, Innis. How long would it take to get the glass carted in?"

"That is the iffy part of the whole thing. It could take a week, it could take a month."

"A month. Shit! Not sure I could wait that long." Ed brought his hand up to his face and rubbed his chin as he thought about it for a moment. "Ah, to hell with it, go ahead and order it up, Innis. If it is a month, it is a month, I guess. Not much, we could do about that. I reckon it would have taken the same amount of time if we ordered another pane of glass at the size that the window is now?"

"I'll order it up today if you want to go ahead with it. We can keep our fingers crossed and hope that it arrives next week. In the meantime, I can get to work framing in the window opening and building the frame for the glass panes," Innis said with pleasurable jubilance.

"You bet, go ahead, and order up whatever it is you need, Innis. Tomorrow is probably best to get started, since it is already late in the day. I'm so damn busy Innis that I think I'll be closing up shop early today," Ed joked. He wasn't busy at all, but he was going to close up shop early.

"What's a matter? Have you guys rounded up all the hood-winks and riff-raff?" Innis teased.

Ed shook his head and chuckled. "I don't think that could ever happen. I have men scattered all across the area and one bounty coming in. It is the same for us every year. During the fall and winter, the bad guys don't seem to be around, and business slows down some. I think most probably head south to the warmer climates. Anyway, I'll see you tomorrow, Innis." Ed made his way to the shop exit.

Returning to the office, Ed closed up shop, saddled his horse, and headed for home. He had good news to share about Brady and was quite excited to share it with Beth. She would be ecstatic and he knew it. For the past while since Brady had been gone, she had been somewhat withdrawn, distracted, and full of worry. The news he was bringing her though, Ed hoped, would bring back the sunshine for her.

Even their little excursion that past Sunday wasn't the same as ones that they had in the past. Beth wasn't herself. She rarely smiled or laughed at his jokes as they travelled across the plain to their favorite picnic spot. The excursion was for two things, some time alone and together and to make sure their horse buggy was operable. The widow Donale had asked to borrow it. She was planning something for Riley. Ed and Beth were sworn to secrecy. He chuckled as he thought about the recent conversation he had with Riley that very day a few hours earlier.

Finally, making the distance home, he spotted Beth in her garden. Tethering his horse, he walked over to her. By now, she was standing with her hands on her hips, wondering what he was doing home so early.

"Has something happened, Ed?" she asked with concern.

"Nope, everything is fine," he responded.

"What brings you home so early then, it can't even be one o'clock yet."

"We got a wire this morning from Travis. He's in Chase and Brady is heading home with Matt. They should be here by the end of the week," Ed was smiling when he said that.

Beth, though, wasn't. She marched over to him, and went up one side him and down the other. Wondering why he hadn't gone to meet him. Even after he told her, that Riley was doing exactly that. It didn't matter to Beth, Brady was their son, and, he was heading home with a killer and was alone. She practically packed him a bag and sent him running.

"Innis is coming by in the morning Beth to get started on that window fix. I have to be there."

"No, Mr. Ed McCoy! You need to get on that mule horse of yours and go meet our son! I will meet Innis in the morning. No more excuses. Get going and go now!"

"I ain't even got anything packed yet, Beth. I need a minute to do that," he hadn't even finished that sentence and Beth was storming toward their house. Slamming the door, she went about stuffing things into a gunnysack not even sure what it was, she was packing.

Before Ed could even make the distance himself, she was standing on the front porch, gunnysack in hand and tossed it to him. "Now get going, Ed, and don't waste any time. I want my boy home in one piece!"

Trying to catch the gunnysack Beth threw to him, he fell, stood up quickly, and headed for his horse. He was getting the hell out of there. He looked back once to see Beth still standing on the porch her arms crossed and tapping her foot.

"You've gone mad woman!" he yelled as he sped up his horse. *Damn woman probably didn't even pack the shit I need, crazy...* he thought to himself as he went around the bend. He stopped when he was out of view of their house so he could look through the gunnysack. Sure enough, the only thing of use inside was an extra pair of pants, a box of matches and a woollen blanket.

The rest of the stuff didn't even make sense, a candleholder, a small dishcloth, dirty and stinky at that, a knick-knack of an elephant and some other nonsensical things. Ed shook his head and chuckled.

"Damn, am I glad we have gear at the office," he said quietly to himself as he carried on.

Finally packed, he followed behind Riley, who was already a few hours ahead. Riley he knew wouldn't stop riding until there were stars in the sky and he could no longer see in the dark. In order for him to catch up to Riley, he'd have to ride longer and harder than that. "It's going to be a long haul, Sampson. Hope you're up for it, you old bugger." After he heeled Sampson's flank, the horse sped up to a running gallop.

At the Chase Hotel, Tyrell was waking up from the few hours of shut-eye that beckoned him. Now, ready for what was left of the day, he donned his hat, slipped on his boots and headed outside. It was a warm evening and he walked over to the stables where Brady's horse was being taken care of. The stable master was cleaning up a few empty stalls and the two men had friendly conversation.

"Good evening, Mr. Sweet. How are you this fine evening?" the man asked as he added another shovel full of manure into the old rickety wheelbarrow.

"I couldn't be better. I'm cleaned up, shaved, and rested. How has the horse been behaving?"

The man smiled. "He's a good horse," he commented as he carried on and dumped the load of manure onto the pile outside. Making his way back, he leaned the wheelbarrow up against the wall and walked over to Tyrell. "There has been dog hanging about. Is he yours?"

"That would be Black Dog. Yeah, he's mine. He ain't caused you any trouble, has he?"

"No, not at all, he's kept me company most of the day. He was here a few minutes ago. Ain't sure where he's got to now."

"No need to worry about him. He comes and goes. Most times never travels far from where, he knows I'm at. He'll likely sleep in the stable with the horse too. I hope that ain't a problem."

"That'll be fine, you weren't expecting me to charge you for his stay were ya?" the man joked.

"If it were going to cost me, I'd of paid."

"Nah, he can stay here for free, Mr. Sweet." The man looked down the narrow passage of stalls to the back open sliding door. "Aw, shit, there is my daughter, Lori. I was supposed to be home an hour ago. I guess I best get. Have a good day, Mr. Sweet," the man said as he started to walk toward his daughter.

Tyrell looked on, surprised to recognise the young woman as the lady he met earlier on when he arrived in Chase.

"You are late. What has been the hold up?" the man's daughter asked.

The man swatted a fly away from his face. "Well, you know how I feel about these galdarn family get-togethers, besides I got busy cleaning stalls. We'll get there, Lori don't worry so damn much all the time."

The woman now looked at Tyrell. He smiled and tilted his hat. For a moment, their eyes locked and she smiled back.

"Who is the handsome man?" she whispered as she looked again at Tyrell.

The man turned and looked, then looked back at his daughter. "That's Travis Sweet. We're stabling his horse for a couple of days, and a dog, too."

Lori's heart fluttered a bit. "Travis Sweet? You don't mean the same Travis that we've all heard about, do you?"

The man shrugged his shoulders. "I don't know if he is or isn't, Lori. Why don't you ask him?" he replied.

"No, I can't do that. That isn't proper. Let's go, the rest of the family will be waiting. Come on, Dad."

"I'm right behind you, carry on."

Tyrell smirked. He had heard a bit of the conversation. He watched as father and daughter exited into the late afternoon sun. Around that time, Black Dog came prancing over with a ground squirrel dangling from his mouth.

"I see you got yourself dinner," Tyrell chuckled as he bent down and scratched him behind the ear. "The stable master says you're welcome to stay in the stable with Horse, if you like. Says you've been keeping him company all day. You must've impressed him some 'cause, he ain't even charging for your stay."

Black Dog wagged his tail glad to know it seemed that, he was welcome to stay with the horse. He crawled between the rails and found a comfortable spot in the clean stall on a pile of straw, where he went about eating his dinner. Tyrell could hear the bones of the varmint being crunched and crushed as Black Dog went to work on it. It was a sickening sound.

"You go ahead and enjoy that. I'll swing by later and bring you some jerky to wash it down with."

The dog looked at him briefly then licked his chops and continued finishing up what was left of the varmint. Tyrell shook his head and made his way back to the hotel... All was well.

Chapter 9

Stopping off at the hotel laundry, he gathered his clean clothes and paid the fee for the wash, then headed to his room. He put the clothes back in his saddlebags. Finding the leather satchel with Black Dog's beef jerky in it, he tossed it on the bed and helped himself to a couple of pieces.

Hearing some soft music and singing in the distance, he walked over to the window and looked on. There was a pig on a spit being roasting over the open flames of a fire and his mouth watered. *Huh, that must be what the old codger from the stable was trying to stay away from,* he thought as he looked at the piece of jerky in his hand and then back to the small crowd of people who would soon be sitting down and enjoying roasted pig. *Some are lucky and some get jerky.*

He pulled his pocket-watch out and looked at the time. It was early enough to slip into the hotel's saloon and have a whiskey, maybe even order up one of the free meals that came with the price of the two-night stay he paid for. Exiting his room, he headed downstairs.

The saloon was mostly empty with only a couple folk scattered here and there. Tyrell made his way over to an empty table near the back wall and sat down. The barmaid came by, a fine looking woman with black as night hair and eyes so blue that they distracted him from her ample bosom that she practically planted right in his face. She took his order of whiskey and steak dinner.

"You a guest of the hotel?" she asked.

"Yes ma'am, room 4, a two-day stay."

"The meal is free, but the whiskey ain't. You want a whole bottle or a glass?" she questioned in the most uptight manner.

He was actually surprised that such a fine looking woman could be so boisterous to the point of rudeness. "I'll take a half bottle. I think it is going to be a long night."

"A half bottle, are you kidding me, mister, you either get a full bottle, or, a glass. Whatever you don't finish here, you can take with you when you leave. What's it going to be?"

"I ain't got much choice it seems. I guess it is a full bottle then," Tyrell answered.

She turned her head and hollered across the saloon, "one steak dinner, and a bottle of whiskey for room 4 guest! You got that, Joe. Joe, did you hear me?"

A grey-haired man poked his head out of the kitchen opening. "Come again!" he hollered as he tilted his head so he could hear.

"Goddamn it, Joe. Hang on a second, mister."

"No hurry, ma'am. I can wait," Tyrell said as she pranced away over to the counter.

"Joe! Can you hear me now?"

The man stuck his head back through the opening. "I can hear you fine now. Go ahead, what was it you wanted?"

"One steak and fixings and I'll get the damn bottle of whiskey myself now that I'm here. You got that, Joe?"

"Sure do, yep, one steak. I'll have that for you in a few minutes," Joe replied as he ducked back into the kitchen. The barmaid went around the back of the counter and grabbed an unopened bottle of whiskey. She looked at it and scribbled out something on a piece of paper. Traipsing back to where Tyrell sat, she put the bottle and clean glass on the table.

"Enjoy your whiskey the steak will be ready whenever Joe figures out what it is he's supposed to be doing." She was about to walk away when Tyrell stopped her.

The Missing Years- Part IV
A Tyrell Sloan western adventure

"Hold on a second, ma'am. Why are you so hard on that ol' codger?" he asked as though she was going to give him a reasonable answer. He should have thought twice about that.

"What's it to you, mister?" she responded with scorn.

"It's off-putting and damn rude, don't you think?"

"Look, mister, I've been running this saloon for ten years. My husband ran off with a goddamn chambermaid, left me damn near penniless and in debt up to my tits. Now if you have anything more to say about how I run this place, I suggest for your own damn benefit that you keep it to yourself."

Tyrell, hadn't gotten a tongue lashing like that, in a long time. He was left speechless. Inhaling deeply he nodded to her and poured himself a whiskey.

"Good, now, if you don't mind, mister, I have a business to run."

"Yep," he replied, as he kicked back the first shot. He watched now as the woman went about her duties, cleaning this, mopping that, yelling at Joe, conversing with patrons that came and went, and it was only Monday. He was slowly getting the picture.

His steak showed up fifteen or twenty minutes later and he felt the need to apologise to the woman for perhaps stepping out of line. He understood now her frustration. He didn't have the chance, though. She simply set his steak down and scooted off to finish whatever it was she was doing before his steak was ready. *It is what it is I guess,* he thought as he dug into the first hot well-balanced meal he had the pleasure to eat since leaving the Fort weeks earlier.

It took him a few minutes to finish and he savoured every mouthful. Even the whiskey, something he usually avoided or at the least shied away from, was going down smooth. With the last piece of steak on the two-pronged fork, Tyrell finished his meal. Civilisation and convenience weren't so bad after all. Sliding his plate off to the side, he poured another whiskey, his fourth or fifth. He had lost count somewhere along the way. One thing was for certain, he was starting to feel it.

As with every other time when he sat in a saloon and drank whiskey alone, someone was tapping him on the shoulder. He rolled his eyes wondering if what he was about to face when he turned to look would be the muzzle of a pistol. With caution and trepidation, he slowly turned with one hand already on his own .45. He almost fell out of his chair when he realised it was Bannock.

"Bannock! Jesus Christ! I would never have expected to see you in these parts," he exclaimed as he stood up.

"Travis! How the hell are you?" Bannock responded as he winked at Tyrell, hoping he was using the right alias for his old friend. Tyrell nodded assuring him that he was.

"C'mon, sit down, Jesus this is quite the thing," Tyrell said as the two of them sat down. "Got us a partially finished bottle of some damn fine whiskey and the steak here is damn fine too. When the nice woman comes and gets my empty plate, we'll get her to bring us another glass, and who knows maybe even another bottle to wash this one down with," Tyrell chuckled. "What brings you way up here, Bannock?"

"I was passing through. Got a wagon load of squealing piglets in the back of my wagon and we are heading back to Hell's Bottom. Goddamn, I tell you, Travis, it sure is nice seeing you. I was going to pass right by here, but was getting dry and figured I could swing in and have a quick draft. I don't think that is going to be the case now, though. Now you know why I'm here. What about yourself, what is Travis Sweet doing here in Chase?"

"Drinking whiskey with my old friend Bannock for the time being, that is what I'm doing here," Tyrell replied as the woman finally came by and took his empty plate and, of course, set a fresh glass down. She wasn't stupid.

"You two all right here or what?" she asked.

"We're fine for the time being, thanks for asking."

"If you need anything give me a shout. I'll check back with you though when I have the time." With that, she darted back across the saloon floor and slipped into the kitchen.

"Something is a bit off center with her, don't you think, Travis?" Bannock questioned as he poured a whiskey.

"She's estranged from her husband, has been running this place for ten years, and is in debt up to her tits." Tyrell looked over to Bannock. "Seriously that is what she told me when I confronted her about the same."

"I guess that makes sense. She does have nice tits though, don't she?"

"Does tit or I mean too," Tyrell responded. The two of them laughed quietly between themselves.

"This is one of those times that I wish I wasn't in such a damn hurry. I ain't going to be able to stay much longer," Bannock, pointed out as he poured another whiskey.

Tyrell looked at him with disappointment, "why the hell, not Bannock?"

"You forgot about the piglets I have in the back of my wagon?"

"I've already come up with a solution for that," Tyrell poured each of them another whiskey.

"And what might that be?"

"Simple," Tyrell slurred, "I have my horse; well, he ain't my horse, mine is dead," Tyrell poured another whiskey and kicked it back. "I should say I have a horse down at the livery stables..."

Bannock cut him off there. "What do you mean your horse is dead? That big, burly son-of-a-bitch that you had the last time we was together?"

"Yep, Pony, that is the one," Tyrell inhaled deeply and poured another whiskey. "Now shhhs, let me finish my story about this piglet situation we seemed to have got ourselves mixed up in. I have this horse down at the stables. It's a big stable. Now here is my plan. I say we finish this bottle," he looked at the bottle, "or some more of it. I reckon it will be dark by then. What we do is sneak them damn squealing piglets, oh, wait a second," Tyrell said as he brought his hand up to his face and scratched his chin.

"How many of them did ya say ya had, Bannock?"

"I didn't," Bannock replied as he kicked back another whiskey himself.

"Oh, okay so ya didn't say, so how many you got?"

"I figure six or seven leastwise." The both of them were obviously getting drunker by the minute.

"So, so wait a minute, go back a couple paces. Ya have six or seven or sixty-seven?" Tyrell poured another whiskey.

"Shit, I ain't sure I could fit sixty-seven in my wagon. I ain't ever tried that."

"No, no, no, Bannock we ain't even established how many of them damn things you got. Don't go buying anymore until we're sure we can get the ones you do have into that damn stable."

"Well, Jesus, why didn't ya say so," Bannock poured another whiskey. They looked at each other confused, blurred vision and all not even sure what it was they were talking about.

Tyrell pointed at Bannock and shook his finger. "Ya know what, I think the best thing to do at this point since we can't establish how many piglets ya got, that we jus' step outside

94

and count the damn things. C'mon," Tyrell said as they clumsily stood up. Grabbing what was left of the bottle from the table, the two of them made their way outside and over to Bannock's wagon, passing the bottle between them as they went. Finally making the distance, they leaned up against the back of the wagon and looked in. "I can hear the lil' bastards breathing, but can't see a damn thing, Bannock. How are we s'pposed to count 'em," Tyrell slurred as he brought the bottle to his lips again and took a long swallow

"An oil lantern might be a solution."

"An oil lantern, yep, would be a solution. Go get it," Tyrell responded as he handed the bottle over to Bannock.

"Where do I get it from?" Bannock asked as he slugged back a swig.

"You ain't got one, Bannock?"

"Nope," Bannock took another swig.

"Then why'd ya say ya did?" Tyrell asked.

"I didn't say I had one, Travis. Said it might be a solution is all."

"We're goin' 'bout this all wrong," Tyrell fumbled with a box of matches he had in his pocket and was finally able to light one. The little amount of light it produced didn't last long enough for them to count the piglets. It woke them up though. They started squealing and snorting and running around in circles in the back of the wagon. It startled both Bannock and Tyrell and the two men fell over. Lying on the ground with the piglets squealing as though they were being slaughtered, Bannock and Tyrell began to laugh. "Goddamn! I'm thinkin' we jus' fell off the wagon, Bannock."

"Yep, I think you is right." They helped each other up, dusted themselves off, and tried once more to count the piglets.

This time Tyrell lit more than one match. It gave off a bit more light, and they tried to count them. "Damn things keep swirlin' in circles. Get 'em to stop, Bannock, so we can, get their numbers."

"How am I gonna do that?"

Tyrell shrugged. "I dunno they're your damn pigs."

Hearing a voice that was familiar to him, Black Dog darted out of the stable and headed up the street to where the god-awful sound was coming from. Satisfied that Tyrell was all right. He sat down behind the two drunken men and looked on. It was quite the fiasco. Finally, realising what it was they were trying to do, he simply jumped up and into the wagon. This caused both Tyrell and Bannock to jump back themselves and, of course, they both stumbled and fell over again.

"Didja see that, Travis? What the hell has jumped into the wagon with my piglets!" Bannock exclaimed, as he reached for his pistol.

"Hold on, Bannock, hold on. I think it was Black Dog," Tyrell slurred as he struggled to get up off the ground for the second time. The two of them cautiously approached the back of the wagon, not sure, if it was Black Dog or not. They were about to look in when Black Dog poked up his head. He was looking at the two of them as though they were crazy.

"It's okay, it's Black Dog," Tyrell said as he reached over and patted him on the top of the head. "You couldn't have let us known you was 'round Black Dog. Shit, you almost made Bannock crap hisself," Tyrell chuckled. "Here is our solution, Bannock, you ain't got to worry about them piglets. Black Dog is here. He'll watch over 'em," Tyrell looked at Black Dog. "Now you stay put and protect them piglets. They is Bannock's, and, he don't want nothin' to happen to 'em. Ya got that Black Dog?"

The Missing Years- Part IV
A Tyrell Sloan western adventure

Black Dog looked at him, turned around, and lay down on the wagon floor among the piglets that, it seemed, had calmed down and were once more sleeping.

"Ya think that dog of yours will keep them piglets safe?" Bannock asked as he tilted the bottle of whiskey up to his lips.

"I don't think it, Bannock, no sir, I know it. He'll watch over them, they're safe. C'mon let's get us another bottle of whiskey." Tyrell looked at the bottle that Bannock handed over to him. "This one is near empty." The two walked back inside, sat down at another table away from the growing crowd, and ordered more whiskey. Before night's end, they had finished the one bottle and drank their way through more than half of a second. They were drunk.

"Travis, did I tell ya, I have a wagon full of piglets?" Bannock slurred.

"Bannock, we's already discussed that. You got sixty-seven of 'em."

Bannock's eyes got big. "Do I? Sixty-seven?" Bannock was shocked. "How'd I pack 'em all into my wagon?"

"Shit, I ain't known how." Tyrell shot back another glass of whiskey. "We better go check."

In the morning, they found themselves sitting up against the wheels of the wagon, not knowing how they even got there in the first place. Folks who were walking by looked at them and chuckled. Still too drunk to move quickly, they helped each other up.

"Jesus, we must've tied one helluva drunk on last night, Travis?"

"It is the only thing which makes any sense, yep, I'd say so." Tyrell picked up his hat that was on the ground. He ran his fingers through his hair and then donned it, "one word, Bannock, c*offee*."

"Yep and lots of it, too," Bannock agreed. He looked into the wagon to make sure his piglets were all accounted for. They were. Black Dog was lying on the floor still, surrounded by a half dozen pink piglets. "Look at that, Travis. Your damn dog is still here."

Tyrell made his way over and looked in. "I knew he'd stick around; told ya he'd protect them. Good boy, Black Dog, well done." Tyrell pat him as he counted the piglets. "Six of 'em, is how many there are."

"Yep, six of 'em," Bannock replied. "I think last night you were trying to convince me that I had sixty-seven." They began to laugh as bits and pieces of their evening began to bounce around in their heads.

"Goddamn, we were drunk. I'm still feeling it now. C'mon, your pigs are safe, let's get us some coffee and breakfast. I'm buying," Tyrell said as he picked up the empty bottle of whiskey that was lying on the ground and tossed it into a garbage barrel that was along the street.

It was while they ate breakfast that Tyrell told Bannock what it was he had been up to and where, he was heading now and the reason why.

"You're a damn bounty hunter?" Bannock said as he put another mouthful of eggs into his mouth and washed it down with a slurp of coffee.

"That is what they tell me. Quite the thing, ain't it?"

"Sure is, I'd never have thought that, good for you. Least you're making an honest living," Bannock smiled as he finished his breakfast.

"Since we're heading in the same direction for a spell, leastwise are you going to tag along with me?"

Tyrell nodded. "I reckon. I'm pretty much done with this town. My room is paid up for though 'till morrow, but to hell with it. I'd much rather tag along with you some. We still have a lot of catching up to do."

"No whiskey this time, though. I reckon I've had my fill of that for a spell."

"Nope, no whiskey, the thought of that actually makes me kind of sick. I've had my fill too." Finishing their coffee, they stood up. "All right, Bannock, I'll settle our breakfast bill, gather my gear from upstairs and meet you outside. I'll hop up on that wagon of yours and we'll head down to the stable."

"I'll meet you outside, Travis," Bannock said as he turned and exited. Making his way over to his wagon, he once more checked on the piglets in the back. Satisfied and with Black Dog still in the back, he jumped up onto the seat and waited for Tyrell who came along a few minutes later.

He tossed his gear into the back and hopped up next to Bannock. "We're good to go, Bannock; let's get."

Bannock snapped the reins and they headed down the street to the livery stable. Tyrell gathered Horse and dropped a couple extra coins into the soup can that was wired to the stall. Then, off he and Bannock set. That was Tuesday, September 22, 1891.

Meanwhile, Ed was trying to catch up with Riley so the two of them could escort Brady and Matt back to the Fort. He had travelled hard to catch up, but his old horse Sampson wasn't as young and agile as he used to be. It was going to take some time, but he'd catch up sooner or later. Whether he caught up with Riley before Riley caught up to Brady and Matt didn't matter much. If he didn't catch up with Riley before then, they'd run into him as they made their way back and closer to the Fort and home.

The Brubakers and Colby were gathering up their gear and getting ready to saddle up. Their hope was that there was a nice sum of money waiting for them at the Mounted Police station in the Fort. The law owed them near seven thousand dollars, for the bounty of the Ridgeback gang they had slain a few days earlier.

"I sure hope Bash and Cannon have all their ducks in a row. That money which is owed to us has been burning a hole in my pocket," Alex said as he swung up onto his horse.

"We ain't even got the money yet and you're already spending it. What kind of economics is that?"

"It's called Shut up Martin Economics One," Alex teased.

"I bet it is," Martin responded as he looked at his cousin and shook his head.

"We get that cash today, we best make tracks west is all I got to say. It would be nice to reap the ten thousand dollar bounty that is on the head of that Matt Crawford fella too. We'd then for certain have a nice pocket full," Cape said as he cinched up his horse's saddle and swung up.

"Could be Crawford might already be apprehended by McCoy's men. They is tracking him as well, fellas. Don't forget about that," Colby said as he leaned forward on his saddle waiting for the others to get ready to ride.

"If that is true, we know it'll be only Brady that will be traveling with Matt. That is one man, Colby," Alex pointed out.

"What the hell do you mean by that, Alex, and how do you know it'll only be Brady McCoy traveling with Matt?" Colby asked forthright.

"What do you think I have been doing whilst you were snuggling up with that McCoy bunch? Think I was sitting around with my thumb up my ass. I've been watching that bunch. I know that Travis Sweet and Brady McCoy headed west alone. I also know Travis is heading to Willow Gate, but he ain't going there for Crawford, he's going there for that Gabe fella that runs the town. Now, Brady on the other hand, well, I heard conversation that he'll be bringing Matt in alone if'n he and Travis are able to throw a rope over him. I also know that Tanner fella who works for McCoy's is heading north. As for Ed and Riley, well they're still here in town. Are you getting the picture, Colby? What more is needed to be said?"

They couldn't know then that Ed and Riley both had already headed west themselves to meet up with Brady. It wouldn't be only Brady, the five of them might face.

Colby was shaking his head. "If you think, I'm going to be a part of what it is I think you are thinking; think again, Alex. I won't be a part of that," Colby pointed out with sincerity and fact. There was no way he'd be a part of that.

"That is too bad, then, I reckon. That has always been the plan, Colby."

"Bullshit to that. I don't recall ever talking that kind of shit with you."

"Well that is how it is going to go down should we run across Brady McCoy and Crawford together."

"I ain't going to be a part of that, Alex. C'mon, give your head a shake. That is murder one. Folks hang for shit like that and a bounty hunter on top of that. Forget about it."

"There is always the possibility that Brady ain't caught up to Crawford, in which case we ain't going to have to find out if we'd hang. There are five of us, Colby. Who is going to stop us? Besides, we could get lucky and catch him off guard, grab Crawford, and turn him in ourselves. No bloodshed or bullets, jus' wit and smarts."

Colby was silent for a few minutes as he thought about it. Somehow, he knew that wouldn't be how it would play out.

He was in a predicament. It was true, there was a possibility that Matt was still free and a possibility that he wasn't. Ten thousand dollars was a lot of cash and he could certainly use his share of the kitty. He decided then that he'd carry on with Alex and their cousins and if by chance Crawford were free, they'd track him down, but if it turned out they came across Brady toting Matt, he'd switch sides quicker than bull trout swimming upstream and the first person he'd put lead into would be Alex.

The others, well he'd send them running back to whence they came. It was the only way, he could assure, that Brady McCoy didn't die over some stupid bounty.

"Fine, you've convinced me, Alex. We'll carry on and hope that if Brady does have Crawford, we can catch him off guard without bloodshed. I reckon though if it comes down to it, we'll do what it is we need to do."

"That's the spirit. For a minute there, I thought you was growing chicken wings and was 'bout to fly the coop. I'm glad that ain't so."

"When there is a load of money at stake, sometimes one has to decide what it is they might need to do to get it and I've decided." That is all Colby said and if Alex couldn't read between the lines, then too bad for him.

"All right are we all set to get?" Brett asked as he tied his bedroll down to his saddle.

"I reckon so," Alex said as the five of them turned their horses and headed into the Fort. It didn't take them long to make the distance.

Constable Bash met up with them at the front counter. "Morning, Colby, Alex, the brothers three. I bet you're here to gather your bounty," Bash said with a smile.

"Ain't no other reason we'd be here. You got some cash for us or not?" Colby asked as he leaned on the counter.

"The good news is, *"Yep"* the bad is not until Cannon gets here can I give it to you."

"What kind of bullshit is that? The five of us deserve that money and you're telling us that we can't have it yet?"

"Sorry, Colby, Lieutenant Cannon is the only one who can authorise the payment. He'll be along shortly."

"We'll sit and wait then, I suppose. The dead were the Ridgeback gang then?" Colby questioned, already knowing the answer.

"The two you and Alex stopped from robbing the Southwestern Fort Bank and the twelve the five of you brought in together have all been identified as the riders of the Montana Ridgeback gang. Yes sir, job well done."

"Getting a compliment like that from you, Bash, still don't make me like you any better," Colby joked.

"Trust me, Colby, the feeling is mutual," Bash responded as he heard the back entrance unlock and open. "Cannon is here now. You might as well all have sit down, it's going to be a couple more minutes I'm sure. If you like there is coffee," Bash pointed to the pot. "Help yourselves. I'll go meet Cannon and make sure the paperwork is in order."

"Don't take your time; we've got places to be," Colby said as he walked over to the coffee pot and poured himself a cup. The others followed suit.

"You know, for a dirt bag lawman, Bash knows how to make some fine coffee," Alex said as he slurped.

A few minutes later, Bash and Cannon approached the front counter. In Cannon's hand was an envelope with seven thousand dollars cash. He tossed it on the counter. "Here is the reward money for that bunch you brought in dead. I hope this isn't something, the five of you are going to take up as a hobby," he was sincere. "Either one of you want to count this?"

Martin stepped forward, picked up the envelope, and opened it. Dumping out the bills onto the counter he counted it out and at the same time made five equal stacks. "Yep, it's all here," he took his stack and tucked it into his pants. "Grab your money fellas and let's get," he said as he turned and headed for the exit.

"There you have it. If Martin say's it's all there, then I reckon it is all there," Cape said as he stepped forward and grabbed a stack himself. He was followed by Brett, then Alex.

Colby was the last to gather his money. He looked at Cannon. "What you said about us taking this up as a hobby, what is it to you, Cannon? We ain't breaking any laws."

"Nope, you aren't, but it could get you killed."

Colby put his money in his pocket and walked away.

"There is your answer, Bob," Bash said as they watched Colby and the others exit.

Cannon, nodded. "Yes sir, a bunch of hotheads who now think they're invincible. Too bad for them, I guess." Cannon shrugged his shoulders. There was nothing, he or anyone else could do about it unless laws were broken. Colby, Alex and the others were free to do with their lives whatever it was they wanted to do, whether it was wasteful or not. The choices they made were their own.

"I guess we now head west, boys. There is ten thousand cash dollars waitin'," Alex said as they swung up onto their horses.

"Goddamn right, let's get," Brett, said.

Turning their horses west, the five of them headed out of town. With fourteen hundred dollars, each in their pockets, they were feeling good. They had taken down the entire Montana Ridgeback crew, a gang of hoodwinks that not even the law had been able to stop, *'they did'*, and on their first attempt too. For the moment, life was good.

Chapter 10

It was mid-afternoon when Ed finally caught up with Riley. He was quite surprised when he did. He had thought for sure that old Sampson wasn't going to keep up the pace, but goddamn it he did. Riley heard the horse approach and turned to see who was coming up on his tail. A grin from ear to ear crossed his face as he made the rider out to be Ed. He stopped his horse and waited.

"Holy Jesus, look who it is," Riley said as Ed drew close enough to hear.

"Afternoon, Riley. Glad we were able to catch up with ya. We've been riding hard since yesterday. It has been quite the haul actually."

"Your misses must've given you the go ahead then, eh?"

"Not so much. More like she chased me away with her broom once I told her Brady was heading home. I'll tell you, Riley. She went up one side of me and down the other, cursing me for not tagging along with you in the first place."

Riley began to laugh. "So it was the opposite of what we thought. Instead of spanking you for wanting to meet up with Brady, she done spanked you for not doing so. That is pretty funny."

"For you maybe; for me it wasn't so pleasant. You go ahead and laugh, though," Ed chuckled. "She threw a gunnysack at me filled up with nonsensical items. Then scooted me off with that damn toe tapping she does when she gets all cantankerous, I would have rather faced a pissed-off hornet's nest," he sighed. "Anyway, I'm here now and damn happy to be so."

"Sure sounds like. I was about to take a rest up yon some. There is a creek there and I reckon our horses could use a drink. C'mon, it ain't much further." The two men continued for another mile, conversing about this, that, and the other thing. Finally, the creek came into view and they swung off their saddles and led their horses over for a drink.

Riley looked up to the sky and took a finger measurement on how many hours of daylight they still had. "The days are getting shorter and the nights a lil' chillier I think, Ed."

"I noticed that last evening. I was wrapped up in a couple of wool blankets and a fire snapping nearby too and I was chilled. The further we get into the mountains the colder it is going to get, Riley."

"Yeah, well, fall is coming. We can't expect it to stay warm for much longer. Soon enough snow is going to fly."

"Yep," Ed agreed. A few minutes later, they were once more on the move. "Wonder how close, Brady and Matt might be?"

"Without knowing where they are coming from, it is hard to say, Ed. I don't reckon they're around the next bend, but I think they're close. We'll have to keep up the pace. Might run across them tomorrow; might not too."

They carried onward. By early evening, both men were tired with aches and pains. Finding a nice clearing near the trail, they dismounted and set up for the evening. With a fire snapping, and beans and coffee on the flames, they made themselves comfortable.

"I'll tell you, Riley. These excursions on a saddle make my lower back throb and my damn ass numb."

Riley snickered, "I know. It's the same for me, too. This kind of gallivanting ain't for the aged. It is a young man's race. Years ago, you and I both would have been able to travel this far and not even break a sweat. Today," Riley shook his head and spit to the ground. "Today, that ain't the case. We travel ten miles and it feels like we've been mowed over by a buffalo," Riley was solemn.

Silence enveloped them as they stared into their evening fire, coffee in hand and empty plates at their sides. It seemed lonely and peaceful all at the same time.

It was funny how men began to feel when they sat around fires with friends and reminisced. It was the same for every man who forged his life out on the trail. Even those who simply sat around fires for the sake of doing so, there was something about the flames, the way they danced in the mild breezes of both youth and the aged. It was a universal language and anyone who had ever been out on the trail understood it. It was called serenity.

Men like them spent their entire adult lives forging out a living by upholding the law in one form or the other, whether it was bringing in wanted men for their bounty or simply kicking the shit out of those that deserved it. Upholding the law and right versus wrong will always come in many different forms. One thing that will always be true: once a flame burns out or gets extinguished all that will be left are ashes and maybe a few simmering coals. That was how both Ed and Riley were feeling. They were simply simmering coals, not quite ash and certainly not flames.

"I have to admit, Riley, that over the last few weeks, hell, months if I were true, I've often thought about what it is I'm still trying to do. With the changes to law enforcement approaching and the new way things are going to have to be done, I sometimes think that maybe it is time to step away and let the younger generation with their fancy training, fresh ideas, hopes and desires step up. Ya, know what I mean?"

"I do. The thing is, what do fellas like you and I do after we hang up our guns and toss our credentials saying who we once were into a drawer?" Riley questioned.

"I ain't sure. I guess that is why we continue doing what it is we're doing," Ed shrugged his shoulders and looked again into the flames of the fire.

A short distance west, Brady and Matt Crawford continued heading east. They hadn't slowed down since earlier that morning and with an hour of daylight left, there was no reason for them to stop. They were close to the Fort and with every mile they trod they were that much closer.

It was Matt who took notice to rising smoke in the distance how far away it was one could only speculate. "Take a look," he gestured with his chin for Brady to look up. "Smoke."

The two men slowed their horses to a stop. "I see it," Brady replied as he looked on. "It ain't close. Still a distance away, I reckon."

"Good to know, though."

"That it is, Matt, yep. Either someone is coming our way or they're heading east. I hope the latter. Since we can't know which, we ain't got to worry, not yet at least." Brady took a swallow from his canteen and passed it over to Matt. "I say we get down near the flats and call it a night."

It didn't take long for them to make the distance or to find a place to set up for the evening. The western horizon slowly turned pink and the first stars of night began to flicker, smoke from their own fire lifted gently toward the sky.

"We put on some good miles today, Matt. I reckon near twenty." Brady added another stick to the fire, and warmed his hands.

"I'd say at least that." Matt wrapped his hands around his tin cup. "The weather is changing. I think fall is on the way."

Brady nodded. "I think you are right." He brought his coffee up to his lips and took a drink. Like every other night

around the fire, their conversation was meagre. It likely had
to do with the fact that they were two men not much different
from one another except circumstantially. One had a licence
to kill, the other had his licence revoked by the same laws
that trained him, and he killed anyway, making himself a
coldblooded killer in the eyes of some. Unfair as it seemed,
this is how the world worked. The corrupt corrupted, the rich
got richer, and the poor along with the righteous working
men died trying to make a living. There was no in-between.

Fifteen miles west of Chase, Tyrell and Bannock were
battling the trots from all the whiskey they had drunk the
night before. "Goddamn it, if I have to run into them bushes
again tonight, I'm going to tie a noose 'round my neck,"
Tyrell said as he sat down near their fire. "How come ya let
me drink so much whiskey, Bannock?" he joked trying to
making light of their situation.

Bannock shook his head. "Hell, all I wanted was one draft
beer, but no, there sat Tyrell Sloan, going by the name of
Travis Sweet. He says to me, stick around have a whiskey,
it'll be okay. So I do. Then I drink another, and another and a
dozen more after that. I'm so drunk by then that I'm led to
believe I had sixty-seven piglets in my wagon," Bannock
chuckled. "Don't blame this one on me, Tyrell."

Tyrell looked at him and smiled. "And there I was, sitting
alone in a saloon in the middle of nowhere. Had a nice cosy
bed to sleep in and a bottle of whiskey, that I had no
intentions of drinking. I had my eyes on the stable master's
daughter, and in walked my ol' friend and compadre Bane
Nock, still going by the name of Bannock.

I cordially invite him to have a whiskey with me, he
complies, and so we had a shot, then another, then another
and a dozen more. After that, he tells me he's got piglets in

his wagon. He ain't sure how many he has, six or seven he says, but 'cause he's slurring it sounds to me like he's saying sixty-seven, so I suggest we go count 'em," Tyrell grew silent for a moment as he tried to think of how he could finish the story with the finger pointing at Bannock, but he couldn't. "You know what, Bannock, it was my damn fault."

They began to laugh and as quickly as their laughter came they stood up and darted into the bushes. The two of them were squealing louder than the piglets that day.

"Damn, it burns. Feels like I have a hot coal where it shouldn't be," Bannock complained from behind his spot.

"It sure does. I ain't ever drinking again, Bannock. I'm done with it. It ain't worth the agony of the afterwards," Tyrell remarked from behind his spot.

"I've heard ya, say that a time or two in the past, Tyrell. I don't believe it for a moment."

"I suppose I have said that a few times and in all likelihood, I'll probably say it again. As of right now though, I'm done with it."

Finally making their way back to the fire for the third time since stopping for the night, they slumped down and rested their heads on their saddles. Their guts churned, not even the water they had been filling themselves up with seemed to take away the dehydration. "You know what, Tyrell?"

"What?"

"Looking up to the stars gets a man thinking. What do you think the odds were that we would've come across each other in Chase of all places?"

"Not sure, when ya think about it, the odds don't seem very good. I mean really, Bannock, who the hell travels the distance you did to buy six pigs?"

"They ain't jus' any kind of pig, Tyrell. There's an old fella somewhere 'round here, who studs out a big ol' boar hog, some kind of special pig of one kind or the other..."

Tyrell flipped his hat off his face and looked over to where Bannock was lying. "Does this ol' fella you're talking about go by the name of Harv, by chance?"

"As a matter of fact, he does. Now how the hell do you know that?" Bannock questioned with surprise.

Tyrell began to laugh. "Jesus, you've got yourself in way over your head, then? There can't be more than one Harvey 'round these parts. I've met him and I've met them piglets' old man too. He's got tusk eight, maybe ten inches long. Harv calls him Chops. The old fella even has a mule named Buffalo Chips. The mule and the hog, as a matter of fact, are barn companions."

"Shut up, Tyrell. Quit bullshitting me."

"I ain't. It is the God honest truth, Bannock."

"Well then, what do you suppose the odds of that are?"

"Again, I'd say pretty slim," Tyrell answered.

"How the hell did you ever meet this Harv fella?"

It took Tyrell a few minutes to tell the story from when Pony died to his first encounter with Chops and Buffalo Chips to finally meeting Harv.

"That part about Pony must've really done a number on you. I know how close you were with that horse. I recall you mentioning that last night, but ya kind of skipped a step, so I didn't question. The rest though about your friend Brady and that hog with his hat in his mouth, that right there was damn funny. I hope these fellas don't turn out like that."

"Get their nuts snipped when they are young then, otherwise you could end up with a something you might not want," Tyrell warned with a smile.

"I only got the one male and had plans to stud him out. These pigs, from what I've heard, are hearty and one doesn't need to spend a lot of money on feed for 'em. That, was one of the reasons I picked them up. The females have already been spoken for."

"These ain't eating pigs for you, then?"

"Not for me. Their offspring, though, could be. I wouldn't know. Once I sell them as piglets, folks are quite welcome to turn them into ham," Bannock smirked.

"If that's the case, Bannock, you better reinforce any pen you plan on keeping that male in. Once he grows into a boar, he ain't no piggly-wiggly. I can assure you of that." Tyrell flipped his hat back over his eyes and softly chuckled to himself. Bannock was certainly in for a surprise.

"Goddamn it, Tyrell, you're making me have second thoughts about this whole pig rearing thing I was going to embark on."

"Huh, what do you think the odds of that were?"

Chapter 11

Ed and Riley were up at the crack of dawn that Wednesday. The sun hadn't even crested the eastern sky when they were once more on the move. They travelled steadily for most of the morning stopping every now and again for only brief stints. There were men travelling towards them from both the east and the west. The ones coming from the west were Brady and Matt; those coming from the east were Alex, Colby and the brothers three. The only riders they knew with certainty that they were going to meet up with were Brady and Matt.

"Damn, I'm starting to feel this ride already," Ed, said as he pulled up beside Riley. "We ought to stop along here somewhere and rest."

"I wouldn't complain one bit about that. We've travelled a good distance since morn and I feel the saddle sores. Right up here is a good as any spot," Riley gestured toward a log that was shaded and to the side of the trail.

Ed nodded. "That's good enough for me," he said as they made the distance. Swinging off their horses and not quite ready to sit down yet, they paced around stretching their backs trying to get all the knots out, even going as far as trying to touch their toes, to no avail of course. "We ain't as limber as we once were, eh Riley?"

"Hell, my limberness left me a long time ago."

Finally, they made their way over to the log and sat down. Ed pulled out his pocket watch and looked at the time. "Almost eleven, shit, we've been at it for near five hours, Riley," he pointed out as he wound the watch up.

"Hope we can last for a few more hours," Riley commented as he took a swallow from the canteen and handed it over to Ed.

"Me too. The further we get, the closer we'll be to Brady and Matt and the better off we'll all be." Unknown to them, Brady and Matt were not more than a quarter of a mile away. Their horses alerted them of oncoming riders.

"Hey, Ed it looks like the horses got a bit of spook in them." Riley pointed out as they looked on.

The two men stood up and listened. In the distance, they could now hear the clip-clop. "Do you hear that, Riley?"

"Sounds like horses. We best saddle up we can't be sure who it might be." They swung up onto their horses and cautiously rode forward. To their surprise a few moments later, the riders came into view.

At first sight, Ed wasn't so sure the riders were Brady and Matt. If they were, then Brady was riding a different horse and wasn't wearing a hat, which in itself seemed odd. Finally, he could make out his son. "Goddamn! Look at that, Riley. That is Brady. Hey, Brady," Ed yelled as he sped up his horse.

"Hey, old man," Brady answered back as he and Matt slowed their horses to a halt and waited for them to make the distance. Brady looked over to Matt. "That's my old man and Riley Scott approaching."

"I figured as much. That is some relief, ain't it?"

"I reckon it is Matt, yes, indeed," Brady responded as Ed and Riley pulled up alongside them.

"Sure good to see you, Brady," Ed said as he looked over to Matt next and tilted his hat. "Mr. Crawford," he acknowledged.

Matt only nodded, and sat quietly on his horse with indifference.

"The two of you come to babysit?" Brady questioned, unsure why exactly they were there.

"I don't reckon you're in any need for babysitting, Brady. We're here, though, to escort you and Matt back to the Fort and home to be on the safe side of things."

"You know something that I don't, old man?" Brady questioned, as the four of them continued onward.

"Could be Alex Brubaker and three more Brubaker brothers along with Colby might be heading this way. And, as you know, Brady, safety is in numbers."

"There are more Brubakers?" Brady was surprised.

"Yep, they're also likely full of themselves. This past Sunday the five of them took down the Montana Ridgeback gang. Killed them all," Ed informed.

"How is it those punks managed that?"

"The ol' ambush and shoot trick," Riley explained.

"Ah, I see. Good for them, I guess. That gang of horse thieving, cattle rustling, bank robbing, woman beaters, deserved every shot the Brubaker's and Colby slammed into them, I reckon," Brady remarked.

"Not many would argue that point. The fact that Alex and Colby ain't riding alone anymore is worth some concern. The two of them together, weren't so threatening. They are now, though. Add three more assholes and we have five assholes that are full of themselves and you might have a concoction of trouble."

Brady shrugged showing little concern. "Maybe, that aside, how have things been back at the Fort?"

"Since you and Travis have been gone, we've sent Tanner up Hazelton way to look into Emery's murder. The bank was robbed on Sunday, but Alex and Colby killed the two would-be robbers, which apparently might have turned out to be members of the Ridgeback gang. After that took place, Alex showed up in town with the brothers three. He, Colby, and the brothers three were heading west, looking for you, Matt, and we assume you too, Brady. Anyway, they came across the gang, set up an ambush, and killed them. Other than that it's been slow," Ed said half-heartedly with a chuckle.

"Interesting stuff," Brady remarked.

"Next question I have for you, Brady. What happened to your horse and where is your hat?"

Brady told the story.

"Son-of-a-bitch, I bet Travis was some upset about that?"

"I reckon no different than any man that loses his horse. I think he was more upset at having to ride a mule for a couple of days," Brady smiled. "It turns out that Harv knows you, old man."

"Yes sir, I once knew both Harv and Gustev. Had no idea the two of them were still kicking. It's been many years since I last saw either one." The riders grew silent for a few minutes while they carried on.

"Up yon is a good place to take a rest, I'm getting sore," Riley pointed out.

"I reckon a rest is in order," Brady agreed. Dismounting and tethering their horses in the shade, the four riders rested. "So, old man, how'd you ever convince ma to let you come this way," Brady asked.

Ed told the story.

Brady laughed. "Sounds like ma. I bet you ran out of there quicker than ol' Sampson could go."

Ed nodded. "You know how your ma gets once she crosses her arms and starts that foot tapping. It is time to head for the hills."

Even Matt chuckled.

"Anyway, I reckon we've rested long enough. Got at least two-days ride ahead of us. Let's get," Ed said.

For the next few hours, they traveled steadily and by early evening decided it was time to stop for the night. Setting up camp, Riley got a fire started, and threw a couple cans of beans into a pot and added some salt pork to a frying pan. The coffee pot bubbled and perked and he set it on the ground next to the fire. All four helped themselves to a coffee as they waited for the beans and salt pork. The rest of the evening slipped away as they conversed. Finally rolling out their bedrolls the four of them slept. Early Thursday after a quick coffee and biscuits, the four men once more hit the trail.

Ten miles east and heading west was a handful of trouble. Alex, Colby, and the brothers three were getting close. "Are you still figuring that Brady fella and Crawford are coming this way, Alex? We ain't saw no telltale sign of 'em yet," Cape Brubaker questioned.

"It is the only way back to the Fort as far as I know. If Brady is coming this way and he does have Crawford, this is the only route," Alex responded.

"How much longer before you figure we'll see 'em?"

"Not one of us can answer that question, Cape. We can't be sure they are even coming this way yet. It is all speculation and second-hand information," Colby responded.

"Hold on, fellas," Brett began as he tilted his head. "Did ya's hear that?" The five men slowed their horses to stop and listened.

"Might jus' be a deer crashing through the bramble," Martin pointed out.

"You might be right, Martin, I don't hear anything now," Brett responded.

"I think you're getting jittery. I didn't hear a damn thing."

"Nor did I," Colby pointed out.

"It don't matter no more, whatever Martin and I heard ain't making no sound now," Brett cautiously looked around. "Ah, I reckon we is good to go. Let's get."

They travelled only a short distance when once again Brett slowed his horse and looked around. "I heard something again fellas. There is something following us I think. Keep vigilant whilst we carry on," Brett pulled his rifle up and set it across his lap. "I suggest the rest of you make your side-arms and rifles accessible. I do believe we have some redskins about."

"Indians? What the hell are you talking about, Brett. I ain't heard a damn thing. You got some kind of magical ears or something?" Colby tilted his head. "Oh, wait. I think I did hear something jus' now," he looked around and into the bramble from which he thought he heard the sound, but saw nothing. "I hate shit like this. I think Brett is right, though; something is about."

The first arrow whistled by Cape slicing his shirt and nicking his left shoulder. "We're under fire, boys! Head for cover!" Cape yelled as he jumped from his horse. The others did the same as their horses spooked and took off at a gallop heading west. Now undercover, the five men looked around.

"Do you see anything, Cape?"

"Not a damn thing Brett, what about you, Martin? You see anything?"

"Hang on and stay down," Martin responded as he slid up the bank and looked across the trail, his rifle cocked and ready. "I do now."

"What do you see?"

"Alex and Colby, huddling down the trail some," Martin chuckled. He had looked around, but saw only them.

"Jesus Christ, Martin. It ain't time to be making jokes. You see any redskins?" Brett asked as he looked over to Cape and shook his head.

"Like I said, Brett, I only see our cousins. They are crouched and coming our way now. I don't see any redskins. Not a one."

"Keep looking, Martin. Arrows don't jus' come out of nowhere."

"I am looking, Cape, there ain't anything I'm seeing 'cept for Alex, and Colby."

The arrow that Crying Wolf had set loose was meant to do exactly what it did. It startled the five men and sent them and their horses running. If he had wanted to harm them, they would have already been slaughtered or captured and hung upside down with honey slathered across their faces above a red ants nest. That, however, was not his intent. All he wanted was one horse. The only way to get one out of five was to steal one at night. That, however, wasn't nearly as much fun as startling the riders off their saddles and watching in which direction their horses ran. And after some fun, he could choose which one he wanted.

Of course, the riders on the other side of the trail naturally assumed that there were several braves lurking. The white man was stupid that way. He lay in wait for a few minutes long enough for the riders to believe that perhaps the braves had taken off, then slung another arrow, and sent it into the dirt a short distance from where he saw a hat emerge.

"Shit, they ain't left. They is still up across the trail somewhere!"

Crying Wolf chuckled. Now was the time to gather a horse. With agility and speed he darted west, through the brush and bramble until he could see three of the five horses, he watched them as they regained their calm. Then he simply

walked up and made his pick deciding on a sleek, red dun.
Removing the saddle and belongings, he tossed it all onto the
ground and tethered the horse. He did the same with the
others, then gave them one more spook and watched as they
headed deeper into the woods. Satisfied and smiling to
himself he swung up onto the one horse he had kept and
proceeded north.

He had been away from his tribe, the Athabascan, on a
spiritual quest since June. For three months, he wandered the
land, horseless for the past month. Now with the red dun he
had chosen, he could once more travel great distances. Within
a month's time, he would be back among his people, his
spiritual quest complete.

"Martin have you seen anything yet?" Brett asked again.

"When I see something, I'll let you know."

By now, Alex and Colby made the distance to where the
others were huddled.

"Did either of you see anything?"

"About as much as Martin," Colby replied. "It seems odd
that there ain't no more arrows flying don't ya think?"

"I'm beginning to think this whole thing don't seem quite
right," Cape pointed out as he looked over his superficial
wound.

"How much longer do ya's figure we're going to have to
sit here before we go after our horses?" Alex questioned.

Colby looked at him. "Feel free, Alex. They headed west
last I saw."

"What? We're going to sit here then?"

"For the time being, I don't think we have much of a
choice. We ain't sure where the bloody redskins are or how
many there might be. Use your head, Alex."

"That's chicken shit, I think, Brett. You fellas sit here and
keep watching all you want. I'm going after our horses."

Alex slipped down the bank even at the protest of the others and scooted westerly.

"Shit, he's going to get himself killed. We better go after him. C'mon, single file, one at a time, follow me," Colby instructed, "and Martin keep your rifle at the ready. I'll do the same. We see anything that ain't Alex, we'll shoot it."

Martin chuckled. "Damn right, Colby, damn right."

It took them a few minutes to finally, catch up to Alex, he was crouched behind a log and looking across the trail. "I figured yous would be by shortly. I've been watching and looking and ain't saw one damn Indian. I haven't even heard a twig snap. I reckon wherever they may have been, they ain't there now."

"We ain't seen a damn thing either. What kind of a frigging Indian attack was this?" Cape wondered.

Martin was peering over the log when he spotted a saddle on the other side of the trail.

"Hey, have a look over yonder. Is that a saddle I see?"

"I do believe so. It actually looks like yours, Colby."

"Goddamn, you're right, Alex. That is my saddle. So, where the hell is my red dun horse?"

"Where are any of our horses?"

"Jesus, I think we've been bedazzled, goddamn," Brett shook his head feeling foolish.

"What the hell do you mean, Brett?"

"I think we've been fooled like greenhorns. The only thing making any sense to me right now is it was a ploy to steal our horses. We should have clued into it earlier."

"I hope not. I'd rather have it out with a band of renegade redskins than have my horse stolen," Martin said with concern.

"What the hell would we do without our horses?"

"Walk," Colby remarked. "I'm going to jump up here at the count of three and head over to my saddle. You sons of bitches better cover me if arrows start flying. Ready, one, two, three," Colby jumped up and ran across the trail. Then, lying on his stomach next to his saddle he looked around. Oddly enough, he saw three more saddles a distance away. With no arrows flying or war cry yells, he simply stood up. "Looks like it is what ya said, Brett. Your saddle, Alex's and I think Martin's is just over yonder, our gear is scattered too. The Indians is long gone. Took our horses and skedaddled."

"Son-of-a-bitch that was the last thing I wanted to hear," Alex remarked as he walked over to his saddle.

"Where the hell is my shit?" Cape asked as he looked around.

"Looks like your saddle and gear is over here in them bushes, Cape," Alex said as he pointed.

Gathering up their saddles and gear, they sat down in some shade and stewed over their current situation.

"Here we is with no damn horses out in the middle of some damn forest, two and a half days ride west of the Fort. How the hell did we get fooled so easily?" Alex commented as he looked around. "Disastrous, is what this is."

"Bellyaching ain't going to help none. We got our gear and saddles, horses well... we can always pick up more," Colby pointed out as he put a piece of grass between his teeth.

"We know this much. A solution is coming our way, only problem is we ain't a clue when."

"You mean, Brady and possibly Matt?"

"I do so, Colby. That'd be two horses more than what we have now."

"Means one fella would always be walking, and three saddles short of horses. You really ought to learn some mathematics, Alex," Martin said with a smirk.

Alex looked at him with derision and shook his head. "Switching riders and having one fella always walking wouldn't be nearly as bad as five fellas walking carrying saddles and gear. With horses, it'd be easy enough to figure a way to haul that shit. Maybe it ain't mathematics I need to learn, and you, Martin, need to learn common sense."

"Touché, Alex," Martin replied with a wink and smile.

Time dragged on as the Brubaker crew and Colby pondered. It was too late in the day to start walking. To kill time they built up an evening camp. With some hours of daylight left they whittled sticks, arranged their gear for easy transporting in case they did have to walk out. They even got into an old favourite they played as kids called 'Spread'. It was a simple game where two of them would stand facing each other, and throw a knife into the ground as close to the other's foot as possible. It didn't matter if it was left or right, the object was to make the other fall over by doing the splits.

If it stuck in the ground, it was one point and the other had to move his foot to where the knife had stuck in. If it hit the other's foot the thrower automatically lost and of course the other ended up with a knife sticking out of their foot if they weren't quick enough to move it. Whoever was left standing at the end with the most points was the winner.

It was Cape, who pulled off the win that day. He walked away as the 'Spread' world champion.

"That brought back memories," Colby said as he thought about how much fun it had actually been. "Damn, I still got scars from when we was kids. You fellas always aimed for my feet."

"You was jus' not fast enough to move your foot, that's all that was," Brett said as he looked at the others and winked.

"Bullshit, usually ya had one or the others distracting me and then you'd make your throw. It was like yous all did it the same bloody way, every bloody time."

"That is called unlucky odds."

"I'll show you unlucky odds, Martin," Colby said as he jumped up and the two began to wrestle. Finally, winded and sweat-ridden, they lay on their backs and looked up to the sky. "That brought back memories, too. We used to wrestle like that a lot. I used to stick dried-up cow pies in your mouth," Colby chuckled.

"Every time you left, I always had a shitty taste in my mouth." There was no holding back the laughter after that. That night out in the middle of nowhere without horses and in the company of each other, the five of them realised that although their lives had been different, with one side of the family being dysfunctional while the other plain crazy, they shared some pretty amazing memories.

The twists and turns their lives took, as they grew older had whisked away their innocence of youth. Who they were today had been forged during that time. That was their reality, good, bad, or otherwise.

Chapter 12

It was Riley, who spotted the first of the unsaddled horses. "Look at that," he said as pointed at the horse that stood nonchalantly a short distance off the trail.

"Jesus, I think that is Alex's horse," Ed pulled up his rifle while Riley and Brady did the same. "We best get Matt undercover. Not sure, what this is all about, go on, Brady, get undercover, and stay with Matt. You hear shooting, don't hesitate."

Brady led Matt's horse into the bramble off the trail. Swung off his horse and helped Matt down from his. Then, stepping forward with his rifle cocked and shouldered, he was ready to cover both Ed and Riley should anything go awry. The two men slowly approached the horse and as they drew close, it walked right out into the open over to them.

Riley slipped a piece of rope over its neck and led it back to the trail. Ed stayed back for a few moments until Riley and the horse were in the clear. Riley now sat vigilant and ready to cover Ed as he made the distance back to the trail himself. They were half expecting an ambush, and for a few minutes they waited ready to give whatever it was that might be given, but nothing transpired.

"This is a bit off, Ed. What do you suppose is going on?"

Ed shook his head. He wasn't sure himself. "Whatever it is, Riley, it can't be good," he looked again at the horse. Sure enough, it was Alex's, he could tell by the single diamond shape on the horse's forehead. "This is Alex's horse; I'm certain of that." At that moment they heard the neigh from another horse and quickly turned in that direction, their rifles shouldered. They saw another horse lurking in the bush and same as the first, no saddle, or gear.

"This here for certain is starting to get weird, Ed," Riley lowered his rifle.

"Yep, we can assume that is likely another one of the horses belonging to one of the others. I don't reckon it is Colby's as his is a red dun. It could be one of the brothers' horses. What I'm finding interesting is they ain't saddled. No reins, bridal, or nothing, not even gear." The two of them continued scouting the area. It didn't take long to see yet another horse stripped of all accessories the same as the first and second.

"That's three, Ed. I think I'm starting to get a picture of what is going on here."

"Me too, we find one more, but not another, then I think we're looking at the old Indian 'grab a horse shoot' trick, often referred to as *grabahorseshoot*." The two men chuckled.

"What's going on, old man?" Brady asked in a hushed voice.

"Awe, shit, sorry, Brady. Yeah, yous can come on up. This ain't what we were expecting."

"Couldn't you have mentioned it earlier? I've been standing here ready to give you cover and you're telling there's no damn reason for it," Brady shook his head as he turned and helped Matt onto his horse. Then, leading both horses, he walked over to Ed and Riley. "If this ain't what we were expecting then what the hell is it?"

"Grabahorseshoot," Ed responded.

Brady tilted his head, confused. "Huh, say again, a frigging what?"

"Grabahorseshoot," Ed repeated as he continued looking into the horizon.

"Oh, of course, one of those... Exactly what is one of those, old man? Do we kill it? Can we eat it?"

"Nope, can't kill it, can't eat it," It was Riley who responded this time.

"Don't you start with me too, Riley. One old senile coot is enough. Now which one of you'd is gonna give me an understandable explanation on what it is we're looking at here?"

"It is called 'grab a horse shoot'. It's an old Indian trick," Ed began to explain.

"Is this gonna take a while? Should I set up camp?" Brady asked sarcastically.

"It is getting late. I reckon here is as good as any place. Sure go ahead, set up."

Brady looked at Ed with a frown. "Are you serious, old man?"

Ed finally broke his gaze of the horizon and turned to look at Brady. "Sure, nothing wrong with this place at all. Anyway, as I was explaining to you, Brady, what is likely going on here is an old Indian trick used to steal horses or a horse. Usually it is only one or two lone renegades, who pull the stunt off. Instead of stealing one horse off of you at night, they have a little fun. First, they wait until the moment is right, then they sling a couple arrows at a rider or group of riders, scaring the shit out of most white men.

The riders usually dismount quickly, and head for cover thinking that they are under attack. The Indian's true intent ain't to kill or maim, jus' to scare ya. Staying hidden, they take note in which direction the riders' horses are going. They sit and wait a while longer then they sling a couple more arrows at you and take off after the horses.

Most riders stay undercover thinking that the Indian's are still about, but they ain't. They likely already have your horses and have picked out the one or two they want. They strip all of them of their gear, saddles and such, since they ain't got no use for that kind of shit. Then, they spook the others off into the bush or wherever, and ride away on the ones they've kept, hence 'Grabahorseshoot'," Ed explained.

Brady rolled his eyes.

"Sure...okay. Now why didn't you say that in the first place?" *It's like they have brain worms, or something, geez...* Brady thought as he carried on setting up their evening camp, while Ed and Riley continued to look for horses.

"We gonna, lead these animals with us when we leave in the morning?"

"I don't know, Riley. We know whom they belong to and we know that they are likely coming this way. I say we let them know where they can find their horses if we come across them. Chances are a couple might follow behind us as we head east."

"All right, then," Riley said as he slipped the rope off of Alex's horse. The horse pranced a distance away and stopped to feed on grass. "I don't reckon them horses is gonna go far."

"Nope, I don't think so either," Ed swung off his horse and tethered him. Then he gave Brady a hand in setting up for the night. He helped Matt get comfortable and loosened off the handcuffs. "Does that feel better, Matt?"

"A bit, thanks, Ed," Matt shrugged.

Riley strode over and dismounted, "I ain't saw more horses, I guess we could say that there might be two renegade Indian's running 'bout," Riley sat down and sighed. "Tomorrow is five-day. I guess that puts us back at the Fort by seven-day, eh Ed?"

Brady raised an eyebrow and looked quizzically to Riley. "What? Five-day... have both of yous lost some brain function since I've been gone. Tomorrow is Friday, Riley."

"How many fingers you got on one hand, Brady?"

"As many as you have Riley, five."

It was then he understood. "I see, Monday in Riley's world is 'one-day', Tuesday, well let me guess is 'two-day' and so on. I'm surprised you can still count that high. I think you and Ed have been drinking shine and have lost a few marbles by doing so. Grabahorseshoot, five-day," Brady shook his head at their antics. "I just might turn around here and head west again. Crazy bastards," he commented as he gathered wood for their evening fire. Finally, with the task done, he sat down with the others. "Did I mention to you old man, that we was hired by a longhair?"

"What are you talking about, Brady?"

"I was approached by a fellow goes by the name of Leif Vanfell whilst Matt and I were heading this way. He'd like for McCoy's to hand over this five hundred in gold nuggets." Brady reached into his saddlebag and tossed a satchel to Ed. "To... get this, Whiskey Tooth George. He's paid us five hundred in nuggets too, for doing it."

"Why would the longhairs want to do that?" Ed questioned as he fumbled with the satchel. By weight alone, he knew it was easily worth five hundred dollars. "Since when do longhairs talk to valley dwellers?" Ed shook his head dumbfounded.

"When you sent Tanner, Travis and me to track ol' Whiskey Tooth down and we came across them dead longhairs? It wasn't Whiskey Tooth, who did the killing of the longhairs. It was Indian's, Whiskey Tooth sent the Indians running though. Anyway, Vanfell wants to reward Whiskey Tooth with that five hundred in nuggets for doing so."

"Who do you reckon is going to want to chase after that old codger?" Ed questioned.

"I don't know," Brady shrugged. "That is your call. You know what else old man, Travis, and I ran across Whiskey Tooth when we were heading west. Had a coffee with him and all, anyway, after our sit down with him and he's leaving, you know what he says to me?"

"I ain't got a clue Brady, what did he say to you?"

"He says 'say hello to that nephew, Ed, of mine', referring to you old man. Anything you'd like to add to that so I get a clear picture?" Brady asked with curiosity.

"So he let the cat out of the bag. All right, yep, he's my uncle. He's your granddaddies brother, makes him your great uncle, Brady. That is all there is to it," Ed shrugged with indifference.

"I know what it makes him to me, but why didn't I know beforehand?"

"For the obvious reasons Brady. C'mon, we're law enforcement type, he's a law breaker." That was all Ed wanted to say about it. Brady didn't question again.

"All right, I guess, like Travis would say, it is what it is." Brady stirred the coals and looked to the horizon, wondering what other kinds of secrets had been kept from him. It was no reason to feel slighted and, he knew that, if there were other family secrets and, he didn't know about them, in all actuality it didn't matter 'cause, he had lived without knowing for this long already.

Brady didn't know it, but Ed was looking at him from across the fire, a solemn look on his face. Brady wasn't a kid anymore and Ed knew he had to come to terms with that. There were things Brady didn't know about, some of it may have been important, a lot of it though wasn't. He decided then to start taking mental notes of things that he thought in time might be important to Brady and once they made it back to the Fort, he'd write it all down on paper. From that day on anything that came to his aging mind that was of relevance, he'd write down too. That way at least if things never came up, there'd always be a handwritten record by his own hand that one day Brady would discover. *A memoir...* Ed thought with inspiration.

Chapter 13

Riley warmed his hands above the flames of the fire and looked to the horizon. A pallid sun slowly crept into the placid blue sky. He added another stick to the fire to fuel the flames. Mingling with their horses were four others. They had counted only three the night before.

Riley chuckled softly to himself, *yep, a good ol' grabahorseshoot,* he thought as he poured a coffee and stood up. With coffee in hand, he walked closer to the four stray horses to get a better look at them. The red dun that Colby owned was the one that was missing. He brought the tin cup up to his lips and took a swallow. *A learning experience for each of them greenhorns, I reckon.*

He looked down the trail as far as the misty morning allowed and made an educated guess that Colby and the others were likely between five to ten miles away. He made that guess on his experiences when he had lost a horse or two. Most times the animal didn't go further than that. Chances were, neither would have the four strays.

Matt woke up next and pulled himself out of his bedroll. Making his way over to some bushes, he relieved himself. That done, he gave it a shake and did up his fly, then walked over to the fire where Riley sat.

"Morning, Matt. It was a cold one last night, wasn't it?" Riley said, as he offered Matt a coffee.

"It was."

That is all he said. Riley understood his reasons for not speaking too liberally. Anything he said could be used against him in court. Riley, though, never put too much thought into that horseshit. Being alone with Matt, while the others remained sleeping, Riley asked why his name was listed in the notebook Tanner found.

"It's all right with me if you don't talk much Matt, the three of us get it," Riley began referring to himself, Ed and Brady. "As you know, one of McCoy's men found your notebook, which ultimately put us onto your possible whereabouts, and lo and behold here ya are. My name was in that book, Matt. Why?" Riley asked, as he slurped from the cup in his hand.

Matt looked over to him.

"How can I be sure anything I tell you won't jeopardize my current situation?" Matt asked, as a matter- of- fact.

"Shit, most of us in this business, don't care too much about reporting every conversation which we have with our prisoners to the upper laws. Right now, my question and your answer is off the record. I'm only wondering why my name is in that book. I can't think of any reason at all, 'cept the fact that I've tracked you for some time now, whenever the mood struck me. Other bounty hunters have done the same, but we don't see their names in that book, so that can't be it."

"I'll tell you. You were the only one that ever got close. When I discovered who you were, I wrote your name down. That way I knew if you were on my trail, I had to be extra vigilant. That, Mr. Scott, is truth."

"I have to tell ya, Matt. That made me a might flush. I can't believe it is that simple, though," Riley commented with doubt.

"You don't have to believe it. It is that simple. Now I don't reckon I'll be speaking much more."

Matt and Riley continued with their stare down for a few brief seconds then each turned their head. It would be left at that. Finally, Ed and Brady woke up. They made their way over to the warmth of the fire.

"Morning Ed, Brady. Last night was a cold bugger eh?"

"Only going to get colder, too, but yeah, damn chilly," Ed agreed as he warmed his hands.

Brady poured himself and Ed a coffee and offered up more to anyone else who wanted one. Setting the pot down, he looked over to where their horses were tethered, and saw the other four milling around.

"Looks like another joined the others, eh?"

"Colby's red dun is the only one missing out of the five," Riley said as he stood up and walked over next to Brady. "I reckon that puts the riders five maybe ten miles west of here."

Brady looked on as he contemplated.

"Really? How'd you come up with that?" he asked.

"You ever lose a horse, Brady?"

"Have so, more times than I'd like to think. What of it?"

"How far did you have to hike to find it and round it up?" Riley questioned as he took a swallow of coffee.

"Likely no further than them distances you mentioned."

"There you go. There is the answer," Riley smirked, he felt smug.

"The horses I lost, Riley, were still packing saddles, gear, and whatnot. You don't suppose that has a bearing on how far a healthy horse can travel?"

"Of course it does," Riley responded as he brought his hand up to his chin and thought about it. Goddamn it if Brady didn't have a point.

"These four ain't packing anything like that. A horse with no gear or rider is obviously going to be able to travel further and faster, ain't he, Riley," Brady smirked as he looked at old Riley who was brooding.

"Ya, jus' ruined my day, Brady. Thanks."

"Shame, that is. Anyway, I'd say the riders could be anywhere between ten and twenty miles east, that be my guess," Brady challenged.

Riley dumped out what was left of his coffee.

"Yep, you're probably right. I never considered gear and shit. Come on, Brady. Let me buy you another coffee, ya punk-ass kid," Riley chuckled as he and Brady returned to the fire and sat down.

Ed waited until the two of them filled their cups before he began with his speech. He wanted everyone to be on the same page, since there was no way of knowing, what might lie ahead with Alex, Colby, and the 3 brothers. "It's going to be an interesting day today as we head east."

"True as that might be, how about giving me a refresher on these three new Brubakers that have come about? Do either of you know anything about them?" Brady wanted to know. He couldn't be part of the team without knowing the rules, or who, his opponents were.

"Only thing I know is the obvious. They're Brubakers. I know the one kid Martin, the youngest of the bunch, packs around a Marlin rifle, kind of, like the one Colby has. From that take down of the Ridgeback gang, one can assume he knows how to use it. The others, Brett and Cape, well, they sport nice looking pistols." That was all Ed knew of them. Riley knew less.

Brady was unimpressed. "That adds up to what, that they're all shooters, have practiced ambushing, and are Brubakers. Hmmm, that is a nice assortment of nothing."

"Keep in mind, Brady, there wasn't much time with them arriving at the Fort and Riley and I being here. They rolled in Saturday evening and by Sunday had moved to a camp outside the Fort. The way Colby was talking when your ma and I ran into them late Sunday afternoon, it sounded like they were staying put 'till mid-week. I never saw them again after that and Riley only saw them on Saturday. By Monday we were heading west," Ed pointed out.

"It don't matter either way. The point of the matter is the fact that we know where they are and what it is they're likely doing there. Conjecture or not, it's a known fact that Alex and Colby were both going to be coming after Matt for his bounty. Whether McCoy's was looking for him or not, if we hadn't found Matt first, Colby and his bunch would have every right to do so. All they know is that we're looking for Matt, too. They don't know we have him. Nor do they know that we're here with you and Matt right now. What they are expecting to be coming down this trail, is one rider, maybe two," Riley wanted to make that clear. "And that is our ace in the hole," he added with a smile.

"Then let's send one rider down that trail. If they see only me riding back they'll keep right on thinking we ain't got our hands on Matt, in fact I'll be certain to let them know that Matt managed to slip through my fingers. You old man and Riley can keep me covered from a distance should things go awry. I'll be sure to let them know, that I spotted their missing horses or at least four of them, up yon somewhere feeding.

Once they get their panties untied that their horses are nearby, chances are they'll go looking for them. Timing here though I reckon is going be important, after you see me continuing east, that be your signal to send one more rider down the trail, the Brubakers and Colby probably ain't going to give a shit on who might be traipsing by, they'll be too concerned in regard to gathering their horses. After that send the last two and we'll all meet up down the trail some. We'll be hours ahead of the Brubakers and Colby. Who knows maybe they'll continue west."

"Problem with that though as I see it what if they recognise one of us," Riley questioned.

"Don't get close enough to let that happen, the only one needing to be recognised is me. Or the three of you can head northerly through the bramble and we can rendezvous same as before down the trail some. The four of us doing that don't make much sense, since we wouldn't be able to send them off with false hope that Matt Crawford is still at large," Brady offered as a second solution. It was the one that both and Ed and Riley favoured.

"I like that idea of heading northerly cross-country. The forest down that way is easy to travel through with enough obscurity to slip right by. Riley, what do you figure?" Ed asked as he looked at Riley for an answer.

"I'm with you, Ed. I also like the idea of letting them think we ain't got Matt," Riley smirked.

"All right, that is how we'll play it," Ed responded. With a solid plan, they finished their coffees, gathered their gear and began their journey along the trail heading east. It was a few hours later when in the distance they could see a crew of men huddling in a clearing. The distance though prevented them of any clear picture on who they were. Chances were it was Colby and crew.

"Right up yonder I reckon are the Brubaker's and Colby."

The four men looked on. "I reckon that is them," Brady said with certainty. "I'll carry on alone from here. Yous can make yourselves invisible for now. Get in a good position of rifle range and keep an eye on me. Once I continue to head easterly, that'll be the signal for you to head north." Brady inhaled deeply. "Here we go," he said as turned his horse and continued onward.

Ed and Riley, leading Matt and his horse, took to cover. They found an area that was within rifle range and from which they could see the five men they were avoiding. Tethering their horses and helping Matt get comfortable, they set up for the long shots if they were needed. It seemed like forever before they could see Brady gaining distance on the men in the clearing.

It was Alex, who heard the clip-clop of a horse and rider approaching. "Hear that, fellas? There is a horse approaching. Brett, you got that spy glass ready?"

Brett reached into his saddlebag and pulled the scope out. Making his way to a spot where he could look up the trail, he lay down and brought it up to his eye.

"There is a single man is approaching. Have a look Alex. Is that Brady McCoy?" he handed the scope over to Alex who peered through it.

"Damn it, that is Brady, all right," Alex looked beyond Brady to see if there were any others following. There wasn't. "No one else is about either, that I can see."

"What do you suppose that means?" Brett asked.

"It simply means that Brady is alone. No Matt, no Travis. This kind of throws a kibosh into our plan," Alex handed the scope back to Brett. "I guess we wait and see what he has to say."

"We ain't gonna take his horse?" Cape questioned.

"He being alone ain't worth killing for one bloody horse. Not to mention that would be all we gained. If Matt been with him there would be more at stake," Alex answered.

"Ten thousand reasons to off him then, now though, not much point," Martin added.

Alex, Colby, and the Brubaker's sat down on their saddles waiting for Brady to approach closer. There was no point in trying to hide. Brady being who he was would likely send help in the form of a wagon or something to pick them up. They'd just have to wait a few days longer. They had enough gear and supplies to manage that long, not to mention the numbers to take on almost anything that might come their way.

Finally, Brady made the distance. He slowed his horse down and with a look of surprise got his horse to stop. "Alex, Colby, what the hell yous doing out here, and who is that you got with you?" he asked as though he had no clue.

"Glad to see you, Brady. These are our cousins, Brett, Cape, and Martin," Colby said as he approached. "We were heading west and got over run by some Indians which then stole our horses. They left our gear though."

"I ran across some horses south-east of the trail, ten or so miles ago. I was wondering what they was doing out here alone and such. I know they ain't wild ponies, could be they're yours."

"How far away you say?" Alex asked.

"I'd guess ten or so miles. Saw only four though."

"Did ya notice if there was a red dun in the mix?"

Brady brought his hand to his chin as though he were in deep thought. "Shit, I can't say for sure, Colby. There were four horses for sure. There might have been a fifth that I didn't see."

"Damn, why would any redskin leave horses about?" Cape asked as he stood up. "That doesn't make sense. Maybe they are wild ponies after all."

"Nope, there ain't been wild ponies in this area for as long as I've been alive. These seemed well behaved like they were trained. Didn't even spook when my horse and I drew close, followed us for a bit too, then they kind of stuck together and headed southerly." Brady hoped he was convincing enough.

"So the redskins took our horses, stripped them of their gear, and set 'em loose. That don't sound right to me, none," Martin pointed out.

Brady shrugged, "I don't know what else to tell ya, I wasn't here when they was about, didn't see none as I travelled this way either. It does seem kind of odd. I'll give ya that. If you want, I ain't got a problem with doubling one of yous back to the Fort, to pick up some horses if you don't think the ones up yon some ain't yours."

"Probably would take us less time to gather up those you saw, if they're ours. If they ain't though, then I guess we're kind of stuck between a rock and hard place. Shit, I dunno, what do you fellas figure?" Alex asked as he looked up the trail.

Colby looked at the others.

"I say we split up, and go looking for our horses. If there ain't been wild ponies in this area for a while, I don't reckon there'd be any now. Chances are them be our horses. Why the Indians never took 'em is a bit troublesome and don't make much sense. Maybe they wanted to divert us from one thing or another."

"I think I agree with Colby. I say we go find our horses."

"Yeah, I reckon that is best. All right, well, Brady thanks for letting us know. I guess we got some horses to round up."

"You folks have enough gear and stuff? It could take a day or two to find them, Alex."

"We got all we need, Brady. Thanks for asking," Alex responded. "By the way, we heard you and Travis was out looking for Matt Crawford. Did ya's have any luck?"

Brady chuckled and shook his head as though it were a fair question.

"That son-of-a-bitch slipped through our fingers more times than not. We got close a couple of times, but it never came out in the wash. He evaded us somehow."

"And Travis, where is he?"

"That is confidential information," Brady smiled. "Nah, not really, he's headed west where we have another job pending. Why you ask?"

"Curious is all, I reckon."

"Well there you have it. If you folks is all right, I need to get back to the Fort and business as usual. Hopefully the old man and Riley ain't killed each other by now."

"Yeah, I reckon. All right, let's split up and find them damn horses," Alex said as he tilted his hat at Brady. "We'll see you around, Brady."

"Good luck, fellas," Brady responded as he heeled his horse. His heart beat fast as he turned his back on them and continued east. He was half expecting a bullet. Ed and Riley watched as Brady continued east.

"There is our signal looks like he's convinced them. Let's get while we can," Ed said as he and Riley helped Matt back onto his horse, swung up onto their rides, and headed north.

Brady had only travelled a short distance when he saw the arrow laying there in the dirt. He swung off his horse and picked it up. *Indians eh, and one arrow...* Brady chuckled, as he looked back, the way he came, *yep, the one renegade sure fooled them,* he thought as he slipped the arrow into his rolled up bedroll for a keepsake. *I guess I shouldn't make fun. Likely would have fooled me too, if I didn't know what a 'grabahorseshoot' was,* he smiled as he climbed back onto his horse and continued east.

It was mid-day when the others made the rendezvous with him. He heard them coming through the bush before he saw them. He slowed his horse down and waited with his rifle ready in case it wasn't who he thought it was. Sure enough, though, the three riders cut up the bank and onto the trail.

"That right there is some exceptional timing, old man," Brady smiled as he made the distance to where they waited for him.

The Missing Years- Part IV
A Tyrell Sloan western adventure

"It was easy going. Saw you a few minutes back, but couldn't quite catch up with you then. I take it that Colby and the Brubakers ain't any wiser on where Matt may be."

"Nope, they figure I lost him. The plan went well, I reckon. They're miles west looking for their horses and we're miles closer to the Fort. I picked this up on my way." He pulled out the arrow and showed it off.

Riley looked it over and chuckled. "It's Athabasca made. Don't usually see them 'round here," he looked more closely. "I think it is actually Crying Wolf's."

"And who might he be?" Brady questioned as Riley handed it back to him.

"He's one hell of a scary son of a bitch, I can tell ya that. His arrows always have purple feathers. It's kind of like his signature. Colby and the others are damn lucky he only wanted a horse. Him being 'round here, if indeed that is whose arrow I believe it to be, then we better keep our eyes peeled," Riley pointed out. "He's more of threat than Colby and the others."

"One Indian, Riley, come on. How can he be more of a threat than five hoodwinks with pistols and rifles?" Brady wanted to know as they continued east.

"Fearlessness and cunning, that's how. We would be lucky to see him before he pounced. He once slaughtered fifteen Crowfoot in one day singlehandedly."

"Did you see it happen, Riley?"

"That I did not, Brady. I was told about it though by one of the Crowfoot who managed to get away."

"So it is hearsay."

"Sure, if you wanna believe that. I, on the other hand, believe what I was told. I know this much with certainty. I wouldn't want to run across him on a good day."

"Then let's hope we don't," Brady remarked candidly.

Chapter 14

"We spent all evening trying to gather our horses. Found four, but not mine. Goddamn!" Colby said as he added a stick to their morning fire.

"Are you still harping on that? You ain't shut up about it since last night. Who knows once we continue west, we might run across that red dun of yours, Colby. In the meantime, I guess we double. I ain't got a problem with that," Martin pointed out.

"Of course you wouldn't. You have your damn horse." Colby shook his head, as he looked westerly.

"I figure the best thing to do is head back east to the Fort. There are horses can be bought in that shithole. Or we can carry on westerly and hope we come across your red dun or a place that we could steal or buy a horse from. I reckon we have the same chances of maybe running into your red dun, as we would going west," Alex made argument.

"The Fort is guaranteed to have horses. That part is sensible. Heading west, we ain't sure there'd be any horses to steal, buy, trade or otherwise. That is the gamble. I think heading back east under these circumstances deals us a better hand," Colby agreed.

"We might even be able to pick up more info on whereabouts Brady might have lost Crawford. I don't reckon the McCoy's are caring too much 'bout him no more. They've been trying to bring him in for a while," Alex smirked.

"That there is a good thought too, Alex. Shit, what happened to you over night? Get some smarts back, did ya?" Martin teased.

Alex looked at him, "I always had smarts. I reckon you lost some, punk," he teased back.

"So the geniuses of the crowd here have come up with the five of us heading back east and get Colby a horse. We have four horses and five cowboys. Now, why can't it be that three of us continue west and one horse and two riders carry on east," Brett pointed out as he took the last slug of his morning coffee.

"I don't reckon there is any reason that can't happen. We could always meet up down the trail some. Colby and whoever rides him into the Fort can always do some snooping regarding Crawford."

"That's what I'm talking about, Alex. Since your friend's the McCoy's ain't got Crawford and we know that he was heading west to that place you called Willow Gate, ain't it likely then that Crawford is still west. You get where I'm going with this."

"Do so, and I like it Brett."

"I don't give a shit either way as long as one of yous rides me back to the Fort. Don't care which one either, if we end up separated by too many days we'll meet up in Willow Gate. That doesn't hurt my feelings one damn bit."

"I'll double you back," Martin offered. "It'll take us three days give 'er take. Anyone know how far that damn place Willow Gate is?"

No one did.

"All right so, we ain't sure how far away it is. Like what Colby says though, we end up separated by too many days, we'll eventually meet up at the Gate. Simple."

"Makes sense, sure. All right I say we pack up and get." An hour later, Brett, Cape and Alex headed west, Colby and Martin east.

"It is going to be a damn pain packing this saddle as we carry on, Martin," Colby pointed out as he tried to get the saddle into a more comfortable position across his lap.

"Ah, quit your cry-babying. We only got three days to go," Martin chuckled.

"I see how this trip is gonna turn out."

"Ya never know, Colby, we might come across that red dun of yours jus' as well as the others might too."

"What do you suppose they'd do, if they did?"

"I'd hope they'd throw a tether over it and run it back this way."

"Brett and Cape might suggest something like that but Alex wouldn't give a shit. He's a bit of a dink in case you don't know, Martin."

"I know all about Alex, and yep, he's a dink."

Tyrell and Bannock had been travelling together for four days. Soon the trail would fork off in different directions. One led west to Hell's Bottom and the other, the less-travelled trail, headed northerly toward Willow Gate and Mac Rider's place. Tyrell could continue on to Hell's Bottom with Bannock, though he knew it would slow him down and he had already been slowed down enough.

"Another few miles of travel, Bannock, and I'll be heading north-westerly," Tyrell said as, he, and Bannock stopped at a nearby creek to let their horses drink and to water the piglets in Bannock's wagon.

"Ya ain't coming to Hell's Bottom?" Bannock asked with disappointment.

"I thought about it and figure I'm so behind that I best carry on straight through to Willow Gate."

"Ya could head that way from Hell's Bottom," Bannock pointed out.

"I know, but it'll slow me down a few more days," Tyrell began, as he looked north, "I'll head up north. Could knock off a few days ride; might make Willow Gate by early

October. I do have one more stop to make. I'd like to stop in on Mac and Rose Rider's place. They live about ten miles from here. From there I'll head up through Big Little Creek and cut back west near there."

"Ya gonna go up through that territory alone?" Bannock asked with concern. "That area is full of renegades and not jus' Indians either."

"I know that, but it is the quickest route to Willow Gate from Mac's place. I reckon I'll be okay, I know the area a bit."

"I don't know Tyrell. One man alone going up that way don't sound like a very good idea to me."

"Shit, Bannock, you, and I have travelled through worse areas in our time. One only has to be careful," Tyrell tried to convince himself. He knew heading up through Big Little Creek could be perilous, but he needed to make some distance and that route so happened to be the quickest from where he was now.

"I only wish you weren't going alone. Damn, if I didn't have a wagon full of piglets, I'd go with you. Two men travelling through there is better than one," Bannock said as he and Tyrell once more hit the trail.

"Ah, no worries, Bannock, I'll do okay."

"I sure hope so. Once you get done with Willow Gate, how 'bout coming to Hell's Bottom. That way I'll know you is still living," Bannock invited.

"When I'm done with the job, I could do that. It might not be 'til next spring."

"Makes no never mind to me, as long as I know you are living."

Tyrell chuckled. "All right, Bannock, I'll do that."

"Good," Bannock replied as they continued onward.

The Missing Years- Part IV
A Tyrell Sloan western adventure

Before the warm September sun was at its peak that day, the two riders came to the fork in the trail.

"Here we are, Bannock," Tyrell said as they stopped.

"I guess this is where we part ways for now." Bannock said, as he looked at Tyrell.

"It is too. I'll tell you though, Bannock, it was sure nice running into you and all. Even though it was only for a few days ride together and couple bottles of whiskey. I'll never forget the sixty-seven pig incident or the time we've spent together on this trail. I'll always remember it as a 'few days with an old friend'," Tyrell chuckled. "Next time we get together let's hope there ain't trail riding involved and we can sit back and bullshit rather than bullshit and ride."

"We'll make it happen, Tyrell." Bannock looked west, then back to Tyrell. "You get done with your business up there in Willow Gate make damn sure you stop by. I'll be waiting, Tyrell Sloan," Bannock said as he snapped the reins and he and his wagon full of piglets headed west.

"You can count on it, Bannock, indeed you can. Be safe." Tyrell watched Bannock and his wagon crest a hill and vanish from his sight. He sat there for a few minutes somber and saddened as he looked on. Black Dog sat nearby. His gaze too was west. "One day, Black Dog, we'll get back to our roots. C'mon, let's get."

Tyrell heeled his horse and headed north toward Big Little Creek his final destination being Willow Gate. First, though, he wanted to see Mac and Rose. He travelled steadily stopping only once. It was late afternoon when he and Black Dog turned up the trail to Mac Rider's place. Mac's old house still stood, but was silent. It meant one thing. Mac and Rose had managed to build their dream home a few miles further up the trail. It was he and Mac, who had horse-logged the area where it was that Mac, wanted to build. It was also, where, he, and Earl Brubaker, had their confrontation that ended up costing Earl, his life. Tyrell thought back to that time. *It seems so long ago...* he thought.

It took only a few minutes to make the distance to the big log house. Mac stood on the top veranda and looked on.

"Is there something I can help you with, mister?" Mac asked as the horse and rider drew close. "This here is private property."

Tyrell had his hat slightly tilted over his face a big smile across his face. He stopped his horse, tilted his hat back, and looked up.

Mac took a second glance. "Jesus Christ, Travis Sweet!" he exclaimed with surprise.

"Howdy Mac," Tyrell spoke as Mac called to Rose.

"Rose, look who it is," Mac yelled for her as she came darting out and stood next to him.

"Travis! Oh, my God! Go Mac open the bottom doors!" she shooed Mac off. "Come, Mac is opening the bottom door," she scooted back inside and darted down the stairs.

Tyrell swung off his horse and tethered him by the watering trough. The big solid wooden door opened and there stood both Mac and Rose.

"Goddamn, let us have a look at you. It is nice to see you, Travis. You were the last person I'd have ever thunk that I'd see again. How have you been?"

"Been well, Mac. And you and Rose?" he looked over to Rose and smiled. She had tears in her eyes. "Ah, shit, come here, Rose." She stepped forward and he gave her a hug. "It sure has been a while, or seems like. I have to tell you, Mac, it is good to see you both and that your dreams have come to fruition. Nice looking house you have built up here."

"It wouldn't have happened without you. I'd still be clearing the land. We only finished it up this past summer.

Some of Rose's family gave us a hand. The Blackfoot, I tell ya, know how to build. Once they started helping, things went up fast. Jesus, Travis, I can't express how damn happy I am to see you. C'mon, I'll show you around inside." Following Mac and Rose inside, he took off his hat and looked around.

"Whew, a lot of nice work done here." Tyrell said as he looked around. The house was magnificent both inside and out, it took a few minutes for Mac to show him around. The tour ended on the top veranda. He put his hands on the railing and looked out across the land. Mac and Rose's place was a fortress. "I'd have to say Mac, that this is one hell of a nice build."

"Thank you, Travis. Rose and I like it too. Tell me what is new with you?"

"I've been working with McCoy's Bounty Hunting Service out of the Fort. I've been with them for the past while. I'm heading to a pending job north of here some. I figured since I was passing by I'd stop in and make sure you were still kicking."

"The McCoy's, I've heard of them. Well good for you then, good for you indeed, Travis."

"It is a good cover, Mac, for... well, you know."

"I do and trust me I ain't spoke a word about the fact. I still believe and always will that Heath Roy, and of course Earl Brubaker, both deserved what they had coming. Nope, I do not know any man named Tyrell Sloan; I know Travis Sweet," Mac assured.

"I thank you for that, Mac. I'm glad you have kept the truth quiet," Tyrell said with sincerity. "I'm getting closer to proving my innocence of any wrong doing regarding Heath Roy's death and this pending job I spoke of might be what does it."

"There is nothing more you need to tell me, Travis. I already know you are innocent."

It was then that Rose called out.

"I have biscuits and coffee now. Come, you two, before they cool," Rose called from the bottom of the stairs.

"Yum, coffee and biscuits made by Rose; let's get, Mac. No use lollygagging. Lead the way," Tyrell said with a smile as he and Mac headed down the stairs. "It sure smells good, Rose, let me tell ya. It's been a while since I ate your biscuits. I ain't ever ate, a better one." The two of them sat down at the table while Rose brought them coffee and set down a basket of fresh cornmeal biscuits.

"Help yourselves," she gestured to the biscuits. "I will bring jam." Turning, she darted back to the cooking area and returned with the jam. "It is wild raspberry and cloudberry, sweet and tart. I made it last summer before this place was finished. I will make more too next year. Travis what is there new with you?" she asked as she spread jam on a biscuit.

Tyrell waited to finish chewing his biscuit before he answered. "First off, that jam is very good, and the biscuits, geez they're perfect," he took a swallow of coffee. "I've found work with McCoy's Bounty Hunting Service's out of the Fort. I've been working with them since leaving here." Tyrell spread jam on another biscuit. "It isn't too bad, I suppose. The pay is good and I'm happy with it for now."

"I'm glad you have found happiness. With us here when you worked, you weren't so happy. You were missing something."

"Trust me, Rose it wasn't because I was here with you and Mac working. The work I was doing did make me happy. I was maybe a little lonely, but I wouldn't say I was unhappy. I grew quite attached to you both. You are like family to me.

Always have been and always will be." Tyrell finished his second biscuit.

"It is nice of this for you to say. I will get you more coffee, would you like?"

"Yes, thank you, Rose." Tyrell handed her his cup and looked over to Mac as she pranced away. "Same as always; that Rose of yours is a busy body."

"It is in her blood, I think. Blackfoot, are always in need of doing one thing or another," the two men chuckled. How true it was.

"Here is more coffee." Rose handed the cup to Tyrell. Mac was looking at her as though he were saying where is mine. "Mac, you know where coffee is; you get." She looked back to Tyrell. "Travis is company. I get for him."

Tyrell snickered as Mac stood up and poured his own coffee while Rose sat down. "I will cook big meal tonight. You must stay. Is late now," Rose, said as she began knitting at the table. "I'm making quilt for baby Mac."

Tyrell was surprised to hear that. "What, you are with child, Rose?"

"Yes, child will be born in winter." Rose continued knitting. "The magic pendant swung over belly says it will be a boy." By now, Mac had returned with his coffee and was sitting down grinning from ear to ear.

"How come you never mentioned this earlier, Mac?" Tyrell questioned with excitement for the both of them.

"Hadn't the time. I was too busy showing you around. I would have told you. It is quite the thing isn't it?"

"Yes, it is. Congratulations! I'm happy for you both. You'll both make damn find parents, I reckon. Geez, a baby Mac! That made my day! I'm sure glad I swung by when I did. I'll have to come up with a gift for yous and him. What is it the child might need?"

"No worries, Travis. We have all we need," Mac assured.

"Regardless, the next time I come this way, I'll be bringing gifts. What kind of uncle would I be if I didn't?"

As late afternoon turned to dusk, Mac gave Travis a tour of the outside. A barn and a shop were still being built, but Mac was doing a fine job in finishing them. The only livestock Tyrell saw were a couple of chickens, a milk cow and calf and Mac's three horses. The steam bath he and Mac put together when he worked with him remained and was still being used by Mac and Rose. They walked over to where Tyrell's teepee once stood. The fire pit was over grown some, but nonetheless, it too remained as it was.

"Huh, I tell you, Mac, standing right here in this spot sure brings back memories. Even Black Dog remembers this place," Tyrell said as Black Dog visited the area and pissed everywhere. The two men chuckled.

"I bet it does bring back memories, Travis. I remember quite well the nights we spent sitting right here, a fire flickering in the wind, coffee brewing, and work waiting for us in the morning." Mac inhaled deeply as he reminisced.

Tyrell found both of them a piece of wood to sit on and they sat. "Yep, we sure worked." It was Tyrell's turn to reminisce and the two men sat in silence for a few minutes.

"I noticed you ain't riding that big ol' horse you had. What happened to him?" Mac asked out of curiosity.

Tyrell told the story.

"I'm sorry to hear that. Damn, he was a fine horse," Mac shook his head. "Crazy a lil' bit maybe, but he was a damn fine one. Not many horses have or ever will be quite like that old boy was."

Tyrell nodded. It hadn't been so long since he last sat on Pony's back, a few weeks at most. "Yeah, he was damn unique. Had his quirks that is for sure and he died due to one of them," Tyrell shrugged. "I can't deny that I wish things didn't happen as they did, but it is what it is, I reckon."

The ding of the dinner triangle saved them both from the awkward moment. Ding! Ding! Ding! It sounded as Rose rang it. "That be dinner, c'mon, Travis, let's go eat," Mac said as the two men stood up and made their way back to the house.

They ate dinner on the top veranda and as it grew dark, coal oil lanterns gently flickered on each corner of the veranda's railing giving them light. It was a beautiful evening, dark, quiet, and calm. Mac couldn't have picked a better spot to build his house. The vertical fence that skirted the house with the one-way entrance only added to the magnificence of the landscaped yard and house design.

"You sure came up with some good ideas when you built this up, Mac. Damn impressive," Tyrell pointed out as he brought his after-dinner coffee to his lips.

"It all worked out as I visualized. Rose's brother Half-Moon is the one that came up with the fence. He didn't see any reason to waste some of the poles I needed out of the way, so the barn could go up. I was happy with the way he built it. It is strong, tall, and a might tough to climb. It makes for a good defense if there is ever a need. I'm building a heavy gate too that I'll put up. Got rifle ports all along the four sides of the house too," Mac chuckled as though his efforts to make the place secure may have been over-exaggerated.

"There isn't anything wrong with that, Mac. Don't ever think otherwise. Out here in the boonies, one never knows what might be or who is about. Best to have all possibilities covered and 'specially, since the two of you are out here alone and have a new one on the way," Tyrell said referring to Mac and Rose's baby.

"Ah, we've been out here for a number of years already, first down at the old house and now up here. We ain't seen much that we weren't able to handle with the help from distant neighbors or by ourselves." Mac took a swallow of coffee. "Those of us up here, as you know, keep an eye out for each other."

Tyrell nodded. "I know," he agreed. With the chill of night settling in, they made their way inside and sat down in the spacious couch room of the house. A woodstove emitted heat and lanterns lit the room. Rose sat in her rocker sipping tea and knitting while Mac and Tyrell told stories, laughed and joked. Although they weren't related in any way, the sense of family was undeniably in that room. It was their past, that had rooted that relationship and the roots were deep.

Chapter 15

Early next morning as the rooster crowed, Mac and Rose stood next to Tyrell's horse as he checked over the saddle and his gear.

"I reckon I'm good to go. It was nice seeing yous. You can count on me dropping by soon after that baby is born; I promise you that," Tyrell smiled. It was a promise he would keep.

Rose handed him a bag of biscuits and two jars of jam. "These are for you as you go."

"Thank you, Rose. I love you for it," Tyrell smiled and winked at her.

Rose blushed.

"You be safe, Travis. There is always a spot at our table for you, yes." Rose spoke softly as she bent forward and kissed his cheek.

"Indeed there is, Travis. You remember that. Don't ever hesitate to stop by."

"Nope, I'd never do that," Tyrell put the biscuits and jam in one of the saddlebags. Reached out his hand and shook Mac's, "You keep Rose and that baby of yours safe, Mac. I'll be coming back this way once the job in Willow Gate is done," Next he gave Rose, another hug, "Rose, you keep Mac on the straight and narrow. Put him to work helping with the newborn when the time comes, you hear," Tyrell smiled as he stepped back and swung up onto his horse. Tilting his hat in respect and admiration, he turned and with Black Dog headed northwesterly toward Big Little Creek, destination Willow Gate and the job that awaited him.

The McCoy's and Riley Scott led Matt Crawford into the Fort early evening that Sunday. While Brady secured Matt and helped him settle in a holding cell, Ed and Riley made their way into the backroom and slumped into chairs. They were, beat, rolled over, and busted. Every bone in their bodies ached, but they had made it. They had escorted Brady and Matt home. Together with Brady, they fooled the Brubakers and Colby Christian into thinking that Brady had been alone and that they did not have Matt Crawford.

"We did it, Riley. We finally did it," Ed said as he found the strength to get the woodstove going. It was going to be a long night for someone. By law, they couldn't leave Matt alone. There had to be a twenty-four hour watch, seven days a week for as long as Matt was their prisoner.

"Not so much us, Ed, but that boy of yours and Travis. They got 'em; they sure did. I tell ya, now that we are here and he is in there," Riley pointed with his finger toward the two holding cells that the McCoy's had, "I'm damn glad it is over. The ten thousand that McCoy's will get will never compare to the feeling of satisfaction I have, even though the only part I played in the end was escorting Brady home."

"I couldn't have said that better," Ed, sighed. "It sure does feel good, doesn't it?"

"Uhuh, it does," Riley agreed.

Brady finally made his way in and sat down. "Matt is comfortable. I told him we'd bring him a coffee once it was cooked." Brady ran his hand through his hair. "We're going to need a watchman and I'll tell yous right off the bat, it ain't going to be me tonight. No sir. I'm going to have a coffee, unload the company gear, and head for home and my own damn bed. Come morning I'm sleeping 'til the cows come home and then I'm gonna wake up, and sleep some more. I might make it back this way come Tuesday," Brady made clear.

"That is fine by me, Brady. You've put on a lot of miles and are deserving of a few days of rest and recovery. Riley and I will sort out which one of us will stay here for now. You and Travis both did a good job with this. Matt has been tracked by a lot of men for a lot of years and you and Travis managed it."

"We had some luck and good timing on our side. We ain't any more deserving praise than any man who would have brought him in. Sooner or later one would've, so let's be clear on that."

"That is mighty humble, Brady."

"Humble or not, it is the truth. We don't need no ribbons, or awards, for doing our job. No one who thinks they do has a place in this business. Besides, it was Travis and that dog of his that managed to get Matt. All I did was kept him safe and brought him here."

Ed inhaled deeply. He understood where Brady was coming from, but as far as he was concerned, it was a team effort and Brady and Travis were the team.

"No matter how it was played out, both you and Travis will always be acknowledged as the men that brought Matt Crawford in. No one else managed out of all the men that have ever tried. That is something you need to take into account and accept."

"I accept it all right, old man. I can assure you of that, but I don't see any reason to be jubilant 'cept for the fact that I'm finally home and I'll be able to wash weeks of sweat, dirt, and stink, off my body and sleep in a real bed... my own damn bed."

The coffee had perked by now and Ed poured the three of them a cup and took a fourth to Matt. "Here you go, Matt." Ed handed Matt the coffee through the bars.

"Thanks, Ed," Matt took it, returned to his bunk, and sat down.

"Are you hungry, Matt?"

"No so much, nope. The coffee is good for now."

"Just so you know it'll be me or Riley that will be on call all night for you if you need anything or want to talk."

"As of right now I ain't got much to say nor am I in need of anything."

Ed nodded, understanding Matt's need to be alone. He had a lot to think about, "that's fine. One of us will check up on you in a bit." Ed turned and made his way to the table and his cooling coffee.

"Matt has his coffee. Says he ain't in need of nothing else. Which one of us two is going to be the unlucky bastard that gets to spend the night on the cot?" Ed brought his coffee to his lips and took a swallow.

"If you stay here long enough for me to fetch a bath at the widow Donale's and let me gather clean clothes, I'll take the cot," Riley offered.

Ed took out his pocket watched and looked at the time. "You even sure the widow would have any baths available at this time?" Ed smirked and raised an eyebrow. "I forgot you are special to her."

"Am not," Riley, said, as he grew flush. "Curse you, Ed."

Brady looked over to Riley, surprised, but not shocked. "Let me guess. You finally managed to sweep that ol' woman off her feet, eh, Riley?"

"No! That's just your old man's bullshit coming out. And by the way, she ain't that ol', younger than me as a matter of fact."

"If you aren't special to the widow, Riley, how would you know that?" Brady teased with a smile. Riley sat there shaking his head with no words to say.

"Go on, Riley, I'll wait for you to clean up and stuff," Ed winked at him.

Riley stood up. "Goddamn it, Ed, I told you there was no stuffing goin' on. Now, I'm gonna go get cleaned up and such and I'll be back," Riley turned and started for the exit. "You and your damn jokes," he muttered as he went.

Ed and Brady sat back and laughed as he stormed out.

"He don't know it yet, but the widow has a surprise for Riley. She wants to borrow our buggy and take him on a picnic," Ed chuckled. "Can you see the look on ol' Riley's face when she shows up at his coach and hog ties him?"

"I see him kicking and screaming," Brady laughed. "It's good see though. The widow and Riley I reckon would make a good pair. They have that thing in common."

Ed looked at Brady somewhat confused.

"What thing is that, Brady?" Brady shook his head and snickered. "Old age, of course; they're both ol' folk."

"Can't deny that," Ed agreed, with a smile.

"'Course you can't deny it, old man. You're as ol' too, ain't ya?" Brady dumped out the rest of his coffee. "I reckon I'll see you Tuesday," he turned and headed for home.

"See you Tuesday, Brady. Make sure you let your ma know we are back. I'm sure she'd like to see you to make sure you is alive and all."

Brady turned and looked back at Ed. "C'mon, ol' man, I wanted some sleep not answer a bunch of unnecessary questions." He waved his hand through the air. "I will, though. See you later."

"Thanks, Brady," Ed yelled as Brady headed for the back door.

Brady made his way over to the corral and saddled up a fresh horse, then headed for home. He stopped off at his folks' place as he said he would. Beth saw him approach from the front porch and she stood up. "Brady!" she darted over to meet him. "Get off that horse, Brady McCoy, and give your ma a hug."

Brady swung off his horse and gave her a hug.

"You've been gone a long time. I'm so relieved to see you. Come, let's have a tea and you can tell me all about it."

Brady stood still. "Sorry Ma, I really need some sleep. I got to get home, lie my head down, and maybe take a steam bath later. I'll swing by tomorrow, how's that?" Brady asked with hope that she'd let him get.

Beth put her hands on her hips.

"If you promise me to come by tomorrow; you've promised that before and you never showed up. Are you going to come this time?"

Brady nodded and swung back onto his horse, "I promise, Ma, I will."

"All right, then. I'll be expecting you," Beth said with authority. "Is your pa going to be home soon?"

"I reckon. He's waiting on Riley to get back from the widow's."

"Okay. See you tomorrow, Brady."

"Yep, will too." Brady turned his horse and headed home.

The weeds in his yard had grown some since he had been gone. Unloading his gear and setting the horse loose to graze, he closed the gate. For now, he cared little about anything except for sleep. Stepping into his three-room house, he sat down at the table and removed his boots and holster. Inside was musky and arid so he opened all the windows to let some air in. He climbed on top of his bed, dirty clothes, and all, and before he could count to ten, he was asleep.

Ed, still alone with no sign of Riley yet, poured a third coffee and went to his office. He grabbed some paperwork and returned to the table. Sitting down once more, he signed and read a few things, then began the grueling task of writing the report on Matt Crawford's apprehension. There were things he still needed to clarify with Brady, but decided he'd get a start on it anyway. If nothing else, at least he wanted to finish the report, he needed to file in order for McCoy's to receive the monetary reward, for Matt Crawford's capture. It took him a few minutes to fill in the report. Finally, he could check it off the list of things he'd have to fill out in the coming days. He looked it over making sure the, *i*'s were dotted and that the *t*'s were crossed. Satisfied he signed and dated it.

"One down, a dozen more to go," he muttered to himself as he looked at the clock on the wall. It was getting late, almost nine o'clock, and still, no Riley. He stood and did his hourly check on Matt, who was sleeping soundly. Ed nodded, *yep, that is exactly what I'd like to be doing...* he thought as he turned and made his way to the table and once more sat down. This time he stretched out his legs and rested his feet on a chair, crossed his arms and dozed.

The next thing that happened woke him in a hurry. The chair was ripped from underneath his feet and he almost slid under the table. He braced himself before falling under completely and sat up. There was Riley, laughing softly and shaking his head.

"Did I wake you, Ed?"

"Jesus Christ, Riley you couldn't have simply shook me awake?" Ed stammered as he rubbed his eyes.

"I suppose I could've. This here though was more appropriate, considering all your jokes as of late," Riley smiled. "I'm here now if you want you could head for home."

"Yeah, guess I could. I ain't checked Matt since nine. Did you happen to look in on him as you came in?"

"Did so, he was snoring as loud as you. He's fine," Riley assured.

Ed looked at him and nodded.

"So you did manage a bath and shave. Lucky you," Ed snickered as he stood up and stretched. "I guess I'll see you in the morning, Riley. Keep an eye on Matt. I'll bring breakfast."

"Eggs, ham, and toast for me, Ed. When should I expect you?"

"Eight or eight-thirty, I don't reckon it'll be any sooner, but you never know. Good night, Riley."

"See you then," Riley said as Ed headed out and for home. He looked through the mess of paperwork that was scattered on the table that Ed had left out. He sorted through it and stacked it in a pile, stood and made an appearance in the holding cell area. Matt continued to snore and so he headed for the cot. Throwing some blankets down he kicked off his boots, hung his gun-belt up, and set the wind up alarm clock that was next to the cot to go off at 1:00 a.m.

It seemed as though he had only fallen asleep and the damn thing went off. He rose and made his way into the backroom and added a stick to the woodstove, then checked again on Matt. Satisfied that he was alive, he returned to the cot and went through the whole process of getting up every two hours and checking in on Matt. It was going to be a long week.

Ed showed up Monday morning as he said at 8:30. "Eggs, ham and toast for everyone," he announced as he set the food down on the front counter.

"Good timing, Ed, the coffee just finished." Riley said as he made his way over to the counter and set his cup down then grabbed one of the meals. "I'll get this to Matt."

"Thanks, Riley, I'll set ours down on the table." Ed made his way into the backroom and set the two plates on the table. Sitting down he looked at the stack of paperwork he needed to finish up. It would take a couple hours. He shrugged. In time, he'd get to it. Riley returned as he began to eat his breakfast.

"How is Matt this morning?" Ed asked as Riley sat down to his own plate of eggs and ham.

"Still living," he replied as he dug into his eggs. "One-day today, beginning of a new week," Riley stated as he stuffed a fork full of eggs into his mouth. "Damn, these eggs are good," he commented as he swallowed his first mouthful.

"It is the beginning of a new week, Riley, and I have a ton of paperwork to get through," Ed took a slurp from his coffee.

Riley pointed with his fork toward the small kitchen cupboard. "You going to pick up some grub today, Ed, so we can keep Matt fed?"

"Will so. Before lunch I'll put together a list," Ed continued eating.

"Good. There ain't much in them cupboards." Finished with his breakfast, Riley stood up and put his plate into the sink. "What are we going to start off with today?"

"I'm going to finish up the paperwork, get it all sent over to Bash or Cannon, whichever one is there today. Then I guess we'll see what comes of the day."

"That leaves me to tend to Matt's needs for the time being then, I suppose, eh?"

"I know you'd rather be doing something else, but until Brady has rested, that leaves only you and me to make sure Matt is tended too."

"I ain't got a problem tending to our prisoner's needs. I could use the rest. That trail riding we did these past few days has taken a toll on me," Riley brought his coffee to his lips and took a swallow.

"Has Matt spoken much to you, Riley?"

"He ain't said much more than 'thanks' for this or that. I reckon in time he might speak some. So far though; nope, he ain't said much."

"He seems to have shut up about most things. I hope he'll come 'round. I haven't talked to Brady much on what, if anything, Matt has said to him." Ed stood up and poured a cup of coffee. "Has Matt had one of these yet?"

"I brought him one earlier. I'll go see if he wants another." Riley made his way to the Matt's cell. "How was breakfast, Matt?"

"Better than what we've been eating on the trail."

"If you hand me your plate and cup, I'll get you another coffee, if you want."

Matt stood and brought Riley his plate, spoon and cup. "I could use another coffee, thanks, Riley."

"No problem, Matt," Riley took the plate and cup. "I'll be back in a jiffy with your coffee."

Matt nodded and sat back down on his bunk. Riley returned a few minutes later and handed him his coffee. "Hot and fresh," Riley said as Matt took the coffee.

"Any idea, on when I'll be facing a judge?" Matt asked as he sat back down.

Riley shook his head. "Sorry, Matt, I haven't got an idea on that. We might know more later on today though."

Matt gently blew on the hot coffee in his hand and took a drink. "Any news later is better than no news now, I suppose," Matt replied.

Riley put one hand on one of the cells bars as he stood there. Hoping Matt wanted to talk. "Is there anything you need or want to talk about, Matt?"

"Not particularly. McCoy's man, Travis Sweet has heard it all. He'll likely have some answers for you, Riley. There is one thing I would like, however."

"What is that?"

"Been on the trail for quite some time and I ain't cleaned up in a long while." Matt took another drink of coffee.

"You're looking for a bath then?"

"That'd be nice, Riley. Is there any chance that can happen?"

Riley nodded. "I reckon we can allow that. I'll have to run it by Ed firstly and it likely won't happen 'til later. You want some clothes cleaned up too. The widow Donale has baths and will clean up your clothes if you want."

"That would be good, they is pretty dirty too. I appreciate it, Riley."

"I'll gather you when the time comes, until then, if'n you need anything else or want to talk, I'll be here. Just holler out."

"I will, thanks, Riley."

"I'll check up on you in an hour or so, 'less something comes up." Riley turned and made his way to the kitchen and sat down again with Ed. "Matt is wondering if he can get a bath and some clothes cleaned up."

"I don't see a problem with that. Best wait, though, until I get the paperwork off to the Mounties. That way they'll know Matt is with us, in case something goes awry."

"That is what I figured. Best to let them know that we got Matt before I take him over to the widow's."

By 11:00 a.m. that Monday, Colby and Martin were only a few miles west of the Fort.

"We're getting close, Martin. We should be there in an hour or less. It's going to be nice to get my own ride. You're a gaseous son of a bitch, and sitting behind you hasn't made this trip pleasant."

"My gut is all garbled, Colby. The only relief I get is when I pass wind. You're quite welcome to swing off and walk." Martin was smiling when he said that.

"Jus' tighten up your belt some. Maybe then I won't get splashed none."

Martin began to chuckle.

"There ain't anything funny about that at all, Martin. What are you giggling about?" It was then he knew why, Martin had passed wind again. "Jesus, Martin, I smell now why." Colby took Martin's advice and jumped off the horse with his saddle still in his hands, and swung it over his shoulder. "I reckon for now, I'll walk some. I'm gonna have to rinse my mouth out with whiskey once we make the Fort, you stinky bastard."

Martin slowed his horse down so he could keep pace with Colby as he walked.

"So, all I had to do was fart to get you off my horse? It ain't been any more pleasant for me than it has been for you. I got some kind of gut thing going on. It damn hurts."

"Beans do that, Martin, and that is all we've been eating, cooked or cold out of the can. Beans, beans and more beans. Tonight I'm eating steak with all the damn fixings."

"We ain't just gonna grab a horse for you and head west?"

"Hell no! We're going to stay a night at the Snakebite, eat steak, and drink draft, maybe whiskey. We'll head after the others 'morrow some time."

"A real bed sounds like a damn good plan, might as well clean up before we head west, too. Is there a bathhouse at the Fort?"

"There is. The widow Donale has baths. I like that idea, some food, a real bed, and a bath come morning. I'm on that like the flies on your backside. Which makes it obvious to me that indeed you need a bath," Colby laughed as they continued east.

It was noon, when they made the distance, but finally there it was. There was the Fort. "There it is, Martin, and here we are. First things first, let's head over to the Mounted Police station. Maybe they have a horse I can buy."

Sure enough they did. Constable Rick Bash was surprised to see Colby and Martin, but he didn't hesitate in selling Colby a horse. It meant one less horse that they had to take care of. "Go ahead and head up to the stables, Colby. I'll be along shortly."

"Thank you, Bash, we'll see you up there," Colby said as he and Martin turned and exited. They made their way up to the stables and waited a few minutes. Bash grabbed the list of horses that he could sell, then turned, and headed for the stables himself. It took a few minutes for Colby to pick out the one he wanted from the list of five that Bash could sell.

He finally decided on a buckskin stallion. "I like this one here, Bash. What's he gonna cost?"

Bash looked through his list. "I can sell that one it looks like for one hundred dollars. It's been here a while. Says here it was brought in as a stray. He's been here longer than a month and no one has laid claim to him. One-hundred and he's yours, Colby."

"Damn right! I'd pay double that for a fine animal like this," he reached into his pocket and pulled out his money satchel, and handed Bash the money, Bash in turn handed him a receipt with the horse's description and whatnot.

"He's yours now. No one can argue," Bash, said as he put the money Colby handed him into the booklet.

"That is good enough for me, Bash," Colby said, as he looked the piece of paper over.

The Missing Years- Part IV
A Tyrell Sloan western adventure

"Thanks for the receipt. I guess I'll get him saddled," he led his new horse out the gate and Bash closed it behind him and leaned on it as Colby saddled the horse.

"Are you and Martin sticking around for a few days, Colby?" Bash was curious is all; he didn't care either way.

"I reckon we'll head out come morning or there about. We got to catch up with Alex and the others. You heard yet that Brady McCoy is back?"

Bash shook his head. "Nope, didn't know that."

"He passed us up the trail some Friday, I think. He was riding alone."

Colby gave the saddle the once over making sure it was cinched up.

"That means Matt Crawford is still fair game." He swung up onto his horse, tilted his hat and he and Martin headed to the Snakebite Hotel.

Bash watched as the two riders rode off, their horses kicking up dust as they went. Turning he made his way back to the station and whatever the day was going to bring with Colby and Martin being back in town. He could only hope that the two of them kept the peace. For now, there wasn't a damn thing he could say or do about them being there.

At 1:00 p.m., Ed showed up at the station with all the paperwork he needed to provide the Mounties with regarding Matt's capture. Bash was confused as he looked through the documentation. "So, McCoy's does have Matt?"

"Yes, we do, Bash. We brought him in last night, early evening."

"Sorry if I seem confused. I just sold Colby Christian a horse. He said he and the others passed Brady up the trail some on Friday. He said Brady was alone."

"What the hell is Colby doing here?" Ed asked with surprise.

"Lost his horse, I guess. I never really questioned," Bash, continued reading what Ed had given him.

"Brady did pass them, Bash. Me, Riley and Matt headed north and rode right pass the Brubaker bunch."

Ed told the story.

Bash laughed.

"They think Matt is still at large. Colby told me that he and Martin would be heading out tomorrow to catch up with the others and I guess to continue looking for Matt. That is damn funny. That made my day, Ed."

Ed chuckled, "I reckon they'll figure it out soon enough," he said as Bash continued looking through the paperwork.

Bash flipped over the first page Ed handed him and continued reading the second.

"It looks like it is all here, Ed. Good job, by the way, in bringing Matt to eventual justice. Cannon will likely want to swing by the McCoy's to give him the once over. I'll send a wire to the Ottawa detachment today and find out how long it'll take to get a circuit judge to reside. Depending on how close one may be, it could take a few days to a week."

"I'll make sure we look after any of his needs in the meantime," Ed rapped his knuckles on the counter. "I guess that is it for now, Bash. I'll be seeing you."

"We'll be seeing you, Ed," Bash brought the paperwork over to his desk and sat down, as he continued looking through it, chuckling softly to himself every time he thought about how the McCoy's fooled the Brubaker bunch. *That is the coy, at the end of McCoy,* he thought with a shake of his head and a smile.

Stopping off at the Fort Grain and Grocery, Ed picked up kitchen supplies to keep Matt fed. He bought the usual, paid the usual price, and headed back to his usual spot in the backroom of the McCoy's office. He set the sack of grub down and put it away, with Riley's help.

"Glad you remembered the grub, Matt hasn't eaten yet. What took so long?" Riley asked as he opened a can of stew and poured it into a pot to heat up for Matt's lunch.

"I got talking with Bash. Colby and Martin are in town."

Riley was as surprised as Ed had been. "What do you suppose they is doing here?"

"I guess they learnt that Colby needed a horse," Ed chuckled. "He bought another from the Mounties earlier on, not sure when. He and Martin must've turned around and headed here the day after we saw them. Colby told Bash they'd be heading out for Crawford tomorrow. I guess we've fooled them so far."

Riley smirked. "Damn, are them boys gonna be pissed when they learn Matt is already here with us. Wonder how long it'll take for them to find that out?"

"If they don't find out before tomorrow, they might not find out until it is in the newspapers. It could be months." Ed put the last of the grub away and sat down while Riley scooped out Matt's lunch and buttered a couple pieces of bread. He walked over to the holding cell area and handed off Matt's lunch.

"Sorry about the delay in getting this to you, Matt. Ed had a meeting with the Mounties so he was late getting back with the grub. It is jus' stew, a couple pieces of bread and butter and another coffee to wash it all down with."

"That is all right. I wasn't quite hungry at noon anyway. I assume it is later than that now?"

Riley peeked around the corner and looked at the clock on the wall above Brady's desk.

"Yep, almost two o'clock, I'll try to get supper to you around six."

Matt nodded as he sat down on his bunk with his platter of food and coffee and began to eat.

"Any word on when I can get cleaned up?" he asked before Riley disappeared.

"I'll see what Ed has to say. Likely, after lunch some time. How is that?"

"That works. Thank you, Riley," Matt continued with his lunch as Riley left.

"Matt's asking about his bath," Riley said as he met up with Ed.

"You can go ahead and take him after he eats. Best keep your eyes opened though for Colby and Martin. We don't want them learning we have Matt, not yet leastwise."

"About that, they know the last place Matt was heading for and that was Willow Gate. That kind of puts Travis in a predicament, doesn't it?" Riley pointed out as he sat down.

"Huh, don't know why I didn't think of that. I'll send a wire, I guess to Willow Gate, and fill Travis in. Can't do that though 'til I know he is there and depending on where about he is now, we can't even assume when he'll make the distance. Good point you bring up there, Riley."

Riley nodded and shrugged.

"I figure we got that first wire when he was in Chase. We can be certain he ain't stopped, riding since. That'd put him closer to Willow Gate than the five of them will be by 'morrow. I don't imagine they'll make the distance to Willow Gate before Travis does. We wait, I guess, until Travis sends us a wire from there, hopefully in the next couple of days." That was really all they could do for now.

At 3:00 p.m., Riley took Matt for his bath.

"Here we are, Matt, the widow Donale's bathhouse." Riley swung off his horse and tethered him, then helped Matt down from his. Opening the walkway gate the two men made their way to the front door. Riley knocked.

A few minutes later, they were greeted by the widow. "Evening Mr. Scott, are you both here for baths?" she asked as she gestured them to come in.

"Not I, Malinda. Matt here though is in need of one. I brought some of his clothes with us. I hope you don't mind giving them a wash. There is no rush. Someone from McCoy's could pick them up tomorrow."

"That is fine. Set them down there, Riley. I'll have them ready for tomorrow, follow me." She pointed to a door, "go on inside, Matt it is, correct?" she questioned as she looked at him.

"Yes, ma'am, it is."

"All right, Matt, go on inside and get into a tub. I'll send Riley in with some hot water. The soap and stuff is on the counter inside. Help yourself, Matt."

Matt tilted his hat in acknowledgement.

"Thank you, ma'am," he said as he opened the door and made his way inside. There were two claw-foot cast iron tubs inside. He sat down on the stool next to the one he was going to use and waited for Riley and some hot water. He was still cuffed and so stripping down would have to wait until Riley took them off.

It took a few minutes for Riley to bring in the first tubs of hot water.

"A couple more tub full's, Matt and you'll be good to go. I'll take off the handcuffs then," Riley turned and gathered more water. It took three trips to fill the tub. Removing the handcuffs, he told Matt to go ahead and bathe and that he'd be outside the door. He stood guard outside and waited for Matt to finish.

"Is that Matt Crawford, Riley?"

"Yes, it is, Malinda. For now, though, please don't let anyone know. The less folk who know he is here in the Fort, the better off we'll all be," Riley insisted.

"I won't say a word, Riley. You should know me by now better than that."

"I do, Malinda. It is just business. I trust you won't say a word," Riley smiled at her and winked.

"That is better. Would you like a tea while Matt bathes? I can bring one to you."

"Thanks, Malinda, but not now; I'm fine."

"Since you are working, I won't bother you again. While he bathes, I'll get started on his clothes. Let me know when you are leaving."

"Thank you, Malinda, I will," Riley nodded his appreciation to be left alone while he did his job and waited for Matt to finish. He watched as she gathered Matt's clothes and pranced off to the laundry room.

Thirty minutes later, a clean and shaved Matt Crawford stepped out of the bath. He folded up the towels he had used, put the soap and straight razor back where he found it, surprised in all actuality that, Riley, had left it behind. After dressing, he stepped out into the hallway where Riley waited.

"Jesus Christ, Matt, you look like a brand new person," Riley commented as he looked at him.

"Thanks. It sure felt good to wash the trail off. Thanks also for leaving behind the razor."

"No problem, Matt. I trusted you. I got to put the cuffs back on you now though," Riley pulled them out of his back pocket while Matt put his arms out. Secured now, Riley yelled down the hallway to the widow. "We're all done here now, Malinda," he gestured for Matt to start walking.

"Okay, Mr. Scott. I trust Matt had a nice bath?" she hollered back.

"Yes, ma'am, I did. Thank you very much."

"That is fine, Matt. Will I see you later, Mr. Scott."

"I'm stuck at McCoy's for the unforeseen future. I might see you tomorrow though for my bath."

"We'll see you then, Riley. Have a good evening," the widow responded from down the hall.

"You too; bye for now," Riley said as he and Matt exited. He helped Matt onto his horse, swung up onto his own and the two men headed back to McCoy's.

"You didn't see Colby or Martin hanging around anywhere did you?" Ed asked from the front counter as Riley and Matt entered from the back.

"Nope, didn't see 'em."

"Good. The widow ain't going to say anything is she."

"I asked her not to. She won't," Riley assured, as he led Matt back to his cell and locked him up again.

"Are you hungry yet, Matt?"

"Not so much."

"I'll bring you supper in a couple hours. Would you rather have beans or stew?"

"Food is food, Riley. Whatever you bring will have to do."

Riley nodded as he turned and met up with Ed at the front counter. "One-day has almost come to an end, Ed. Wonder what two-day is goin' to bring. Today was pretty slack."

"We'll likely see Cannon tomorrow. Not sure when, but we can be expecting him. He's gonna want to have a look at Matt to make sure, I suppose, that he is Matt, but that is tomorrow."

Chapter 16

It was 9:00 a.m. Tuesday, when Lieutenant Bob Cannon showed up at the McCoy's office to have a look at the infamous Matt Crawford and to confirm his identity. Ed and Riley met him at the front counter.

"Good morning, Bob."

"Good morning, men. Finally, McCoy's brought in Matt Crawford, eh?"

"We did, indeed. Travis and Brady are the ones that managed it."

"That is good news. I'm glad his reign of killing has ended. He's been at it a long time and it has taken a long time for any man to finally, bring him in. I'm glad it was you folks. Take me to him, Ed. I need to see for myself that it is he."

"Right this way, Cannon," Ed gestured for him to follow. Making the distance, he opened the holding cell area and let Cannon go on his own to see and talk to Matt.

The lieutenant walked down to Matt's cell and looked in on him.

"Hello, Matt. I'm Lieutenant Cannon of the Mounted Police here in the Fort. Has Ed and his men been treating you all right?"

"I ain't got any complaints," Matt answered back.

"Good, I'm glad they're keeping you happy," Cannon looked at the likeness of the photo he had of Matt in an envelope. Satisfied it was Matt, he put the photo away.

"You are entitled to legal counsel, if McCoy's hasn't mentioned that to you yet."

"I'm well aware of what I'm entitled to. Not sure, I'm looking for such though. Not much point in that, I'll take

176

what I have coming without counsel," Matt responded with dislike.

"That is totally up to you. If you change your mind, let Ed or one of the others know and the Crown will provide you with one. That is your right and Canadian law. You might want to consider it."

"Already said, I don't want counsel at the moment."

"That is your right, too. Anyway, Mr. Crawford, I have identified you. My job here is now done. I'll see you in court," Cannon said as he turned and exited. Ed locked the door to the cell area as Cannon stepped out.

"Good news. That is Matt Crawford. He doesn't seem interested in the Crown providing him with legal counsel, but he was asked and that is all that matters. Good luck with him. I'll make sure you folks receive the reward. I guess that is it. Is there anything you folks need?"

Ed shook his head. "Nothing comes to my mind. We'll keep him safe and healthy until court. No worries there, Bob."

"He may be with you for a while. We haven't heard back from Ottawa regarding any circuit judges in the area. Means there likely isn't any for now, at least. It could be a while."

"Then I guess we wait," Ed shrugged, there was nothing anyone could do about that.

"That is the only choice, isn't it?" Cannon stated as he made his way to the exit.

"It is too. Thanks for identifying him, Bob. Have a good day," Ed said as Cannon nodded and exited.

"There we have it, Riley. Matt's been identified. Cannon is going to see to it that we get the bounty. Not a bad start for two-day," Ed smiled.

"It sure isn't. It is a good start if you ask me."

177

The Missing Years- Part IV
A Tyrell Sloan western adventure

It was shortly after Bob Cannon left that Brady finally showed up. Ed, by then, was in his office writing in his journal about the past day's events. Riley was sitting in the backroom his feet up on a chair and resting. They didn't hear Brady come in. The first thing he did was checked up on Matt.

"Hey, Matt how are you doing?" Brady asked as he approached Matt's cell.

"Hello, Brady. I suppose I'm doing as well as can be expected," Matt shrugged.

"How has the old man and Riley been treating you? I see that one of them must've taken you for a bath. It feels good to clean up after the distance and events we've had come our way, doesn't it?"

Matt only nodded in agreement.

"All right, well, Matt, I best go let the old man and Riley know I'm here. I'll probably see you later," Brady said as he left Matt alone. Making his way to the front of the office, he stopped and chatted with Innis, who was there, doing some work to the window.

"Morning, Innis," Brady said as he approached.

"Hey, Brady," Innis began as he set down his tools. "When did you get back?"

"Sunday evening. I stayed away from here and rested. It has been a long couple of weeks. I'm still a bit weary," Brady chuckled. "So, the old man has you fixing that window, eh?"

"We are changing it some though. It'll be smaller by a bit and will have separate panes. That is why I'm framing it in, one of the bottom panes, will open as well. Ed's decided to go with shatterproof glass, which, is lead infused. It is a new type of glass on the market," Innis responded in one breath. That was the way he was, conversations with him, were always long-winded.

"That is quite interesting, Innis. I'll let you get back to it then," Brady smiled. Innis nodded and picked up his tools and carried on. Next Brady headed to the backroom and woke Riley.

"Sleeping on the job, Riley? Really...," Brady smirked as Riley opened his eyes.

"Leastwise I was here at the start of the day," Riley said as he sat up with smile.

"Not too hard for an old folk such as yourself to pull something like that off, 'specially since you slept here. Where is the old man?" Brady asked as he poured a coffee and sat down.

"In his office, I think." Riley rubbed his eyes, "did you hear the news...," Riley started as he yawned and stretched.

"Ah, what news might that be, Riley. I've been back home slewing weeds for the past couple of days, so tell me how would I have heard any news?" Brady shook his head.

"Right, sorry about that, Brady. I'm still half-asleep."

"Uhuh, so, what is this news?"

"One: Cannon has identified Matt, and two: Colby Christian and Martin Brubaker showed up in town yesterday. Colby needed a horse. They told Bash that they'd be heading out today to meet up with the others and, get this, to track down Matt," the two men laughed softly. "You know Brady, I have respect for Colby. It is the others I ain't so sure about but, when this opportunity came about to fool the lot of them, I figured it'd be a good learning experience for them. I reckon though we ain't going to fool them forever."

"As long as Matt has been identified by Cannon, and he's here with us, it don't matter how long we fool 'em. The fact is we have Matt. Even if they had found out already, it wouldn't make a bit of difference. I say we let it play out however and whenever it ends," Brady took a swallow of coffee. "The only problem I see is that the Brubaker's and Colby will eventually end up in Willow Gate. They know that to be the place Matt was heading when we started this last hunt for him. It might hamper Travis's investigation of Gabe Roy when he finally makes it there."

Riley nodded and inhaled deeply.

"I thought about that, too. Spoke about it with Ed. Once we hear from Travis that he's made it to Willow Gate, we'll send a wire back explaining the situation. Least, then he'll be aware of the pending possibility that he might run into them. The Brubaker's and Colby have not broken any laws. They are free to do as they please. There ain't nothing stopping them from going to Willow Gate, whether they figure they is going after Crawford or not."

"I'll feel badly, though, if something comes of it and Travis gets hurt or worse. It'll be due to us sending them, Brubaker boys, and Colby westerly."

Riley waved his hand through the air.

"Chances are, Brady, Travis will be well aware of them fellas heading that way, days, maybe even a week or two before they make the distance," Riley pointed out.

"Yeah, I reckon you're right. We won't concern ourselves too much with that then. Changing the subject now, did Cannon say when there'd be a judge here about?"

"He ain't sure when; could be days."

"There are some things that Matt told Travis. He's got information on Gabe Roy, and some shoddy land deals and some other stuff that will certainly help us as we expose Gabe. He's willing to be our witness regarding the dirt we're trying to expose. If Cannon don't know how long before a circuit judge comes around, then that will help us in the long run.

Ed needs to fill out the legal forms pertaining to witness protection and submit them before Matt goes in front of a judge. Of course, we'll need to convince Matt to write a statement. That is the hard part. If he doesn't want to speak, he doesn't," Brady pointed out.

"Let me get this straight. Travis is a witness to what Matt said, except he ain't going to be available to say otherwise for a time. We bring that up to a judge and he might send a summons to Travis. I ain't sure now which could jeopardize the investigation into Gabe more than the other, the Brubakers and Colby or a circuit judge summoning Travis."

"That is the predicament we're in. If Matt doesn't give us a statement on what he knows, then there is that possibility that Travis may very well be summoned," Brady sighed.

Riley thought for a moment.

"Let's not forget that Matt was once a decorated U.S.A Ranger or the documentation we already have, like the fact that he also witnessed that Pinkerton, Ranthorp, murdering Emery. That makes him a witness to murder. He saved the town folks of Vermillion when Talbot and the Kingsley gang went through and set the place ablaze; that makes him a hero. Plus, he gave you and me, Ranthorp's horse after he shot him for killing ours.

And remember this, too. The only killing that Matt is responsible for up here in Canada is killing that no good Talbot Hunter. Since there ain't much proof of that, it makes it all conjecture. The killing of Ranthorp on the other hand was witnessed by you and me, so undoubtedly that is one killing, we can't say he didn't commit.

The rest of those he killed were all in the U.S.A and were all corrupt, high-profile government players. These are all things that'll favour the judicial proceedings, I think."

"They most certainly will, Riley, and if those facts alone get him exonerated, then we'll be ahead of the game. If it goes the other way though, we'll lose a couple of steps."

Riley nodded in agreement.

"Yep, but we'll always recover from losing a couple of steps as we dance."

Ed finally made an appearance and sat down.

"What is that the two of you are talking about?" Brady and Riley explained it to him.

"Like you both have said, the facts on why Matt should be exonerated are pretty clear. I figure whether he gives us a statement or not, what we have on him and about him, can only go one way and that is complete exoneration. It is more likely that when we get all the dirt on Gabe that we need and proceed with exposing him, it'll be Matt Crawford that gets a summons," Ed was certain of that.

"I sure hope you are right, old man. I'd hate to see Matt hung."

"He ain't going to hang. I'm confident of that and to assure it, I will fill out all the legalities needed to protect him as a witness to our on-going investigation regarding Gabe Roy and, of course, our witness to Emery's murder."

"Without his statement though, it could be pretty tough to do," Riley pointed out.

"Could be, but I reckon we'll cross that bridge when the time comes. Anything he has said to Travis can be kept between us. The law don't need to know. Again, we are protected by the governing laws. Anything he has said about Gabe is confidential to our case. There are some technical legalities going on though, and that is the fact that he both witnessed Emery's murder and killed the man responsible, albeit in an unrelated event. This is the part, which I'll admit is a grey area for me. However, I know a way around it.

Since we are investigating Emery's murder, he is also our witness to that investigation. We have him tied to two legal investigations, which involve both murder and corruption. That ends it pretty much right there," Ed smiled.

"Goddamn, that is the truth, ain't it?"

"It is, Riley."

"I never thought of it like that, either. That is some damn fine two-stepping, old man."

"That is why I have an office and you don't, Brady," Ed teased.

"Keep in mind, old man, that one day I'll be kicking your ass out of that office," Brady teased back.

Riley chuckled and shook his head. "See, Ed, like I've always said, he's a punk-ass kid. He's too damn smart for his britches."

"Right as he might be in regard to that, though, Riley, he's got a long way to go." Ed looked directly at Brady and smiled.

"I don't know old man. You and Riley are both coming to the end of the road, ain't ya, ol' as you both are and all?"

Ed crossed his arms and simply nodded. It was true. Riley sat there and looked into his empty cup wondering if he even wanted a coffee. Brady simply chuckled. "See, the two of you can't make argument to that."

"You know, we were having a fine morning until you went and pointed that out. Damn, punk-ass kid," Riley grumbled.

The rest of the day at McCoy's went as usual, with paperwork being worked, and documents filled out. The three of them kept hourly checkups on Matt, hoping that sooner than later he'd open up and maybe talk some, but he never did. At the front of the office, Innis sawed and hammered.

The streets of the Fort were busy with people. It was a typical Tuesday.

At quitting time, Riley agreed to finish the week off at the office, as long as he could have Saturday and Sunday off, simply because it was damn cold at night and his coach wasn't quite as warm as he had hoped it would be. That is why he wanted the weekend off, so he could winterize the damn thing.

Neither Ed nor Brady had a problem with that. From Friday to Friday, Brady would take over and they'd repeat the cycle until Matt was no longer they're responsibility. With the schedule settled and everyone in agreement, Ed and Brady headed home.

Chapter 17

Tyrell woke that morning to a cold fog that surrounded him. The ground was wet and heavy with dew and he was chilled to the bone. The further he had travelled the night before, the colder it seemed to get. Adding some sticks to the smouldering coals of his fire, he warmed his hands above the flickering flames. *It gets much colder and we're likely to see snow,* he thought as he reached over to his saddlebag and pulled out the old map he carried with him. According to the map, he had another twenty or thirty miles to go before the trail he was on crossed the trail he needed to be on. At that point, he'd turn south-west and carry on to Willow Gate. Big Little Creek was the halfway mark between where, he was now, and the trail that led to his final destination.

Kicking dirt over his fire and making sure it was out, he gathered his gear, saddled the horse, and headed off. The goal he set for himself that day was to make twenty miles. As long as he wasn't slowed down by the unknown, he was certain he could put that many miles behind him. The old trail in some places was overgrown with mountain ash and fern. On one occasion, he had lost the trail due to such overgrowth. Luckily, he ran across it again after a few miles of bush dodging. It slowed him down some and worked the horse more than he had wanted, but they carried on.

By mid-day, they came across Big Little Creek the halfway mark. At that time of year, it was nothing more than a constant trickle, but it was wide and deep, and in early spring as the evidence showed, it roared through there like thunder. They rested for a few minutes, long enough for Tyrell to fill his canteens and for Black Dog and the horse to drink. Continuing onward until dusk, they managed another ten miles. It was there that he set up for the evening. Sitting close to his fire with Black Dog at his side and the horse tethered a short distance away, he had an ominous feeling.

Perhaps it could have been the fact that he was heading into otherwise unknown territory. The route to Willow Gate by way of Big Little Creek wasn't often travelled. It was a lonely stretch of trail at best; at worst it was often travelled by hoodwinks or renegade Indians.

A snap of a twig in the distance alerted Black Dog and he perked up his ears. Tyrell loaded his rifle and laid it across his lap. Black Dog only stared into the darkness of evening. This put Tyrell at ease. Whatever it was beyond his view was not a threat.

"Likely a deer, eh, Black Dog?" Tyrell spoke. He put his arm over Black Dog's shoulders and patted him. "I'd have to say a deer. Otherwise, I reckon you wouldn't be so calm."

Black Dog continued his gaze into the dark wood. Again, there was some rustling in the bush closer than it had been the first time. Black Dog darted forward even after Tyrell commanded him to stay.

"Damn it!" Tyrell said in a hushed breath as he quickly stood up and shouldered his rifle, ready to send lead down the barrel at whatever it was that was coming his way. Minutes dragged on. He was half-expecting to hear snarls and growls as Black Dog sent whatever it was running. Instead, the wood grew deathly quiet and time stood still. Then, Black Dog simply trotted back followed by a man on a horse. Tyrell kept his rifle shouldered, and looked on.

"You on the horse, if you're here to cause trouble, trust me, tonight isn't your night. Come out where I can see you or I'll be sending lead down this barrel quicker than you can turn that horse around and skedaddle," Tyrell was firm and sincere, he wasn't playing games.

"There is no need for that, man who travels with dog. Where is the big horse you once rode?"

There was a familiarity to the voice, he heard, Tyrell tilted his head.

"Who might you be?" he questioned. Finally, the man and horse stepped out of the shadows.

"It is I, Crying Wolf."

"Crying Wolf?" Tyrell repeated.

"Yes," the horseman responded. Tyrell couldn't quite make out the rider yet, although he could see the silhouette of a man and horse. He kept his rifle shouldered.

"Come closer into the fire's light," Tyrell said as he put his thumb on the hammer of his rifle and waited. The man and horse drew closer. A smile crossed Tyrell's face as he un-cocked his rifle.

"Well I'll be! It is you. Come over to the fire and sit." Tyrell gestured as he leaned his rifle on an old log and stepped forward.

"I wondered why I didn't hear Black Dog chasing off whatever it was that was rustling in the wood. How have you been?" Tyrell asked as Crying Wolf slid off his red dun horse.

"I have been well. Where is the big burly man named Buck?" Crying Wolf questioned as he led his horse next to Tyrell's and tethered him.

Tyrell responded with a sigh.

"Buck headed home to the Yukon late this past July."

"The big burly man Buck always wanted to go home. It is good to know. The men you two hunted when we last sat at a fire, what of them?"

"We caught them. Shortly afterward, a couple of weeks I reckon, maybe longer. That is when Buck headed home."

"I told you then you had good help," Crying Wolf said as he and Tyrell sat next to the fire.

"Yes, you did. And you were absolutely right," Tyrell looked at the coffee pot. "Can I offer you a coffee, Crying Wolf? It isn't Buck brewed, but it is as good."

"Thank you. Yes, I will have a coffee. Your big horse that you rode, what has come of him?" Crying Wolf asked with curiosity.

"Some weeks ago he provoked a sow grizzly. He's dead now," Tyrell said with sorrow as he poured Crying Wolf a coffee and handed it to him.

Crying Wolf shook his head.

"He is not dead. Horses like him will always live in the hearts of those who knew him. He was a great horse. I am sorry for you."

Crying Wolf took a sip from the cup in his hand.

"Yes, you are right; this coffee is good." The two friends sat in silence for a few minutes, watching the flames dance to and fro.

"Can I ask, Crying Wolf, what are you doing so far from your home?"

"In June when we sat together at the fire with the big burly man, I was off to see Little Dan of the Kaska tribe. From there I set off on a spiritual journey. That journey has ended and now I head back north, to the Athabasca. And you, Travis, why is a man of law on this trail?"

"I am heading to Willow Gate. This was the shortest route from whence I came."

"The bustling town of Willow Gate, yes, I know of the place." Crying Wolf slurped his coffee. "It is said that it is the place of corruption and sin."

Tyrell nodded. "It is a town like any town, I reckon. There are the good and there are the bad."

"Yes, but it is not the good that you seek, is it?"

"Nope, it certainly is not."

"You will seek the lawless and corrupt. That is what men of law do. I know the man you seek without you telling me."

Tyrell looked across the flames to Crying Wolf. "How would you know this?" he asked.

"Gabe Roy is bad medicine. You are not the only one seeking him," Crying Wolf pointed out.

"What do you know of Gabe Roy?" Tyrell was quite curious now.

"He has exploited for his own pleasure many Indian women. He is protected by the law of that town. They too are corrupt. It is hard for the Indian to prove that he has killed some of our women, but he has." Crying Wolf grew silent for a moment. "He exploited my niece and killed my brother. One day Gabe Roy will pay, through law justice or death or perhaps both."

"You are right Crying Wolf, it is Gabe I seek. He believes that my intent is to protect him. My true intent, however, is to expose him and the corrupt law of Willow Gate and bring justice to each of them."

"You will be spoken of in legends and around fires if you alone can do that."

"It won't be me alone, Crying Wolf. There are others involved too. It is a combined effort."

"Yes, I know. The men you work for, the McCoy's; they too will be spoken of around fires. If you and they can bring Gabe Roy to justice, it will be a good day when that happens."

"How do you know so much, Crying Wolf?"

"I hear and see things and I watch closely," Crying Wolf smiled.

Tyrell smiled back and shook his head. "I guess I couldn't argue that since you seem to know more than what any man should know about my business. I can't, for the life of me, figure it any other way."

"Wisdom and knowledge, Travis, can be sought in the wind and our visions. One only needs to look and listen." Crying Wolf waved his hand through the air.

"Let us no longer talk about Gabe Roy or the corruption that is, but lets us talk now about the good in life."

"Yes, I agree, Crying Wolf that would be best."

For the duration of the night, while they conversed they did not speak of Gabe Roy or the corrupt law of Willow Gate.

In the twilight of predawn, Crying Wolf, silently slipped away taking with him Tyrell's horse and leaving behind the red dun. Stuck in a log was his signature of safe passage and friendship, one of his purple-feathered arrows.

The first thing Tyrell noticed when he finally woke himself was that Crying Wolf was gone. Next, he noticed that his horse was gone and tied in its spot was Crying Wolf's red dun. Somewhat confused and perhaps a little perturbed, he quickly got up. It was then he noticed the arrow. He pulled it out of the log and looked at it, then back to the red dun.

The arrow he understood. Crying Wolf did the same thing when he was first introduced to him through Buck. It was Buck, who explained the message, and what it meant. *Why though would Crying Wolf take his horse and not the one he rode in on the night before?* That part was perplexing.

Tyrell shook his head and shrugged. There wasn't any point in getting flustered. The red dun was a nice looking horse. Sure, he'd have to explain to Brady what had happened to his horse. There certainly must have been a reason for Crying Wolf to have done that. For now, though, it was a total mystery. Tyrell scratched his ear as he tried to make sense of it, but he couldn't. It was kind of funny in a way. *Least I ain't left horseless,* he thought as he added sticks to the fire.

A few miles up the trail, Crying Wolf inadvertently stumbled into a camp of four very unfriendly men, dirty, drunk, and looking for trouble. They pulled their guns on him and made him stop.

"Look at this, an Indian, ridin' a buckskin, now where do you boys suppose an Indian got a horse like that?" the first man taunted.

"Couldn't be his. Don't the Indian jus' ride on the backs of their squaws? I think that horse might be stolen," the second man stepped closer and looked at the horse. "Yep, I reckon we have ourselves a horse, thieving' Indian."

"Let's string him up, Carl. He's jus' a stupid Indian."

"Nope, nope, hold on. I think he's deserving' of a beat down first. Look at his face, looks like he's in need of a few more scars," Carl began to chuckle, "hey, Smitty, knock this Indian 'round some; then we'll hang 'em." Carl stepped back as the man named Smitty stepped forward. He was an ox of a man, but stood no chance against Crying Wolf, nor did the other three.

Before Smitty even reached Crying Wolf and his horse, Smitty fell to the ground with a knife stuck in his throat. Crying Wolf swung off his horse with great agility and with a knife in both hands, he spun around Carl stabbing him in the heart. Then, as quickly, he threw his second knife into the chest of man number three. The fourth man, confused and shocked at Crying Wolf's abilities, tried to fight back, but it was in vain. Crying Wolf slit his throat from ear to ear. Not one shot was fired; not one arrow was spent. Crying Wolf now stood over the dead men and looked on.

"I do not have these scars on my face from losing," he spoke solemnly to the dead. Retrieving his knives, he pulled them out of the dead men and wiped them clean on their shirts.

"Some of you white men are very, very stupid." Standing Crying Wolf removed the saddles, and gear from the dead men's horses and tossed them to the ground.

"You animals deserve much better," he said as he scared them off, he watched them briefly as they scattered into the woods. Swinging back onto the buckskin he had taken from Tyrell, he carried onward, as though what had taken place was as common as ticks in July.

Tyrell was on his first cup of coffee by now and still somewhat perplexed. He looked over to the red dun as he slurped.

"I don't know, Black Dog. This here situation is a bit off center. I don't get it. Makes no sense at all, leastwise, not to me," he said to Black Dog as though the dog could offer up some reasoning.

"I know, you ain't got a clue either. We have a new horse, though. We ain't going to suffer none. I guess, not until we run across Crying Wolf again if we ever do, will we ever know the 'why' in this equation."

He ate a couple of the biscuits with jam that Rose had given him as he sat and thought. "Even cold these biscuits are damn good, ain't they," he, stated as he handed a piece off to Black Dog, than gathered his gear.

"We'll make the trail going west to Willow Gate today, Black Dog," Tyrell said as he saddled the red dun.

"I figure once we get on the better trail, it won't take but a couple days to make the distance, providing, of course, we ain't held up along the way by this, that, or the other thing." He swung up onto the horse and heeled the horse's flank.

"C'mon, Black Dog, let's get," he said as they set off at a slow trot.

It wasn't long after that he came upon the grisly scene of the four dead men, slowing the horse down, he cautiously pulled his rifle from the saddle scabbard and loaded it. Looking around, he determined that the area was clear. The only things he saw were the eyes of dead men. With trepidation, he swung off the red dun. There had been only a brief scuffle. The men were killed up close and personal, throats slit and bodies stabbed.

"Jesus, Black Dog, these men are even armed with pistols. It don't look like that helped them any."

He stood up and made his way to where he saw a saddle. He didn't see only one; he saw four and gear scattered all over. The four horses, he noted, had taken off at a gallop and one horse walked away in the opposite direction going northwesterly.

"One man, four kills... Crying Wolf," he muttered to himself. He looked through the scattered gear to see if there was any identification, on whom the men were. There wasn't. "These men ain't got names, Black Dog. Leastwise nothing in this gear says who they are. John Does, I guess," Tyrell shrugged.

"They crossed the wrong Indian, I'd say. The right thing of course to do is to bury them, and toss their saddles onto their graves and let the law know in Willow Gate where they can be found. Don't that seem ironic, the *law* of Willow Gate. They're about as lawless as these men, I reckon."

Tyrell thought for moment.

"Or we could just bury them, saddles, gear and all, and be done with it. Either way, I best get my field shovel."

Four hours later, he had managed to dig a hole that was big enough to hold the bodies, saddles, and gear. It was off the trail where the ground was soft. It would be hard to see unless one went looking for it.

The mound of dirt of course would be an indicator that something was buried there. He took his time in concealing the mound by tossing some deadfall over it. He stood back and looked on. Satisfied, he nodded.

"That'll do," he muttered as he looked around for a landmark that would be easy to remember in case there ever was a need to exhume the bodies. He decided on the big egg-shaped boulder that was along the trail, he went over to it and paced out the distance to the grave mound in thirty strides. *It is an easy number to remember and not too far off the trail. Perfect,* he thought as he headed back to his horse and Black Dog who lolled in the shade.

"We're all done here now, Black Dog. How about you go over to the boulder and take a piss on it. I might need you to find it for me if I can't," Tyrell joked as he put his field shovel back. To his surprise, Black Dog stood up and pranced over to the boulder. He didn't piss on it, but he did on the tree beside it. Tyrell looked on in amusement. "Atta boy, that'll do. For that, my friend, you get a big, fat piece of jerky." Reaching into the leather pouch where he always kept jerky, he tossed one to Black Dog. He gnawed on one himself as he rested, tired from the four hours of digging.

Looking west, he brought his hand up to eye level and took a finger reading between the sun and horizon on how many hours of daylight there might be.

"Looks like we might have three maybe four hours of riding we can do. We was slowed down, Black Dog. That damn Indian should've buried those men himself." Tyrell shook his head and chuckled. "C'mon, let's put this behind us," he said as he swung onto the red dun.

The Missing Years- Part IV
A Tyrell Sloan western adventure

They travelled fifteen miles that day or so Tyrell speculated. It would have been twenty had they not been slowed down. The main trail now was only ten miles away. "Right here, Black Dog, is where we'll settle for the evening. We've got good views of north and south leastwise. It's flat and there is enough grass to let the horse feed."

He pulled the red dun up to a tree and dismounted. Tethering the horse, he removed the saddle and his gear and then proceeded to gather enough wood to see him through the night. As early as it was, there was a chill in the air. The sun was slowly dropping behind the western mountains. *Yep the days are getting shorter and nights are getting colder,* Tyrell thought as he struck a match. It didn't take long for the flames to warm him or for his evening coffee to start bubbling. Removing the coffee pot from the flames, he set it down next to the fire and retrieved his tin plate and cup, a pot and a can of beans. He thought back to how Pony always got whenever he ate beans. It brought a meek but soothing smile to his face. Crying Wolf was right; Pony would never be dead. He'd always live in the hearts of those who knew him, most definitely in his.

He sat back and waited for the beans, his mind adrift with memories of Pony, of Red Rock Canyon and his home in Hell's Bottom and all those friends he had left behind believing that he was dead. In time, he would resurrect himself and once again go by Tyrell Sloan. Until then, though, he would be content with who he had become and that was Travis Sweet, bounty hunter.

It was a hard thing to pull off, being two different people to protect only one, but it was something he had to do until he could clear his name of any wrongdoing in the deaths of Heath Roy, Ollie Johnson and two other men who he hadn't even met. He had a hunch, though, on who had killed them.

Heath Roy and Ollie, yep, he killed them all right. The other two, though, didn't die by his hand.

Tyrell inhaled deeply as he stirred his beans.

"Sometimes life sure gets in the way of life, don't it, Black Dog?" His beans cooked now, he dumped them onto the plate and dug in with both a spoon and a biscuit. Not surprising to him, Rose's biscuits even with beans were damn good.

"Cold or with beans, that Rose sure knows how to make a biscuit," Tyrell stated as he smacked his lips, broke a piece off and tossed it to Black Dog.

Fed and relaxed now, he poured a bit of water from his canteen into the pot, swooshed it around some, and dumped it out. It was clean enough as far as he was concerned. He did the same with his tin plate and then tucked both of them away in his gear. He nibbled on jerky and the odd biscuit as the sun went down. When the white moon of night finally appeared in the sky, he added a few thick pieces of wood to his fire and warmed his hands. Draping a woollen blanket over his head and shoulders, he huddled close to the orange flames. *It's going to be a frosty one tonight, I reckon,* he thought as he looked up to the clear, star-studded sky.

Colby Christian and Martin Brubaker, were setting up for the evening as well. They had been on the trail since Tuesday afternoon. They were cleaned and shaved, and felt good. "It's gonna be another damn cold one tonight, Colby," Martin added wood to their fire as the two sat close to it.

"I reckon so, it is the first of October tomorrow. If the weather keeps cold like this," Colby spit to the ground, "then, I'd say were in for an early winter, Martin. We might make Willow Gate before the snow flies; might not too."

"We damn better make it there before the snow. I ain't packing no winter clothes and being on a trail like this up and over mountains and whatnot, if the snow comes, we're gonna be damn chilled."

"Only whilst we're up in the mountains. Once we get down lower it won't be so bad," Colby assured him with hope.

"The snow comes though before we get down low, we could freeze up in the hills," Martin wrapped his bedroll around his body and stirred the coals.

"Ah, we ain't gonna freeze, Martin. Shit, we know how to light a fire, don't we?" Colby chuckled.

"Fires don't keep the ground from freezing. Nor snow from falling. We'd still be damn cold."

"We have a week maybe two-week ride ahead of us and chances are, Martin, we're gonna see snow. There ain't a damn thing we can do about it. Not a damn thing. Worrying about it and talking 'bout it is gonna take the fun right out of this ride, so quit your sniveling."

"I ain't sniveling."

"It sounds to me like you is, Martin."

"Making conversation is all, Colby. I only wish I had packed some long underwear and maybe some wool pants. I didn't think though I'd need them. Always seems when you don't think you need something it turns out that you do."

"Maybe we should've thought about picking up some gear when we was back at the Fort," Colby stood up and gathered some wood.

"Figure it is too late to turn back and do jus' that? We'd be behind by a couple days, but we'd have gear. I dunno." Martin shrugged his shoulders. It was just idea.

"Shit, Martin, I hate the thought of heading back to the Fort to pick up gear, but in the long run it might be best. We were in too much of a hurry to catch up with Alex and your brothers that we wasn't thinking straight, I reckon." Colby tossed some wood onto the fire and brought the flames up. He warmed his hands above the flames, as he looked east and then west. They hadn't travelled too far yet. Maybe it was best to turn around and pick up some new gear. Having some warmer clothes and blankets probably wasn't such a bad idea. It was always better to be safe than sorry.

Colby sighed as he looked into the flames of the fire. "I reckon, you is right, Martin. We might as well turn around in the morning and head back to the Fort. We'll get some new gear and stuff, warmer clothes and whatnot. It is a shame that we'll lose a day or two of riding, but I'd hate to be caught in a snowstorm up in the mountains. I ain't packing no warm clothes either. We'll head back east in the morning. We get before the sun rises and we might be able to make the distance by nightfall. Leaves us with Friday to buy what we need and head out again."

"You know it is like we is greenhorns or something. We didn't even think about buying gear when we were there. Nope, we head out onto the trail, travel a day and half and decide, shit, we need gear. That right there is stupidity, Colby, plain stupidity."

"Like I said, we was in too much of a hurry to get. That's all right though, Martin, we'll get what is needed and not look back. It's a minor setback, that's all. No big deal."

"The others are gonna be a week's ride ahead of us. I think that is a pretty big deal, Colby."

"There ain't anything we can do about that unless we keep heading west. It sounds like you ain't so sure now if you want to turn back and pick up gear or not. So, what is it Martin, you wanna head back or not?"

"No, no. I want to get warm gear. We'll head back as you say in the morn. It's just that, well, it seems kind of stupid, don't it?"

"We've already agreed upon that, Martin, and as stupid as it seems, we'll be better off with warm gear as we proceed westerly. I'd rather be a week behind than never catch up."

Chapter 18

Colby and Martin headed east long before the sun rose the next morning. They travelled for a good part of it without stopping, until, out of the blue, Colby slowed his horse down and looked off the trail.

"Hold up a second, Martin. You notice this before when we passed by?" Colby gestured to the side of the trail as Martin rode up.

Martin looked on.

"Looks like three horses rode up here through the bush." He shrugged his shoulders. They both swung off their horses to get a better look.

"Three horses, like you said Martin. The trails old, though. I'd say three or four days. Hmmm, weird that we is noticing it now, 'specially since we've passed by this spot three times," Colby stood up as he looked into the bush.

"It's a trail, Colby. Some riders came through there. What of it. That ain't anything concerning," Martin swung back onto his horse.

"I ain't so sure about that, Martin. Three or four days ago would've been when we met up with Brady heading back to the Fort."

"What of it? You ain't making any sense. Are you still asleep or what?"

"I reckon opposite of that, Martin," Colby said as he led his horse for a bit, looking closely at the ground as he went. He stopped and knelt down. "Look at this, Martin. Those three riders stopped here and were joined by a single rider that could've been Brady."

"What? C'mon, Colby we ain't making much distance looking at an old trail."

Martin was getting a little hot under the collar. Whatever it was that Colby was suggesting wasn't making any sense to him. "Besides, how'd you know they met up with another rider?"

"The stop and turn tracks that horses make tells me that." Colby waved his hand through the air. "Anyway, let's get. It doesn't mean anything, I reckon," he said as he swung up onto his horse.

"'Bout time you came to your senses. You wasted a couple minutes there, for what?"

Colby shrugged. "I was curious more than anything, I suppose."

"No more of that shit, Colby. Who cares if some riders came through the bush. Ain't you ever met up with riders along a trail?"

"Have so. That is why it likely doesn't mean a thing. I tell you this, though, before we leave the Fort this next time, I want to stop in at McCoy's."

"What the hell for?" Martin asked as he looked at him and frowned.

"I have a hunch on something, but I ain't about to get in to it with you right now. You keep your thoughts and insults to yourself for the time being."

"That takes the fun out this second trip into the Fort, but whatever it is you're thinking, Colby, likely ain't worth any contemptuous insulting I could do," Martin chuckled as he sped up his horse, spitting up dirt and dust. Colby heeled the flank of his horse and chased after Martin.

They travelled non-stop for the majority of the morning. Stopping at a creek that trickled by the side of the trail, they rested for the first time.

"Damn, we've been hard at it, Martin, for a lot of hours. We keep up this pace and we'll certainly make the Fort before it gets too dark." Colby splashed water on his face to wash the dust off.

"It is warm today. Nights though, they is pretty cold, ain't they?"

"Only reason the nights is cold is 'cause we was deeper into the mountains. Down here on the flat, the sun beats down hard and heavy."

Martin took a long slug of water. Finishing what was left of his canteen, he filled it up again. Colby did the same with his canteen and a few minutes later, they hit the trail. Riding straight through to the Fort, they finally made the distance as the sun was creeping gently behind the western mountains. Colby drew his horse to a halt and the two of them looked on.

"We can either set up here for the evening or we could get us a couple of rooms at the Snakebite. Which one of the two is your preference, Martin?" Colby asked as he looked over to him.

"I think a couple of rooms for the night, be best. We can have a steak and a couple of draft at the Snakebite. Out here we got beans and water or coffee."

"You think like me, Martin. Let's get us a couple of rooms. A nice thick steak and a couple of cold ones is my preference too."

They heeled their horses and made their way to the Snakebite Hotel. Grabbing a couple of rooms, they headed downstairs to the saloon and ordered their supper and a couple of ice-cold draft.

"I'm glad we decided to get rooms. It makes things a bit more pleasant. We'll be long on the trail again, soon enough," Colby said as they waited for their meal and drink.

It didn't take long before Kitty brought them their order. Thanking her as she pranced away, the two of them dug in. Finishing up their steak and draft, they ordered another round of cold ones. By the end of the evening, they had drunk a half a dozen each. Not quite drunk and not quite sober, they retreated to their rooms.

"If'n I ain't awake by first light, Martin, and you is, wake me. And if I is and you ain't, I'll wake you," Colby said as the two of them climbed the stairwell up to their rooms.

"Sure, what happens if neither of us is up at day break?" Martin smirked, "then what?"

"Then I suppose we get a late start," Colby shrugged. "I'll see you in the morning, Martin."

"See you then, Colby."

Colby sat on the edge of his bed as he pondered. If what he assumed to be true, then the McCoy's did indeed have Matt Crawford. He thought about how they may have fooled him and the others to think Brady was alone, when he had passed them that past Friday.

Could be they saw us, split up, and had Brady prance by to convince us that he was alone, when he wasn't. That'd explain the three riders coming out of the bush and meeting up with Brady. Damn, that is sly... he thought as he lay down. *I guess I'll know if this stands up when we stop off at McCoy's tomorrow. If it turns out as I think, then they've had the son-of-bitch for a week.*

Colby shook his head and closed his eyes, tired, and beat from the day's ride. The half-dozen drafts that he and Martin had consumed had finally taken their toll. The sun was peeking through the window of his room the following morning, Friday, as he opened his eyes. It seemed as though he hadn't even been asleep. *Damn, morning' already,* he thought as he rubbed his eyes. He sat up in his bed, slipped on his boots, grabbed his saddlebags and rifle, exited, and walked down the hall to Martin's room. He knocked.

"Hey, Martin, rise and shine. We got places to be and shit to do, I'll meet you downstairs."

He waited for Martin to respond.

"Yeah, all right, Colby. Be there in a minute," Martin sat up and stretched. "Are we getting breakfast first?"

"I reckon some eggs and coffee are due," Colby replied as he turned and headed downstairs to the saloon. Sitting at a table, he ordered eggs and coffee for both himself and Martin. A few minutes later, the saloon door opened and in walked Ed McCoy. He noticed Colby sitting at a table and he made his way over to him.

"Hey, Colby, how is it going today?" he asked as he approached.

"Morning, Ed. I'd say it is going. Are you going to join me and Martin for breakfast?" Colby offered.

"I can't stay long. Just here to pick up breakfast for Riley and Brady," he lied.

"I see, all right, well it was nice talking with you."

"It was good to see you too, Colby. I thought you and Martin headed out already."

"We did, but decided we needed gear to traipse through the woods. It is getting cold out. We'll be heading west after some breakfast though. Got to find Crawford before someone else does," Colby smiled.

"I wish you luck in that."

"Thanks. We might need all the luck we can get," Colby said as Martin finally showed up. "There is Martin now. Well, Ed, I guess we'll be seeing you 'round."

"Good luck in all your endeavours; Colby. I'll be seeing you," Ed responded as he turned and made his way to the front counter and ordered breakfast for Matt, Riley and himself.

Martin sat down at the table.

"That was Ed McCoy, wasn't it?"

"It was, said he's here to get breakfast for he, Brady and Riley. I think he was bullshitting though. I think he's getting breakfast for himself, Riley, and Matt Crawford."

"What? What the hell are you talking about now, Colby?" Martin asked as Kitty brought them their breakfast.

Colby looked up to Kitty as she set down their breakfast. "Thank you, Kitty."

"You're welcome, Colby. I hope you enjoy it," she turned and walked away.

"Now that she is gone, what the hell are you saying about McCoy's and Matt?" Martin questioned again as he slurped a swallow of coffee.

"Like I pointed out to you yesterday along the trail, something strange is going on," Colby put a mouthful of egg into his mouth and washed it down with a swig of coffee.

"You never pointed anything out yesterday," Martin responded as he began to eat.

"No, I guess I didn't," Colby shovelled another fork full of egg into his mouth. Swallowing, he told Martin about his assumption.

"You mean to say that McCoy's do have Matt and that they pulled the wool over our eyes?"

"I reckon it is something like that, yep."

Martin shook his head.

"I don't know how you can assume that."

"How many times do I need to explain it, Martin? Here's the gist of it again. Last Friday when Brady passed us, I think he was filling our noggins with BS. I think, and again this is an assumption, I figure Brady and whoever else was with him spotted us in that clearing where we was all huddled after we lost our horses. I think they split up. Brady rode by us intentionally to convince us that he was alone. Whilst three other riders, one of them likely Matt Crawford, decided to head through the bush and meet up with Brady down the trail where we ran across them horse tracks. This way, it would appear that Brady was telling us the truth, since we believed him to be alone," Colby shook his head. "I don't think he was, though. Not now, leastwise. We'll know more after we stop off at the McCoy's, but I'm betting they have Matt."

"It turns out like that, then, this day is shit," Martin responded as he finished his eggs and coffee.

"I would agree. It surely will make a mess out of what we are trying to do."

"If we find out they do have Crawford, we're gonna have to make quick time in catching up with Brett, Cape and Alex. Man, they'll be pissed."

"They as well as us I reckon," Colby finished his eggs.

"We gonna head over to McCoy's then right away?"

"I figure Ed will be telling the others that we're here. They'll be watching for us, I think. We'll gather our gear and such, and when we head out, we'll stop by. It'll give the McCoy's time to think that we have already left. They'll drop their guard down then we'll surprise 'em," Colby smiled.

"All right, well, our breakfast and coffee is done. Let's head over to the Fort Grain and Grocery, get our gear, and see if you is right about the McCoy's having Crawford."

"Yep, let's get."

Colby and Martin stood up and slid their chairs in then exited into the early morning sun. Making their way over to the mercantile, they splurged on buying gear and supplies. Loading it all on to their horses, they slowly made their way across town. Spotting Brady who appeared to be going in the opposite direction, Colby called out to him.

Brady stopped his horse and turned around.

"Colby, I wasn't expecting to see you. How are things and what are you doing here?" Brady asked as he rode over to where Colby and Martin stood.

"We figured we needed gear to track down Crawford 'specially since she's getting damn cold at night. Can't be sure how long it'll take to track him down. Best to be safe than sorry, I reckon. How did you like your eggs this morning, Brady?"

"Eggs, what are you talking about? I ain't had any eggs this morning."

"Strange, we saw Ed earlier at the Snakebite, said he was getting breakfast for you, Riley and hisself."

It was then Brady understood why Ed would say that.

"My eggs I guess is getting cold then, but they'll have to wait. I got some business to tend to before I head to the office."

"We have shit to do too. We best get. It was nice talking to you, Brady. We'll see you around," Colby said as he and Martin continued.

"We'll see you Colby, Martin. Nice seeing you folks. Be careful out there. That Crawford is a bitch to track down."

"I suppose he is, otherwise you'd already have him, eh?" Colby smiled.

"If he didn't evade us as he did, yep, we'd have him, but damn he's cagey. Anyway, take care, Colby, we'll be seeing you," Brady said as he tilted his new hat and continued on his way.

Colby and Martin headed through town at a turtles pace. Stopping off at the McCoy's office, they tethered their horses. With the window boarded off, they couldn't see in, nor could those inside see out. Riley and Ed heard the door open and they made their way to the front counter to see who had come in.

"Hey, Colby, Martin, wasn't expecting yous. What brings you?" Riley asked as he and Ed made the distance.

"We is heading out and I figured we'd stop by to say hello and goodbye. I wanted to talk to Brady. Is he about?" Colby questioned.

"Umm, no, he, ah, headed out," Ed responded evasively.

"Shit, when is he gonna be back?"

"Likely, not for a couple hours, what is it you need to see him about?" Ed asked.

"Just wanted to thank him again for pointing out where he saw our horses, when we were hoodwinked by some Indians along the trail last week. Never did find my red dun, though." Colby tapped his fingers on the counter. "You mind if we sit and wait for him?"

"We have a lot of work to do today. Maybe you could swing by later," Ed suggested.

"Nah, we really should be hitting the trail. I have a question for you though, Ed. Did you folks enjoy your breakfast? My eggs I think were a bit rotten. They gave me a bit of a gut ache."

"Ours was fine," Riley shrugged.

"Good, good to know. How did Brady like his?"

"Just fine, I reckon."

"Uhuh, sure he did. Since he ain't around, I guess we'll head out, let him know I stopped by to thank him again. We'll be seeing yous," Colby said as he and Martin turned and began to walk out. Colby stopped short of the door and turned back. "One other thing, you folks did a good job in making us think Brady was alone. He weren't, though, was he?"

"What do you mean, Colby?" Ed questioned with surprise.

"I think he was with two other riders. I also think one of them riders was indeed Matt Crawford."

"What? We ain't got Crawford. He's still running around somewhere," Riley tried to sound convincing, but he wasn't. Colby could see right through that lie.

"I don't think so, Riley. We spoke with Brady not five minutes ago, said he never had no eggs. Yet, the two of you say he liked 'em fine. Now if he never had no eggs, how'd you know he liked 'em fine? I tell you what I think. I think that third order of eggs you picked up, Ed, was for Matt Crawford. Brady ain't even been to the office yet."

Ed and Riley looked at one another. The ruse was up. There was no point in lying anymore. They had Crawford and he was secured. There was nothing Colby or Martin or any one of the Brubakers could do about it. Ed sighed.

"You are right. We do have Matt. Brady and Travis were able to bring him down. Riley and I escorted him and Brady home last Sunday. He's been with us since."

"That is what I figured. We wouldn't have even stopped off here today if'n we didn't come across four sets of horse tracks, three that popped out of the wood along the trail. I reckon that'd have been you, Riley, and Matt. Am I right about that, Ed?"

"You are, Colby, yep. That was Riley, me, and Matt. We circled around you folks when we spotted you. We sent Brady along the trail to fool yous. I guess you were fooled for a bit," Ed shrugged his shoulders and smiled.

"You played that well, I think. Damn shame though that now we have to chase after Alex and the others to let them know."

"We didn't want any trouble, Colby. That is why we did what we did," Riley pointed out.

"No problem, Riley, I get it. I can understand that. I'm glad we was able to make heads and tails out of it before we spent too much time looking for Crawford. The cat is out of the bag now, though. I guess that is it then," Colby nodded. "There ain't much we can do about it. You folks have Matt and we don't." Colby looked over to Martin, "I guess we best get after Alex and your brothers, Martin."

Martin nodded.

"I reckon so. Damn shame we is gonna be out that ten thousand."

"It is, but I heard a fella once say, *'it is what it is'*, and that is what this is. I guess we'll get out of your hair now, Ed, Riley," Colby tilted his hat and he and Martin exited.

"Goddamn it, Colby, I can't believe them sons of bitches outsmarted us and have Crawford. What are we gonna do now?" Martin asked as he swung up onto his horse.

"Ride out of town and head after your brothers and Alex. There ain't anything else we can do, Martin. McCoy's men ain't stupid. They played their hand and we lost ours. It is that simple. There will be other bounties of opportunity, as we go along," Colby said as they heeled their horses and headed west. That was Friday, October 2, 1891.

Chapter 19

Tyrell, Black Dog and the red dun finally made the distance to the trail that now headed due west and into the town of Willow Gate. Tyrell slowed the red dun down, stopped, and rested. "Here we are. Finally, a decent trail to travel and a less perilous one than the one we travelled to get here," Tyrell sucked on an eyetooth. "Three, maybe four-days' ride and we should be damn near to Willow Gate, if not already there. That ain't going to be so bad. We'll settle for the evening up the trail some. With luck, we'll be able to find some water. My canteen is getting low. I reckon, though, we'll find water. C'mon, let's get," he said as they continued.

A short time later as the sun was going down they found a spot that suited them. He swung off the red dun, took the saddle off, and unloaded his gear. He looked around. A glacial creek ran by and he led the horse over to it. While the red dun drank downstream, Tyrell filled his canteens upstream. A short distance away, he noted a decent clearing that had been used many times by other travelers. Tethering the red dun to a sapling where grass and clover grew, he walked over to the area.

There was a fire pit already made and he gathered some wood and stacked it near where it would be within an arm's reach. An old log that he dragged close would suffice as a place to sit. Striking a match, he lit the strips of birch bark he had peeled off a nearby birch tree, sat back, and watched as the flames to his evening fire slowly came to life. Black Dog came over and sat next to him. Tyrell put his arm over the dog's shoulders and patted him. "Night one on the trail to Willow Gate, eh, Black Dog. That last trail was hellish, covered in thorns, and such. I know now why it ain't used except by the wayward and desperate. From here on though, travelling ain't going to be so perilous," Tyrell hoped as he looked into the flames. He knew that even commonly used trails could often bring unwanted scenarios. In other cases, they could bring pleasant encounters of the friendlier type. Just as likely sometimes, the only encounters were with everyday animals. With Black Dog at his side, though, he was prepared for whatever he might face as he made his way to Willow Gate.

There were two things, he needed, to do immediately when he finally arrived, even before he spoke with Gabe Roy. The first depended on what time of day it was. He had to send a wire to McCoy's to let them know he had arrived. The second and probably the more important, was to look in on Emma to let her know why he was there and to tell her to use his alias Travis Sweet, if, and when she ever needed to address him. Of course, this would matter only if Emma still lived there.

No one else in Willow Gate knew who he was. Gabe Roy knew him as Travis Sweet, not Tyrell Sloan, the man who had killed his son Heath Roy.

Gabe heard of Travis Sweet due to Tyrell's encounter with Earl Brubaker. Tyrell thought back to how odd it seemed that shortly after the death of Earl the made-up name 'Travis Sweet' became notorious as the man who had killed Brubaker. Gabe sent two men looking for Travis Sweet. He wanted to hire him to track down the man who killed his son Heath, not knowing that the man named Travis was actually Tyrell.

Gabe wanted Travis to find and to bring to justice Tyrell. He even offered Travis fulltime employment as a bodyguard of sorts. Of course, Tyrell turned the offer down in a hurry. Now, a year later, he had finally submitted to Gabe Roy's will to hire him. Oddly, one of the men that Gabe sent back then was Tanner McBride, one of Tyrell Sloan's old-time running buddies. Tanner, though, understood Tyrell's need for anonymity and so he played along, calling him Travis. It wasn't until they were alone did they speak like the old friends they were. That friendship was rekindled. Now both of them worked for McCoy's, he as Travis Sweet and Tanner as Tanner.

The whole idea of it was so unbelievable. Tyrell shook his head to snap himself out of the past and back to reality. *Having all that running through my head right now sure makes me wonder how this whole charade is going to play out in the end,* he thought as he wrapped his hands around the tin cup in his hand. Taking a swallow, he nodded to himself. *I have a job to do and I must do it to the best of my capabilities. I must rise up from doubt. I must be Travis Sweet a hired man to Gabe Roy, an investigator of McCoy's Private Investigations and Security.* He repeated that a couple of times in his head. He didn't know why, perhaps it was doubt.

That night, as he slept, a frost rolled in. He woke due to the cold, added wood to the fire and wrapped himself up in his bedroll. The only good thing about waking so early was to be able to warm up at the fire. It was dark as night. The stars were starting to fade, but they still twinkled and flickered. He stood up and extinguished his fire, then gathered his gear and saddled the red dun. Rather than sit and wait for daylight, he figured why not hit the trail? He had slept for about six hours, and was feeling rested, "it might be dark, red dun, but there ain't much use in wasting time. The trail, I reckon, is good enough that we should be able to stick to it."

He looked over to Black Dog, "you take the lead. Stick to the trail. No wandering off. You do that 'til sunrise and I got a piece of jerky for you. You bugger off, though, forget about it." Tyrell smiled as he swung up onto his saddle. "C'mon, we're getting an early start today. We'll break in a bit at the first sign of sun. How'd that be?" It seemed they all agreed.

It was a peaceful ride as they carried on. The trail, as Tyrell had assumed, was easy enough to follow. He started to count the nights and days it had been since he left Brady and Matt. He guessed right down to the date and day.

"I figure we split up the sixteenth of September. I'm damn certain we've been on the trail ten days plus a week. I'd say today is Saturday, likely October 3. That sound about right, Black Dog?" he questioned whimsically, as though the dog would answer," Tyrell snickered. "Four days' ride puts us in or close to Willow Gate by the seventh. That is a lucky number."

By mid-afternoon, they found themselves in the high country. There was another valley to cross before their destination would be found. Slowing the red dun down to a halt, Tyrell decided they'd rest. The sun was hot because they were above the forest on the rocky slope of the trail. It wasn't as bad as it looked. Wagons, buggies, even the stagecoach when in operation, used the trail. It was a good a place as any to rest.

He swung off the horse, and let it feed on the mountain grass, while he and Black Dog shared some jerky and fresh water from one of the canteens. Tyrell inhaled deeply the fresh mountain air and all the scents that came with it. He was grateful for another day of living.

On their way once again, they traversed the switchbacks of the trail that eventually led to the valley floor. The trail was now shaded by the pines that grew on either side. The sun shone through only where the evergreens were sparse. Early as it was, along that trail it felt more like early evening than late afternoon. It was cool and silent, almost eerie, made even more so when the valley winds blew.

An old wooden sign along the trail read, *'Wagon Rest Ahead'*. It was odd to see such a sign way out in the middle of nowhere, but it made sense when he finally, came upon a clearing with tables and a roofed fire pit. There was a rail to, tether horses and mules or what have you. Empty, but obvious, grain bins were in front of the rail so whilst animals were tethered they could eat or drink. Beyond that, was another roofed area, likely used for the horses, and stagecoach in case of bad weather. It was perfectly located and likely had sun all day. He could see the faraway mountains to the east and the closer, yet still distant, mountains to the west. North and south were rock bluffs and forest.

"Here is where we're staying tonight. The stagecoach likely stops here when it heads this way and I assume others, too. Tonight we're gonna use it."

Tethering the red dun and unloading his gear, he removed his saddle and dumped some grain into the bin. He didn't have much, but he had enough to feed the horse a couple of times if needed. Right now, it wasn't needed; it was a novelty thing more than, anything else.

With some daylight still left, he and Black Dog walked around. They found some old cans riddled with bullets and empty rifle and pistol casings scattered here and there. He smiled to himself as he set one of the cans up and walked back some to where he could still view it.

He loosened up his shoulders, took a couple of deep breaths, looked the can in the eye, and smiled. With speed and precision, he snapped his pistol from its holster and pulled the trigger sending Mr. Can tumbling through the air. Before it finally landed in the tall grass, Mr. Can had gained

two more holes. A surprised smile crossed his face. It had
been so long since he fired the pistol or had any reason to use
it, but it appeared he still had the speed and aim to make a
perfect kill or three. He had three shots left, so he set up the
can again this time walking further away than the first.

With the same speed, the can suffered three new holes. He
was satisfied with the outcome of his little expenditure. Sure,
it cost him six bullets, but it was fun. He waited for the
casings to cool before he loaded the pistol with six fresh
bullets. The casings he tucked away into his saddlebags. He'd
reload them in time.

He found a couple of old faded cards, ten cents in coins
and some other small pieces of litter including broken glass,
which he simply tossed into a fire pit. The burnable he'd use
to light his evening fire. It would clean the area up some.

He laid the old casings out on one of the tables. It would
have been irresponsible to leave them scattered, as a horse or
mule could swallow one or more. With darkness
approaching, he gathered up wood and lit a fire. Settling in
for the evening, he set a pot of beans to simmer over the
gentle flames. Sitting at the table, he waited for them to
finish. It didn't take long and he was soon eating beans and
slurping his evening coffee.

"Sure nice coming across this place, eh, Black Dog? Even
if it began to rain, we'd be covered," Tyrell looked around.
The sounds of night slowly came to life. A coyote in the
distance howled and a few birds chirped their goodnight
song. It was a peaceful and relaxing evening. Everything was
as it should be.

On Wednesday, October 7, 1891, the town of Willow Gate
came into view. Tyrell stopped his horse and looked on.
"There it is, Black Dog. There is Willow Gate." After a few

minutes of sitting and looking, he finally made his way into
the town. It was early enough that the telegraph office was
open and he sent a wire off to McCoy's. After paying the
small fee, he carried on to 'Emma's Place', one of the few
eateries in Willow Gate.

Swinging off the saddle, he tethered the red dun and
entered. He sat at a table with his back to the wall. Emma
noticed him and she tilted her head. He looked familiar to
her. Making her way over to his table a big grin crossed her
face. She was about to speak, but Tyrell stopped her. He
looked around to make sure no one was within earshot and
gestured for her to sit down. He explained to her what he was
doing there and that he was using the name Travis Sweet. She
continued to smile. Finally, perhaps Willow Gate would be
once more the peaceful town it had been before Gabe Roy
turned it all upside down.

"Travis, it is good to see you. I often wondered what
became of you," Emma said as she sat at his table. The two of
them talked for a few minutes, bringing each other up to date
on their lives since their last meeting.

"It is good to see you too, Emma. It has been a long time."
Tyrell removed his hat, and set it on the table, as he looked
her in the eyes. She was as beautiful as she was the first time
he laid eyes on her. He could tell she was even happier than
she was when they first met. Things had turned around for
her there was no doubt about that.

"I'm glad to see that you are still running this place. There
was a time, I know, that you were seriously thinking on
letting it all go, but you didn't and that is the best news I've
heard in a while."

"It was because of you that I pulled myself out of that
depressed state. I washed my hands of all the bad stuff and let
it all slide off my shoulders. I now fully own this place. Gabe

Roy has nothing to do with it anymore. It is all mine," she said with pride and sincerity.

"I'm happy for you. I know how much you love this place and all the work you have put into it. It would've been a shame if you had walked away from it."

"I often thought I would, but once Heath Roy was... well, you know, gone from my life for good, I knew then I had a clean slate to do better and I did. I paid off that bastard Gabe, got everything checked, and double checked by a lawyer and signed away. Gabe now has nothing at all to do with this place. In fact, he rarely comes here now, which suits me fine. He's still an ass and I don't like him one bit. The way he and his son Heath constantly belittled me because I owed them money for this place, I'll never have respect for Gabe. I hope you are able to bring justice to Willow Gate."

Tyrell inhaled deeply.

"I hope I can expose him and his shoddiness and bring justice to him as well. It is going to take time though, but I am committed to the job for now. I'll do my best, Emma. That is all I can do. As long as you and I keep what it is we know to ourselves, then I believe there is a light at the end of it all."

"I have kept your last name away from everyone that ever asked about the Tyrell fellow, who killed Heath Roy and his idiot friend Ollie for this long already, and I have no intent on letting anyone know now. You did me a great favour when you put both Heath and Ollie in the ground. From this day on, you will be known to me as Travis Sweet. I don't even know anyone named Tyrell Sloan," she smiled. "Can I get you anything, Travis?"

"I'd love a coffee and one of those sandwiches you make," Tyrell smiled back and winked at her.

Emma stood up and slid her chair in. "I'll bring it to you right away," she said as she pranced off.

Tyrell sat alone at the table and looked around. His mind raced with visions of Heath Roy and Ollie Johnson as they pulled their pistols and wounded him. He could even feel the sting from Heath's bullet as it grazed his shoulder. He shook his head as he snapped out of it. Finally, Emma brought him his coffee and sandwich. She set it down in front of him.

"Here you go Mr. Sweet, one coffee and a roast beef sandwich, with everything on it."

"Ah, yes, the best sandwich and coffee this side of the Rocky Mountains," he said as he looked at it.

"If you want or need anything else, let me know, Travis. I'll be here."

Tyrell nodded.

"Thank you, Emma, I will." Tyrell took a swallow from his coffee as Emma turned and went back to serving her other patrons. An hour later, he paid his bill, asked directions to Gabe Roy's place, and set off. It didn't take long to find the house, big as it was and all. He swung off his saddle tethered the horse and knocked on the door.

A black woman answered and invited him in.

"I'm Travis Sweet, here to see Gabe."

Tyrell removed his hat and fiddled with the brim, while the lady walked up some stairs and knocked on a door.

"Master Roy, Travis Sweet has arrived," she said as the door swung open.

"All right, Neeada, thank you. Now go on and get back to whatever it is you were doing. Send Travis to me," Gabe said as he closed the door in her face.

"Right away, master Roy."

Neeada returned to where Travis stood.

"Master Roy will see you. He's in his office at the top of the stairs and to your left," Neeada said as she scurried off.

Tyrell didn't even have time to thank her. Making his way up the stairs and to the door on his left, he knocked.

"Yes, come in." Gabe stood up and met him, as he stepped in. "Mr. Sweet," Gabe began as he reached out his hand to shake Tyrell's. "I'm happy to see you. Please, please, come and sit down. We have a lot to discuss," Gabe directed him to a chair in front of his big oak desk.

"Thank you, Mr. Roy," Tyrell said as he sat down.

Gabe poured himself a brandy and offered one to Tyrell who declined.

"No thanks, Mr. Roy. I'd like to get on with what it is we need to discuss."

"That is fair enough. You can call me Gabe, by the way."

Tyrell looked at him and shrugged.

Gabe sat down behind his desk.

"How was your trip?" he asked.

"Same as any trip, long, tiring and cold sometimes. I'm here now, though. Ed has told you what it is McCoy's expects to be paid. Five hundred cash a week plus all expenses, right? My first week's pay is upfront so due today," Tyrell, pointed out.

"Yes, indeed. I did agree to that. I figure you are worth it. Anyone who can pull a pistol quicker than Earl Brubaker is worth that amount."

"You can also quit pointing out what happened between me and Earl as though it is a perquisite for this job. I know what went on with me, and Earl. You don't need to keep pointing it out, Mr. Roy. In fact I would prefer if you didn't from here on."

Gabe took a swallow from the brandy in his hand. "Are you ashamed with the fact that you killed him?" Gabe was curious. He didn't want anyone who was ashamed of killing to be working for him.

"I never said that at all, Mr. Roy. There is no shame in killing someone while trying to protect yourself, when it is either you or them," Tyrell affirmed.

"Good to know. I thought perhaps you weren't the man for this job after all."

"You are quite welcome to find someone else, but I'll be expecting five hundred cash before I leave."

"No, no, Mr. Sweet, you're the man I need for this job and we'll get to that shortly. I am curious, though, why you didn't take my offer when I sent Tanner McBride and Buck Ainsworth to look for you."

"Simple. I wasn't looking for employment back then." As far as Tyrell was concerned, there was nothing more needed to be said in that regard and he made it quite clear.

"I see. And now you do need employment?"

"Nope, not really, have you forgotten that I work for McCoy's. You hired them and it so happens I'm the man that Ed sent this way."

"On the contrary, once I heard that the man who sent Earl to hell worked for McCoy's. I requested you. Ed didn't send you." Gabe took another swallow from his brandy. As though what he said meant something. "I requested you," he repeated.

"Trust me, Mr. Roy, whether you requested me or not, Ed could have simply said we ain't interested and I wouldn't be here now. So I say I'm the man that McCoy's sent." Tyrell looked directly at Gabe as he said that. He wasn't intimidated, if that is how Gabe was trying to make him feel.

"Fine, you are the man they sent. We'll leave it at that. Do I pay you directly the wage or do I send it to McCoy's?" Gabe asked, already knowing the answer.

"You pay it directly to me, Mr. Roy. I'll keep track of it and I'll give you a receipt for every expense I incur that is business-related."

"Of course," Gabe agreed as he pulled a chequebook out of his desk drawer.

Tyrell shook his head. "Ah, if you're writing that out to me, don't bother. I only take cash."

"Huh, cash?"

"Yep, cash only, Mr. Roy. You agreed to that yourself. If you need some time to get it, I'll come back." Tyrell began to stand.

"No, no, stay seated. I'll get it." Gabe stood up, and made his way into another room and opened his safe. Pulling out a few stacks of one hundred dollar bills, he counted off five. Returning to his office where Tyrell waited, he handed the money off. "There you go. Five hundred cash dollars for your first week's wage. Now, about the job I need you to do," Gabe poured himself another brandy as Tyrell checked the payment.

"I'm all ears, Mr. Roy," Tyrell said as he looked over to Gabe.

"There isn't much to the job. I only need you to keep my back safe. There are some, who'd like to see me, penniless, and some who would rather see me dead for whatever reason, they can conjure. Your job will simply be to protect me and my wealth until such time I no longer need your services."

"I figured as much. I need to know, though, why would anyone want to see that come of you?"

"Some seem to think they have reasons, but clearly and legally they don't. The Mounted Police in this town have been doing a fine job in bringing justice to those that have tried one thing or the other to see me killed or broke. But, they aren't always available, like a hired man. That is why I need services such as the McCoy's offer."

"We ain't hired gunmen, Mr. Roy. I can offer you protection against the ill fated, but not against the law. In other words, if you need protection from the laws of the land for stuff you have, or have not done, that I cannot protect you from, the law will always win."

"It isn't the law. It is the lawless I need protection from."

"And McCoy's can offer you that," Tyrell assured.

"Good. There is a small house on this property where I'd like for you to stay as my guest while you are working for me. It has a stable for two horses. Feed will be provided. The house has running water, bath, and toilet. I will even provide you with a maid if you like."

"I don't see any reason for a maid, Mr. Roy, but if you haven't a problem with a dog living there with me, I will take the house." Although he would have rather rented a room at the hotel and charge Gabe for it, if nothing else the offered house would put Tyrell closer to the investigation against Gabe Roy.

"You have a dog?" Gabe was a bit curious on why Travis Sweet would have a dog. It was often said that the man that had killed his son, Heath, was running with a dog. However, there was no proof. It was all hearsay. It seemed a bit odd to Gabe.

"He's a trained service dog," Tyrell fibbed. Black Dog had never been trained, but it made the dog, sound official.

"I see, I thought maybe it was a simple mutt. A service dog is a different story," Gabe chuckled as though he were relieved.

"What do you mean a different story?" Tyrell questioned.

"It is nothing that concerns you at the present."

"I'm afraid it does, Mr. Roy. If I'm expected to protect you, I need to know what it is you meant. Is there someone with a dog that is looking for you or vice versa?"

"It has been said that the man who killed my son had a mangy dog," Gabe lowered his head and looked at his empty brandy glass as he thought about Heath.

"Your son Heath, you mean?"

Gabe stood up and poured himself a double shot of brandy. "Yep, Heath and, of course, his childhood friend Ollie were best friends right up until the day they were both killed by a fellow named Tyrell. The only person who was able to give a description of this man was a floozy named Emma. Still lives here, she does, and runs a small cafe here in Willow Gate. She and Heath at one time were an item, then this stranger Tyrell rode into town. I guess he was getting sweet on Emma and Emma was submitting to his desires. I reckon Heath heard about this and went to confront Tyrell, 'cept, well, that man Tyrell shot both of them before Heath even pulled his pistol," Gabe paused for a few minutes.

Tyrell sat there waiting to hear more of the built-up tale, none of which was truth and he would know, but it wasn't the time or the place to tell his side of the story. At the present, he was Travis Sweet not Tyrell Sloan.

Finally Gabe continued. "Anyway, this Tyrell fellow shot Heath and Ollie for the simple pleasure of doing so. I sent bounty hunters, hired guns two of which were also killed. Their throats were slit from ear to ear. I even hired Brubaker to search for him, offered a nice reward, everything, but no one ever saw or heard from that man again." Gabe shrugged. "Could be he's dead by now or never existed in the first place and it was Emma that shot Heath and Ollie then made up some story. What I know for certain is if I can ever prove she did the killing, I'll hang her myself," Gabe sat back down.

"That is quite the tale, Mr. Roy. I knew your son was killed. You hear stuff like that in the business McCoy's is in, I have seen wanted posters of this Tyrell fellow and I can tell you that not even in my travels have I ever seen him. Maybe there is more going on. If you like while I'm here, I can look into Heath's death. McCoy's can offer you that service too for an extra fee," Tyrell was building up a reason now to spend more time with Emma to protect her. Gabe sounded like he was ready to start looking for others to blame and obviously hang and Emma was on his list.

"One of my first points in hiring a private investigation and security firm such as McCoy's was indeed to also look into Heath's death, and at the same time keep my back from bullets and my wealth from being swindled or stolen. That is all part of it," Gabe said with surprise and anger.

"Sorry, Mr. Roy, but no it ain't. You hired McCoy's to protect you and your assets not to look into who killed or didn't kill your son. That is a different thing altogether. We can offer it, though," Tyrell was being honest and firm. Besides, the more he could charge Gabe Roy for McCoy's services the better.

"My understanding was that I could hire McCoy's to work for me and to do whatever it is I wanted 'em to do." Gabe was getting a bit drunk and the drunker he got the uglier he got. Tyrell, though, was aware of this because of what Riley had told him about his own experiences in working for Gabe Roy.

"You have the wrong idea then about what McCoy's offers. We can protect you and your assets. We can privately investigate almost anything under the sun. When you hired McCoy's you hired one man to protect you and your assets at a fee of five-hundred cash a week plus expenses. You didn't hire us to investigate your son's death."

Tyrell shook his head.

"We'd have to charge you for that, Mr. Roy, but we can certainly do it."

"Charge me! Jesus Christ, I'm already paying you five hundred a week. I have even offered you residence for you and a dog, no less."

"Black Dog is highly trained. He keeps me safe. He'll protect you as well if I command him to do so. You might not often see him, but you can bet, he ain't never far from my side. He's not just *a simple* dog," Tyrell made clear.

Gabe waved his hand through the air.

"Whatever, whatever, a trained service dog, he's still a damn dog."

Gabe paused.

"How much more will it cost me to have you or should I say McCoy's privately investigate Heath's death then?"

"Truth is, Mr. Roy, I'd have to wire Ed to be sure. I reckon it might be close to double," Tyrell guessed.

"Double! That's a thousand a week. Holy sweet Jesus! You might as well jump back on that horse of yours and be gone. A thousand a week! That is robbery!"

Tyrell stood up as though he were about to leave. He had Gabe where he wanted him now.

"Hold on, you. You're actually going to leave?"

"Doesn't sound to me like you want me here, Mr. Roy, or want to pay the extra for us to look into your son's death. Now, I'll stay if you only want my services for security reasons at the agreed upon wage. I won't be looking into Heath's death, though. You decide. I think tonight, I'll spend in the hotel. You let me know what you decide in the morning," Tyrell turned and began to walk toward the door.

"Hold on, Mr. Sweet. Okay, I'll pay whatever is extra for McCoy's to investigate Heath's death. I won't assume it to be more than a thousand a week though."

"All right," Tyrell said as he made his way back to the chair he previously sat in. "I can't be sure exactly what Ed will charge. I wouldn't think it'll be anymore than what I said. So, now you want us to protect you and your assets and to also investigate the death of your son, correct?" Tyrell wanted to be clear and he wanted Gabe to understand.

Gabe ran the palm of his hand up his forehead and through his hair.

"Yes, I want to hire you and McCoy's to protect me and my assets as well as investigate my son's death," Gabe stood up and poured another brandy.

"Now that we are clear on that, Mr. Roy, I'll send a wire off to Ed. He'll likely reply by tomorrow."

Tyrell stood up.

"Since we ain't finalized a wage, I think it is only fair to you, Mr. Roy, that until we hear from Ed, that I'll book myself a room at one of the hotels here in town. Do you have any suggestions?" Tyrell asked, knowing that Gabe would likely direct him to one of hotels that he owned.

"The umm, the Willow Gate Nugget is the best, I think."

"I'll go book myself a room there and will talk to you after I hear from Ed, Mr. Roy."

"I'll see you then."

Gabe watched as Tyrell exited, grabbing the entire flask of brandy, he sat down at his desk and drank away his sorrows.

Tyrell made his way back to Emma's place and asked her what hotel she could suggest. It wasn't the Willow Gate Nugget, but the Owl's Nest Hotel, which was directly across the street. Tyrell thanked her and made his way to the Owl's Nest. He paid up front for a two-day stay. His room was spacious and had running water, a toilet, and down the hall was a bath area. The bed was big and firm. A chair and ottoman sat the foot of it and the sitting table was by a window that overlooked 'Emma's Eatery'. *Hmmm, talk about coincidences,* Tyrell thought as he looked on. After some time and before the telegraph office closed, he made his way to it and sent off another wire to Ed to let them know that Gabe was requesting another service and to find out what he should charge for said service. Until he heard back from Ed, he would enjoy his time away from Gabe.

Chapter 20

Ed McCoy made his way to the McCoy's office. His son Brady had been on twenty-four hour watch for almost a week, keeping their prisoner Matt Crawford fed and safe. He entered through the backdoor and was surprised to see that Brady hadn't even woken up yet. Ed looked at his pocket watch. It was 8:00 a.m. Taking, a moment, he looked in on Matt. All was well and he proceeded to the backroom that had the cot. He banged on the wall.

"Rise and shine Brady! It's eight a.m., and you ain't even got coffee going.

Brady looked toward Ed as he rubbed his eyes.

"Jesus Christ, old man, I've been up and down every hour on the hour for almost a damn week. Can't I catch a break?" he said as he swung up from the cot. He rubbed his back. "And this damn cot is in need of a new mattress or we need a whole new cot."

Brady slipped into his clothes and pulled his boots on. Ed, by now, was in the small kitchen stoking up the woodstove. Finally, Brady made his way into the backroom kitchen and sat down at the table.

"Did you hear what I said about that damn cot?"

"Sure did, it needs a new mattress you said. Maybe today you could go over to the mercantile, and see if they have any. I don't think they do, but you could always check."

"Why wouldn't they have any damn cot mattresses?" Brady asked.

"They don't stock them, Brady. You'll have to order it," Ed said as he poured three coffees for himself, Brady and Matt.

"You're on duty, Brady, so go on and take this to Matt." Ed handed Brady the coffee.

"You're standing and I'm sitting why don't you take it to him?"

"You should've had all this done by now. Matt should've been fed breakfast by now, too. I'll get that started and you take him his morning coffee."

"Jesus, this babysitting is really a pain in the ass." Brady stood up and took Matt his coffee. "Morning, Matt. Sorry I'm late in getting this to you. Slept in a bit," Brady said as Matt stood up and reached for the coffee.

"No worries, Brady. It's all right." Matt took the coffee and sat back down on his bunk. "Any word yet on a circuit judge being around?"

"We ain't heard nothing yet, Matt. Sounds like you really want to get this over with."

"I do. I've been stuck here in this cell two weeks this Sunday. I'm starting to get tired of it."

Matt took a swig from his coffee.

"I can understand that. Maybe we'll hear something today," Brady shrugged.

"I hope so. It would be nice," Matt responded.

"You do know that Ed has filled in the documents that make you a witness to two ongoing investigations, don't you?" Brady questioned as he put one hand on the bars and conversed with Matt.

"I assume he ain't heard anything back on that yet either has he?" Matt questioned, although he already knew the answer.

"That'll likely take time. He only sent the documentation in this past Monday. You never know, Matt. That could be what the holdup is in getting a circuit judge," Brady pointed out.

"I suppose it could. I hope we hear something about something soon."

"Let's hope so, eh? Anyway, Matt, I think Ed is fixing you up some breakfast. I'll get it to you once it is ready."

"I guess I'll talk to you later then."

"You will so."

Brady turned and exited the holding cell area. Making his way to the front counter, he watched as Innis put in the last pane of shatterproof glass in the broken window.

"Damn, that does looks quite smart, Innis."

"It does, doesn't it?" Innis clarified as he stood back and looked at the work he had done. "I'm quite surprised that I was able to finish it before the snow. It didn't take as long to have the glass shipped in as I expected. This glass is also obscured, so you can look out but folks can't really look in unless they cup their hands over the glass."

Innis pulled out a rag from his back pocket and wiped the four panes of glass down, removing handprints and whatnot. "There, all done," he said as he admired his workmanship and tested the one pane that opened.

"Are you going to paint our logo on there?" Brady asked.

"I will, but it won't be today. I have another job I need to look at. Have you or Ed come up with a logo?"

"I think all we want is 'McCoy's Private Investigations and Security' or something along that line."

"That should be easy enough to do. I'll come by Monday next week and finish it up. Between now and then, you folks might change your mind, and instead have a sign built that we can hang above the door. I think that might look better, it'll keep the window looking good. It is up to you folks, though." Innis gathered his tools and cleaned up a bit. "Well Brady, I'm off. I'll see you next week."

"Have a good rest of the day. We'll see you next week, Innis." Brady turned and made his way into the kitchen.

Sitting down at the table, he took his first sip of morning coffee.

"Yuk, damn. It's gone cold already."

He stood up and poured a fresh cup.

"Is Matt's breakfast ready yet old man?" he asked as he sat down again and waited.

"It will be in a couple more minutes. Has Innis finished with the front window?"

"He just finished it off now. It looks pretty damn smart too. He said it is obscured as well. We can see out but folks can't look in," Brady took a sip of his coffee. "Yeah, that's better," he said as he looked over to Ed. "Innis mentioned we might want to think about having a sign made up, rather than paint the glass."

"A sign, that sounds all right. Did you tell him to go ahead and do it?" Ed asked, as he flipped the hotcakes, he was making for Matt's breakfast.

"Nope, he'll be stopping by on Monday. We can tell him then. By the way, where in the hell is Riley? He should be here by now," Brady took another slurp of coffee.

"The widow took him out in our buggy last night. I reckon he'll be late today."

Brady chuckled.

"I would have liked to have seen his face when she showed up at his place. I imagine he was quite surprised."

"You can bet he was," Ed said as he flipped the hotcakes one last time. "Here's Matt's breakfast," he tossed six hotcakes onto a plate, scooped up some butter that he set on the side. He added some syrup and jam in two little cups.

"I ain't sure which of the two he likes, so he's gets both."

Brady stood up and took the plate.

"I hope you saved me some of those," Brady said as he looked at the hotcakes. "Looks like you might have even known what it was you were doing, old man."

"I've been cooking hotcakes and eggs for a long while, Brady. I think I know by now what it is I'm doing. I did make enough for you and I as well, and Riley too if he gets here before we finish 'em all."

Ed turned back to the woodstove and added more hotcake mix to the pan.

"These here will be ready in no time, Brady. Give Matt his and you can have this next set."

"That sounds good to me."

Brady turned and took Mat his breakfast.

"Here you go, Matt. Ed made up some hotcakes. He did a damn fine job, too."

"They do smell good," Matt stood up and took his plate through the opening.

"Thank you very much, Brady," he made his way back to his bunk and sat down.

"Tell Ed he did a fine job," Matt said as he dug in.

"I will, Matt. I'm going to go get mine now. We'll see you later."

Matt didn't even look up from his plate. He simply nodded and continued to eat.

"Matt says you did a good job with them hotcakes, old man," Brady sat down and waited for his stack to be finished.

"The secret to a good hotcake is buttermilk," Ed pointed out as he flipped the cakes that were cooking.

"Buttermilk, you must've stopped off at Steve's Farm this morning?"

"I did so. I picked up buttermilk and eggs."

"How is old man Steve doing? I ain't been over to his place since I've been back. Last time I stopped in, he wasn't in the best of shape. He's getting old." Brady smiled, "I guess we all do though don't we, old man."

"Jesus, Brady, why do you keep pointing out old age?"

"Did I? I'm sorry, old man. I didn't realise I had," Brady smirked.

"You know damn well that you did. Now get over here and get these hotcakes. You get the burnt one too, for being a prick," Ed tossed the cakes onto a plate, as Brady stood up.

"Burnt is all right, I don't mind. Hard to believe though that you could cook a dozen hotcakes and only burn one. A fellow your age gets distracted pretty easily I would've expected a few more burnt ones," Brady took the plate and sat down again at the table snickering the entire time as he dug in.

"Keep making jokes, Brady. One day one of 'em is going to bite you on the ass." Ed shook his head and smiled as he flipped the last of the cakes.

They were finishing up their breakfast and the cleanup that followed when the front door opened. The two of them went out to meet whoever came in. It was Bud from the telegraph office. "Good morning, Ed, Brady. I got three telegrams for you."

"Three?" Ed questioned with surprise as Bud made his way to the counter.

"Yes sir," Bud said as he handed the folded pieces of paper over.

"Are any of them from a circuit judge?" Brady asked as Ed opened the first and began to read it.

"They're from your men Travis and Tanner," Bud said as he waited for Ed to decide if he was going to send replies.

"It says here Tanner is in Hazelton. Says we need to look into a man by the name of Jack Calloway. Apparently he lent Ranthorp five thousand cash for a poker tournament."

Ed handed it over to Brady who read through it as well.

"This one," Ed began, "says Travis is in Willow Gate, arrived there yesterday."

He handed that one over to Brady too.

"And this one says Travis sold Gabe another service. Wants to know what we should charge him. I guess Gabe wants to hire us to also look into the death of his son, Heath." Ed inhaled deeply as he looked over to Brady. He was grateful Heath wasn't his son. To lose Brady would be devastating. Even though he wasn't keen on Gabe Roy, he could only imagine the pain he was still going through. "What do you say, Brady? What should we charge Gabe for that service?"

"It depends. Do we need to send another man? Before you say anything, old man, I want you to know, that if we decide to send another man, it ain't going to be me. I've been back two weeks, spent one week at home, and this second week I've spent here. There is no bloody way it'll be me."

"I don't think we need to send another man. I think Travis could pretty much handle it. It turns out later on that we need another man, well, we'll have to decide then, I guess. What do you think is fair to charge?"

"Gabe Roy has more money than the Fort Bank. Let's do some quick calculations, he's already paying us five hundred cash a week, plus all of Travis's expenditures, and that is just for protection services. We add an investigation to that I don't see why we couldn't then charge double. A thousand a week, I'd suggest. It is up to you, old man. You're the one that runs this place."

Ed thought for a minute.

"A thousand I think is a bit much. I figure seven hundred and fifty. That'll give Travis a bit of play money leastwise, two hundred and fifty a week."

Ed looked over to Bud, who was sitting down on a chair near the door waiting.

"All right, Bud, I have one reply," Ed waved him over as he scribbled out a reply that simply read '*Seven hundred and fifty a week, cash only. Colby, Alex, and three cousins, heading west to Willow Gate.* "This goes to Travis Sweet in Willow Gate," he handed the reply over to Bud.

"Well, eighteen words are better than one or two." Bud shook his head. "Like I said before, Ed, these short replies ain't going to make me a rich man," Bud chuckled. "I'll get it sent right away."

"Thank you, Bud. How much are we up to now? You have been billing me, ain't ya?" Ed asked to be sure.

"Yes, I have. You can swing by whenever you like to set it straight," Bud nodded and headed out the door.

Ed and Brady watched as Bud scooted across the street and out of sight.

"Huh, first time I've taken noticed to that window, now that it is finished. Like you said, Brady, it looks smart."

Brady looked at Ed and shook his head.

"We've been standing here for a couple of minutes already old man while we read these wires, and only now you noticed."

"I was too busy reading what was written."

"Uhuh, okay. Anyway, so now we know Tanner is in Hazelton and Travis is in Willow Gate. Tanner mentioned this Jack Calloway fellow. I've heard that name before. He's a loan shark, I think. Tanner says Jack lent Miles Ranthorp five thousand for a poker game."

"I know, Brady, I read the wire."

"What do you make of that? You got any opinions?"

"I think it is like Tanner said. I think Ranthorp tried to get to Matt all those months ago so he could pay off a poker debt.

Here lies the problem, though. Matt also witnessed Ranthorp leaving Emery's room in a hurry, and a short time later, Emery was found dead. Could be Ranthorp went after Matt to off him 'cause he was a witness to Emery's murder. I don't know," Ed shrugged. "We'll have to see what comes of it all. I think Tanner is on the right track."

"One of us I figure needs to get over to the Mounted Police station and see if Bash or Cannon have anything on this Jack Calloway fellow. And one of us needs to stay here. Which of the two do you want to do, old man?" Brady questioned. Hoping it would be he that headed over to the station he was bored with being on guard duty.

"You've been cooped up here for the past while, Brady, so you might as well go ahead and see what if anything Bash or Cannon have. I'll stay here."

"Thank God," Brady said with a smile as he quickly exited without saying another word. It felt good to be in the fresh air and doing something other than being a servant. He stopped off at the telegraph office and paid their bill, a whopping three dollars. Getting the receipt, he continued down the block and crossed another street to the Mounted Police station. Constable Rick Bash was behind the counter as Brady walked in. "Good morning, Rick," Brady said as he made the distance to the front receiving counter.

"Hey Brady, how are things going today?" Bash asked.

"Pretty good, Rick, it is sure a nice morning out. Sure felt good to walk here." Brady leaned on the counter.

"Guard duty, eh?"

"Well as you know, Bash that is what it is all about. Yippee." Brady rolled his eyes and shook his head.

"I hear you. I've been stuck with training two new members this past week. I know how you must feel though doing guard duty. How is Matt doing by the way?"

"He's all right. Getting antsy, I suppose. Really wants this whole thing over and done with. I can't blame him. He's been locked up almost two weeks and not a word regarding any circuit judge being in the area."

"We haven't heard a word in that regard. I can't help you there much."

"I know you can't, Rick, but maybe you can help me with something else."

"What's that, Brady?" Bash asked as he tucked some documents into a drawer.

"We're looking for anything you Mounties might know about a fellow goes by the name of Jack Calloway."

Bash brought his hand to his face as he thought for a moment. "Calloway, Calloway. That name does sound familiar. Give me a minute, Brady. I'll look that up," Bash said as he turned and walked over to a big file cabinet. He looked down to the 'CA' headings and slid open the drawer. "Calloway," he mumbled as he moved his finger along the edge of the document name list looking for Calloway. "Here it is, Calloway, Jack Robert." Bash continued reading the document as he walked back to the counter.

"You got something then, eh, Bash?" Brady asked as Bash approached.

"Hardly the type of criminal I would expect McCoy's to be looking for. He's a petty loan smith. His only crime was drunk in public three years ago. Well, that and of course the moral crime of charging an arm and leg in interest when he loans money." Bash set the folder down on the counter so Brady could have a look.

"I didn't say we were looking to put him in cuffs, Bash. We needed to know if he loans money, which you have already pointed out that he does," Brady said as he looked through the folder. "We got a wire from Tanner McBride up in Hazelton this morning. He came across Calloway on his travels, I guess. Calloway said he lent that Pinkerton, Miles Ranthorp, five thousand for a poker game up that way. It could be why Ranthorp is dead now 'cause he was stupid enough to go after Matt for the reward to pay off the debt. If he hadn't been tracking Matt at the same time as Riley and I and hadn't shot our horses, he might be alive today. We ain't sure where all this fits into Emery's death, but I think there is some kind of correlation."

"That could be, I suppose, but it could have nothing at all to do with it. We all know that Matt Crawford witnessed Ranthorp leaving your man Emery's room, and that shortly after Emery was found dead. Could be Ranthorp went after Matt because he was a witness to that crime."

Brady nodded and chewed on the inside of his lip.

"That too is quite possible and might very well be the only reason. Least we know the name of one other person who has had dealings with Ranthorp, besides Matt, and Emery, and that is Calloway. The icing on the cake, I reckon, is getting the names of any of the gamblers that might have sat at the same card table with Ranthorp before things went awry. Maybe one of them saw or heard something that might have gone on between Emery and Ranthorp. There is definitely something that ties the two of them together," Brady inhaled deeply. "All right, Rick. Thanks for the bits and pieces. We're clear now that Calloway does lend money."

"No problem, Brady. We're always here to help if we can. Good luck with Matt and such. We'll let you folks know as soon as we hear about a circuit judge."

"Thanks a lot," Brady turned and exited. The walk back to the dreaded office and guard duty made him take his time. He was glad that come morning it would be Riley, or Ed who took over the next week. He didn't care which, but it certainly wasn't going to be him. He stopped outside the front of the office and looked at the window. As Innis said, he couldn't see in. He cupped his hands over the glass, but even then, it was dark and hard to see anything past the entrance. Finally, he walked around back and came in through the backdoor, just to kill a couple more minutes.

Ed heard the backdoor open.

"Is that you, Riley?" Ed hollered from the backroom as he stood up to go have a look.

"Just me, old man," Brady responded as he made the distance to where Ed now stood.

"What did you find out, Brady?"

"Calloway is a known loan smith. He was arrested one time for public drunkenness three years ago, I might add."

"So not much then, did you see Bash or Cannon and did either one say anything about a circuit judge?" Ed asked as the two of them sat down.

"It was Bash I saw. They ain't heard anything about a circuit judge, but they'll let us know when they do." Brady took his new hat off and set it on the table. "That new damn hat of mine doesn't fit nothing like my old one that hog of Harv's took," Brady commented as he looked at it.

"It just needs to be worked in. Let your horse piss on it a couple of times. That'll pretty it up and fix it," Ed said with a smirk.

"I didn't say it wasn't pretty old man. I like the way it looks. And no damn horse, is gonna piss on it. The thing cost me fifteen bucks, almost twice of what my other cost," Brady complained. "That reminds me, McCoy's owes me three dollars."

Brady pulled out the receipt he got from Bud and handed it to Ed.

"I'll put it on your next pay, Brady," Ed teased.

"Of course you will."

Brady looked up to the clock on the wall.

"Eleven o'clock almost and still no Riley, one of us should go check on him, make sure he didn't have a heart attack or something."

Brady was simply looking for another way out of the office.

"Maybe you're right, Brady. I'll go check."

Ed stood up and exited, leaving Brady sitting at the table with his head in his hands. *That didn't go as planned,* Brady thought as he made his way to the front counter and watched as Ed rode past the front window waving and smiling. "I should've known that was going to happen." He shook his head as he went and checked in on Matt.

Matt was sitting on his bunk his knees up and his back against the wall.

"Hey Matt, you need anything or want a coffee?" Brady asked as he looked in on him.

"Nah, I'm all right, Brady. Just thinking is all, not much else to do. I know I asked earlier, but any news on a judge yet?"

Brady shook his head.

"Sorry, Matt, I was over at the station earlier and asked, they ain't heard nothing yet."

"Damn it. I'm beginning to think that I'd have much rather been picked up by the Marshals. Leastwise then, I still wouldn't be sitting in a cell. What is a matter with the judicial system here in Canada?" Matt half chuckled.

"A lot has to do with where we are. We ain't near any big city. We're way out in the middle of nowhere. I know it must be a royal pain sitting around, Matt, but there ain't much any of us can do," Brady said apologetically.

"It ain't McCoy's fault, Brady."

"You know what, Matt, when Ed and Riley get back, I'll see if we can't get you outside for a bit. How does that sound?"

Matt's demeanour changed instantly and he smiled with hope.

"That would be appreciated, Brady."

"When they get back, I'll make a point in asking," Brady promised as he turned and walked away.

"Thanks." Matt called out as Brady exited. The thought of fresh air and a stretch outside was more than he would have expected and he was grateful for the consideration.

Brady added a few pieces of wood to the stove and looked through the cupboards for something he could cook up for Matt's lunch. He settled on beef stew. He'd slap together some biscuits as well. Getting all the ingredients together, he went about the task. Hearing the backdoor open, he assumed it was Ed and Riley, but instead it was only Riley, who made his way into the kitchen. Brady turned and looked at him. "So, the old man roused you out of bed, eh, Riley?" Brady asked as he continued mixing the biscuits.

"Huh, what, no, I was, I was sleeping in," Riley said somewhat confused.

"What, Ed didn't wake you?"

"Now why would Ed do a thing like that?"

"Might have had something to do with the time of day it is."

"No, I didn't see Ed."

"What? Hold up a second there, Riley. Were you at home or not?"

"At home, when?"

"God damn it, Riley, when he woke you."

"He didn't wake me," Riley sat down.

The Missing Years- Part IV
A Tyrell Sloan western adventure

"I see, so you weren't at home. You spent the night at the widow's did you, you ol' son of a gun," Brady teased, he understood now.

"I didn't say that," Riley was blushing by now.

"I don't think you need to. The way you're acting and how red your face is pretty much clarifies it," Brady smiled.

"It does not, Brady. I just wasn't at home. I could've been anywhere."

Brady poured Riley a cup of coffee and handed it to him. "You keep telling yourself that, Riley. I hope you had a good time. Your week-long shift starts tonight."

"I'm aware. I ain't looking forward to it. I got my place all cosy now."

"You're going to have to miss it for a week, 'cause there ain't no damn way I'm pulling a double." Brady opened the can of stew and slopped it into a pot. "I figured after I get Matt fed, we could take him outside. He could use some sun. What do you think, Riley?"

"I ain't sure that is proper procedure, Brady. He's a prisoner." Riley took a swig from his coffee.

"He is, but even prisoners in prison are allowed a couple minutes outside. We could sit out back. Hell, we could sit on the back steps even."

Brady stirred the stew and put the lid on the pot. He fished around for a baking sheet, and scooped up some of the biscuit mix and set it in the cook stove oven.

"I think we should wait and see what the boss man has to say before we decide," Riley suggested.

"I suppose that would be best. We finally got word today that Travis is in Willow Gate and Tanner has made Hazelton. He wired us a name of a fellow named Jack Calloway that we are looking into. He lent Ranthorp five thousand cash for a

243

poker tournament up that way. I've checked with Bash this morning and Calloway is a loan smith."

Brady turned and with his back to the counter, he crossed his arms and leaned against it.

"You mean loan shark," Riley butted in.

"I suppose so. That is some good news though, ain't it? That both Travis and Tanner have made their destinations and are alive and well."

"Damn right it is. I know Ed was getting worried about the two of them," Riley responded.

"He ain't worrying no more. We're also getting two hundred and fifty cash more a week from Gabe Roy. Travis sold him another service, 'private investigation'," Brady opened the oven and checked on the biscuits.

"Let me guess, to investigate who killed Heath," Riley predicted.

"That is right," Brady replied as the front door opened. "That might be Ed, now," he said as he set the cooking sheet of biscuits on the counter and removed the stew.

He and Riley went up front. It wasn't Ed. It was Lieutenant Bob Cannon. In his hand, he had two official looking envelopes.

"Morning, Bob. You're bringing us news about a circuit judge ain't ya?" Brady asked with hope.

"It is indeed a legally binding document. It isn't regarding a circuit judge though. We don't get that kind of information from the Police Commissioner and that is where this has come from," Cannon said as he handed one of the envelopes over to Brady.

Brady pulled the document out, his whole face lit up as he read.

"I'll be goddamned! The Police Commissioner, has declared Matt Crawford as a Crown witness for McCoy's. All legal proceedings against him have been stayed. Says, here the Mounted Police have investigated the Vermillion incident and have found Matt Crawford to be innocent of all killings, here in Canada, up to and including Hunter Talbot, and one US Pinkerton, Thomas Lierpp *aka* Miles Ranthorp. And have even suggested he get a Canadian Patch of High Regard for his part in saving countless lives during the Vermillion catastrophe that would have otherwise been lost, if he had not acted as he did."

Brady inhaled deeply he certainly had goose bumps. He looked over to Cannon.

"Thank you very much, Bob, for all the work you Mounties put into this," Brady shook his head. "I don't think either of us was expecting anything like this. Ed is going to shit his pants, as sure as this is signed by the Police Commissioner."

"Matt is free?" Riley questioned somewhat shocked and surprised. Matt hadn't even gone before a judge yet. It seemed odd to Riley.

Bob Cannon nodded.

"He is free to walk Canadian soil all he wants. He isn't protected by Canada Law though in the United States. He goes down south and they pick him up, there isn't anything Canada can do."

"Could the Marshals come up to Canada and arrest him?"

"Not without a lot of red tape. He is protected by the law of the land up here and can't be extradited as long as he remains a Crown witness to Emery Nelson's murder and the pending case McCoy's are pursuing against Gabe Roy. He's as safe as any Canadian citizen until he steps across into the U.S.A," Bob Cannon made clear. "The only legal thing Matt may ever see as long as he remains in Canada and withholds the peace, is a summons. And that would only be, if he can't be sought once you folks have all you need to prove who killed Emery, and bring Gabe Roy to justice. He's a Crown witness so he is and will be expected in court once those proceedings begin," he added.

"Cut him loose, Riley," Brady said as he tossed Riley the keys to Matt's cell. Riley caught the keys in mid-flight, and as quick turned and almost ran to the holding cell area.

"You certainly got a break cut for you today, Matt," Riley said as he unlocked the cell door.

"You folks are taking me outside for some air?" Matt asked as that was the only thing he was expecting.

"Damn right. In fact, Matt, we ain't even going to need cuffs nor are any of us going to walk beside you."

Riley was smiling from ear to ear.

"What?" Matt asked confused.

"You have been cut loose, my friend. You don't even need to appear before a judge. The Police Commissioner has stayed all charges up here in Canada. The Mounties have even suggested you get a Patch of High Regard for your participation in saving the town folk of Vermillion when Talbot and the Kingsley gang set it ablaze."

Matt almost fell over, but Riley caught him.

"What?" Matt asked again not sure, he heard what he thought he heard.

"You are free, Matt, leastwise here in Canada."

"Free?"

"Yes sir. Free as any Canadian citizen. How does that make you feel, Matt?"

"I ain't got any words, Riley. Jesus Christ! I thought for sure I was going to hang," Matt said as he and Riley made their way to the front of the office.

"Not now you ain't, not here in Canada," Riley said with jubilation. "I think Cannon has some shit for you to sign,

Matt. Then we'll have some things to go over with you too."
Riley directed Matt over to the front counter where Cannon
stood.

"Hello, Mr. Crawford," Cannon began.

"Lieutenant Cannon," Matt greeted back.

"Riley has filled you in on what has taken place?"

"Yes sir, he has. I'm at a loss for words to be quite
honest."

"That's okay, Matt. I have a couple of things for you to
sign and I'll need a thumb print from you."

"Sure anything, whatever it is you need, Lieutenant," Matt
said as he leaned against the counter.

Bob Cannon pulled out three documents and read them out
loud to Matt. "You understand what all that means, Matt?"

"Of course I do, Lieutenant. Means I'm protected by
Canadian Law as long as I remain in Canada. It also means I
have to agree to and sign a Crown witness document, and
provide the Mounted Police with a thumbprint. I was once in
law, Lieutenant."

"I know you were, Matt, this, is basically a formality is all.
You'll need to sign here."

Cannon put an 'x' on the line Matt needed to sign, "and
here too," he did the same to that line.

"Then we'll need a thumb print here," Cannon pointed to
the thumb print space.

"Well, let's get on with it, then," Matt said as he took the
pen from Cannon and signed his name on the two places.
"There you go, Lieutenant. Next I take it is the thumb print."

"Yes, indeed." Cannon pulled an inkpad out of his shirt
pocket and set it on the counter. He opened it and pressed
Matt's thumb into the pad. Then took his hand and pressed
the thumb onto the document. He handed Matt a piece of
cloth so he could wipe his thumb. "There you go, Matt. These

documents must be adhered to or you may risk being arrested and the charges that have been stayed could be reinstated. Do you understand that, Matt?"

"Yes, I do," Matt, said with sincerity.

"All right, then. That is it. Brady and Riley are witnesses to this undertaking. You best keep the peace and abide by Canadian law or you could face, like I said, another arrest."

"I get it, Lieutenant. I do have a question though. Am I allowed to work here in Canada? I'll need to somehow make a living."

"Yes, you can work in Canada, as long as you abide by the labour laws and pay taxes. There is nothing stopping you from doing that. In time those laws might change, but as it is right now, you are a fee man, Matt, and the government knows you need to make a living. Do it on the right side of things and in two years you could actually become a Canadian citizen, if you like."

"Huh, well that does give me something to think about."

"Indeed, it does," Cannon looked over to where Brady and Riley stood huddled.

"I have one more thing for you folks, Brady," Cannon said as Brady approached.

"What's that, Cannon?"

"Even though Matt is free, he wasn't when you folks brought him in," Cannon pulled out a bank note and handed it to Brady.

"That is ten thousand dollars for Matt's capture. It is yours."

Brady took it and smiled, "thank you, Bob. You can be sure McCoy's will make good use of this."

"I'm certain you folks will. I also have a wanted poster of you, Matt. It has always been a tradition of the Mounted Police to hand over a wanted poster to the suspects if they are proven innocent of crimes that they were suspected of. You have been, so here you go."

Matt took the poster and looked at it. "Not sure what I'm going to do with it, but it is a nice gesture. Thank you, Lieutenant."

Cannon nodded with a smile.

"In time the rest of the posters that may be scattered about will be taken down and you are quite welcome to tear down any you see," Cannon chuckled.

"The Police Commissioner will contact all police agencies throughout Canada and have your name removed from their most wanted list. Rest assured though it won't happen overnight," Cannon put the signed documents back in their envelope.

"I wouldn't expect it to. These things, I know, take time."

"Yes, they do. One other thing, Matt, I think you should give a big thank you to McCoy's men for their due diligence in keeping clear documentation, of the events that took place, while they looked for you, and their belief in your innocence. Those factors played a significant role in what has taken place here today," Cannon, pointed out.

"I do thank them, Lieutenant. I also thank the Mounted Police and their good work in helping with what has transpired here." Matt nodded with gratefulness.

"Remember this too. You haven't been exonerated of past crimes here in Canada. There has only been a 'stay of proceedings' put on them. They are still documented and can be used in other court proceedings where you are a suspect of any said crime."

Cannon explained the two different meanings.

"Exoneration is a clean slate. All known and current charges are completely dropped and nullified. A stay of proceedings is a clean slate with simple conditions. Are you clear on that, Matt?"

"I understand it, Lieutenant. I am clear. For me it is as good as exoneration and I'm damn grateful for that."

Cannon rapped his knuckles on the counter like, he always did when he was about to leave.

"Good. Okay, my job here is done. Don't spend all that loot in one spot, Brady," Cannon smiled as he walked away.

"Well, that part is over, Matt. We have some stuff we need to go over with you too. We might as well have a sit down," Brady gestured for Matt to follow him, and Riley and directed Matt to the table.

"Go on, have a seat. You want a coffee, Matt?"

"Sure do, thank you, Brady."

"No problem, what about you Riley? You want a cup too?"

"Damn right I do. I think I might slip a shot of whiskey into mine. Today has been one hell of a bounce. Nothing but good news all around," Riley said as he sat down and pulled the small flask of whiskey he always carried from his vest pocket. Brady handed them their coffees and put biscuits onto a plate then sat down himself.

"Help yourselves to those if you like fellows."

Brady took a slurp of coffee.

"And no I ain't going to stop either of you from putting a splash of whiskey in your coffees. We have good reason to celebrate," Brady said with a smile.

"What about you? You want a splash, Brady?" Riley questioned as he offered his flask to him.

"I'll do my drinking when this day ends."

It was around this time that Ed finally showed up. As soon as he stepped into the backroom kitchen and saw Matt sitting at the table, he drew his gun. "What the hell is going on here?" he questioned with surprise as to why Matt was sitting at the table and not cuffed.

"It's all right, old man, settle down." Brady tossed Ed the folder that Cannon had dropped off.

Ed put his pistol back in its holster and began to read. "Holy shit, congratulations, Matt! I bet this was the best news you heard in a long while." Ed made his way over to the table and sat down while he continued looking the document over.

"It is, it was, and I thank each of you for making it happen," Matt said with sincerity as Ed finished reading.

Ed looked over to Matt and nodded. "We were only doing our jobs, Matt. I'm certainly glad to see it has all been worth it. You're a free man," Ed said with a smile. "What the hell are you going to do with yourself?"

"Keep the peace, I reckon. It is only a stay of proceedings, but it is better than any outcome I was expecting."

"It is not quite the exoneration that we were hoping for but, it is damn close," Ed said as he grabbed Riley's flask and took a swig.

"This one is to you Matt Crawford," Ed tilted back the flask again and took a second shot and the flask was empty. "Jesus Riley, you need to get a bigger flask," Ed commented as he wiped his mouth.

"We also got paid, old man."

Brady handed Ed the ten thousand dollar bank note.

"This day just keeps getting better. I say we close shop and head over to the Snakebite. Drinks are on me," Ed invited.

"I'm all for the boss buying me a drink," Riley blurted.

"All right then, let's get to some celebrating."

The four men stood up and headed over to the Snakebite.

The Missing Years- Part IV
A Tyrell Sloan western adventure

In Willow Gate, Tyrell was making his way over to the telegraph office, hoping there was something from Ed regarding the fee they would charge Gabe Roy for investigating his son's death. Sure enough, there was a wire.

The telegrapher handed Tyrell the wire. "Here you go, Mr. Sweet. It arrived a couple hours ago. I was going to deliver it to you, but ended up busy."

"No problem," Tyrell said as he took the folded piece of paper and exited. He read it as he walked back across the street. *Seven hundred and fifty a week, cash only. Colby, Alex, and three cousins, heading west, to Willow Gate.* "So along with three cousins, Alex and Colby are coming to Willow Gate. That is interesting. Wonder what that is all about?" Tyrell softly questioned as he made his way to Emma's eatery. Sitting down at the same table he sat at earlier, he waited for service. It didn't take too long and finally Emma approached.

"Good afternoon, Mr. Sweet. What can I get for you today?" Emma asked with a smile.

"I'll have the same as usual, Emma, a roast beef sandwich, and a coffee."

"Coming right up," she said as she pranced away.

Tyrell sat at the table and looked around. Emma's place was quite busy. The customers had her going this way and that. Tyrell chuckled. *A busy woman she is,* he thought as he watched her work.

A few minutes later, she made her way back to his table and set down his sandwich and coffee. "Here you go, Travis. I'd sit with you for a minute, but we're swamped right now." She was smiling and had a twinkle in her eye. "We haven't been this busy in a long time," she said as she scooted off. Tyrell didn't even have time to comment. Instead, he sat there and watched her as he ate and slurped his coffee.

Finishing up he left a tip and paid at the counter. Next, he set off to Gabe's place a short jaunt down the road. Knocking on the door, Neeada answered.

"Good afternoon, Mr. Sweet. Please come in," she gestured.

"Thank you, Neeada. Is Gabe able to see me?"

"I will check," she said as she scurried up the stairs and knocked on Gabe's office door.

"Mr. Sweet is here, Master Roy. Should I send him up?"

"Yes, send him up, Neeada."

Neeada made her way back down the stairs and informed Tyrell that Gabe would see him. He tilted his hat and thanked her as she went back to dusting and cleaning.

Tyrell knocked on the door and Gabe invited him in.

"Good to see you, Travis. I take it Ed has replied to your inquiry."

"He has, we'll do the investigation into Heath's death as well as keep you and your assets safe, for seven hundred and fifty cash a week."

"So you were off the mark by two hundred and fifty bucks. Seven fifty is fair enough, all right. I will agree to that," Gabe said as he put his hands behind his neck and leaned back.

"Will you be starting now?"

"As soon as you pay the extra two hundred and fifty cash, I'm ready to start," Tyrell nodded.

Gabe reached into his desk and took out the rest of the money, and handed it to Tyrell.

"There you go, Travis. You can gather your gear and move into the guest house anytime," he handed Tyrell a key. "It is the green house behind the stables. You can't miss it."

Tyrell took the key.

"I'll get my stuff stowed and return."

"Nah, you show up here Monday. Get a good start at the beginning of the week. My day starts at seven in the morning. You'll need to be here by then."

Tyrell nodded.

"I'll see you then, Mr. Roy," Tyrell stood up. "McCoy's looks forward to aiding you and keeping you safe."

"Good. We'll see you Monday, Travis."

"Yes sir, you will." Tyrell exited and headed back to the Owl's Nest to gather his gear. An hour later, he was unlocking the door to the Roy's guesthouse, Black Dog at his side.

"Here is home, Black Dog, leastwise for the time being." Tyrell tossed his gear on the bed and looked the place over. It wasn't bad. It would certainly suffice. Black Dog sniffed around outside getting himself familiar with the scents and sounds. Satisfied, he lay down on the front step and dozed.

On that date, October 8, 1891, Tyrell Sloan *aka* Travis Sweet began his investigation into Gabe Roy's illegal business activities, in hopes of bringing justice to the people of Willow Gate, that he had taken advantage of, including the men and woman he had done the same too.

Pay back was coming...

Chapter 21

The table at the Snakebite where McCoy's men sat was the only full table in the saloon. It was too early for most to be drinking draft and swilling whiskey. The McCoy's though had good reason to celebrate.

"Today has got to be one the best days of the year," Riley kicked back a whiskey.

"All crimes committed by Matt, up here in Canada leastwise, have been 'stayed', the Mounties have suggested he deserves a Canadian Patch of High Regard, they have paid us the ten thousand offered for his bounty, and today he is a free man. Now if that don't beat all nothing will," Riley kicked back a second whiskey and slammed his glass down onto the table, "Yes, indeed, today is a damn good day."

"You ain't getting no, argument from me," Matt said with a smile as he too chugged back a whiskey.

"I'll drink to that," Brady said as he took a long deep swallow of his draft beer.

"Everyone fill up your glasses again. I am going to make a toast," Ed said as he handed the whiskey bottle around and they all filled up their shot glasses.

"To the legendary Matt Crawford, a son of a bitch to track and one hell of a shooter. This here Matt is to your freedom!" Ed said as they tilted their glasses in unison and kicked back their swallows of whiskey.

"Fill 'em up again, boys," Matt began as the bottle was passed around.

"This is to the men of McCoy's, a damn fine bunch of bounty hunters. And only second to each of you, the Canadian Mounted Police. To all of you, thank you!" Bringing their glasses together, they downed their shots of whiskey for a second time.

With the whiskey bottle slowly diminishing, Ed ordered another and a round of steaks for everyone at the table, even though it was only 3:00 p.m. By 8:30 that evening, they had finished their second bottle of whiskey among the four of them. The only action the Snakebite was seeing that night was the antics and money of McCoy's men. The few patrons that did come and go didn't stay long. It was a typical Thursday at the Fort, with the exception of the new man in town, Matt Crawford. Only a few even knew who he really was, and only those few were the ones that counted.

"Isn't that something, Jim?" Kitty questioned with amusement as she sat down next to Jim, the Snakebites custodian and her part-time husband.

"An ex-US Ranger and Rebel Ranger and wanted man, Matt Crawford, sitting in our saloon with the men who brought him in. It isn't anything we'll likely see again."

"Nope, Kitty, it ain't anything we're likely to see again. I figured Matt Crawford to be sinister and dislikable, but as I've been listening and watching, he's a damn decent man."

"He must be, Jim. I have never heard of a wanted man not standing before a judge."

"Hell, from what I've heard he saved the town folk of Vermillion when that chicken shit Talbot burned the place down. I also heard a while back, he shot some fella, a lawman type that shot and killed Brady and Riley's horses. He then gave them the dead man's horse. It is kind of funny when you think about it."

"There isn't anything funny about a man killing another man, Jim. It isn't funny at all," Kitty said with scorn.

"I suppose you are right," Jim shrugged as he went back to his duties.

By now, the four men were showing their drunkenness. It was a comical show of idiocies of how men got when they over drank and celebrated. Their conversations turned from one thing to the next. Mostly it was a mix of slurs, shouts, and laughter. Kitty sat back for the most part and chuckled.

"Whatcha gonna do with yourself now, Matthew?" Riley asked as he squinted and looked over to Matt who had his head in his hands and elbows on the table.

"Yeah, Matt, what... " Ed burped, "what Riley said, is you gonna do now?"

"Yesterday, I was in cells."

Ed, Riley, and even Brady looked on at Matt confused it really wasn't an answer to the question.

"You were as a matter of fact. You're free now, Matt," Riley pointed out.

"That is what they tell me, so I ain't got a clue what I think I'll do. Hmmm, maybe see if I can't get a job runnin' cows or something. I dunno..." Matt slumped forward and slid under the table.

"Where, where the hell did he go?" Ed asked as he looked at Brady.

"I think, he, he must've fall down," Brady slurred as he tucked his head under the table and looked.

"Yep, yep, Matt is sprawled out under this table. Look you can see him...," Brady stated as he too now fell off his chair.

"Jesus, now they is both gone, Ed. What are we gonna do?" Riley questioned as he frowned and shook his head.

"Look, hey, Riley, look, look, I see Matt under the table and Brady he's laid out on the floor. This brings a whole new meaning to *'drank them under the table'*."

Ed and Riley started to laugh.

"I see 'em now. We gonna help 'em up?"

"Nah, let 'em sleep it off. You gonna double me home, Riley? I can't remember where I put my horse."

"Hmmm, did we ride here, Ed? Or did we walk?" Riley wasn't sure. He was too drunk to remember and it was obvious that Ed was too.

"I think Brady knows," Ed kicked Brady a couple of times.

"Hey, Brady, where did you put our horses?" For one reason or another at that moment, both Ed and Riley split a gut laughing.

"Are we too ol' for this shit, Ed, or what?"

"Brady keeps sayin' so, but he's passed out drunk, so it don't matter," Ed waved his hand through the air.

"I think I'm gonna start walkin' home, Riley. Beth is gonna peel a strip off my backside if I don't show up for dinner," Ed began to stand.

"Dinner, shit, Ed it is almost nine o'clock, I think you missed the dinner bell," Riley pointed out in a slur of words.

"Oh oh, I guess I'm in a lot of trouble then," Ed sighed as he began to stumble out.

"Hold up there, Edward. I'll walk home with ya."

Riley stood up and tripped over Brady.

"Goddamn it, Brady couldn't you have found a better place to pass out," Riley commented as he got his balance back.

Kitty stopped both of them at the door.

"You fellows aren't leaving here until you get those men off the floor," Kitty stood firm.

"But, Kitty, they is drunk. We can't pick 'em up, we're too ol'," Riley said as he looked over to Brady and Matt.

"You fellows brought them here and you can't leave them on the floor like that, Ed, Riley."

The two men inhaled deeply and sighed.

"All right, c'mon Ed, lets pick 'em up and set 'em at the table."

"I got dinner waitin' though, Riley," Ed said as he followed Riley over to their table. They struggled with sitting Brady and Matt up at the table. Kitty couldn't help but chuckle at their antics.

"Is that good, Kitty?" Riley asked as he looked at Kitty who was standing close.

"I guess that'll have to do. They're off the floor at least." Kitty shook her head as she watched Ed and Riley stumble toward the exit and head for home.

The two of them stood on the boardwalk and looked around.

"Hey, Ed, I guess we walked over. I don't see my horse anywhere."

Ed stood there swaying back and forth.

"Well, shit," he said as he leaned up against a post, "I guess we walk."

"We could head back to the office. It's closer. We could sleep there," Riley suggested.

Ed scratched the top of his head.

"Umm yeah, yeah, let's do that Riley. Lead the way."

Ten minutes later Ed was struggling with the backdoor key to the office.

"You even sure that is the right key, Ed?" Riley asked as he sat down on the backstairs, drunk and exhausted, searching his own pockets for the backdoor key.

Ed looked at the key in his hand. It was hard for him to focus. He brought it up closer to his face.

"Jesus, Riley, you is right, been strugglin' with the damn front door key."

They both started to laugh. Finally, Ed managed to find the right key and they entered. The two of them staggered into the kitchen and slumped into chairs.

"Damn, we made it, Riley." That was the last thing Ed said as his head bounced off the table and he passed out.

Riley sat there looking on with a frown on his face.

"Did you pass out or somethin' Ed? You did didn'tja?" Riley scratched his face.

"Well, Ed, g'd night."

Riley stumbled to the cot and as soon as he fell upon it, he passed out himself, with his boots, hat, pistol belt, and clothes still on.

At 11:00 p.m., there was a banging on the front door, and it roused Ed out of his drunken state. He rubbed his eyes and sat up. With cobwebs still in his head, he stood up wobbly and peeked around the kitchen door. Again, there was a banging, then, he heard the voice.

"Edward Ronald McCoy, you answer this door right now!" It was Beth Anne.

"Awe shit. Goddamn it," he softly said as he tried to make himself respectable.

"Hang on, Beth. I'm on my way," Ed hollered as he exited the kitchen and answered the door. Opening it, he saw that she wasn't alone. The widow Donale was with her and their black buggy was harnessed to a horse.

"Evening, ladies," Ed tried to say without too much of a slur.

"Ed McCoy, you have a lot of explaining to do! I was expecting you home six hours ago. Where have you been?" Beth asked without mercy.

"Is Riley with you, Ed?" the widow Donale asked with no-less mercy.

"Jesus, being scorned by the both of you is damn frightening. Yes, Riley is here. We celebrated a lil' bit Beth, Malinda, but we is safe and sound."

"And Brady, did he go home?"

Ed swallowed deeply, and scratched the top of his head. "Well, I ain't so sure. He might have wondered home by now."

"What exactly do you mean 'by now', Ed?" Beth asked as she and the widow forced him back inside. Beth tossed her riding gloves onto the front counter and looked around. By now, Riley was peeking around the corner from the cot room. He was sweating and his eyes were big.

"Oh shit," he quietly mumbled as he fell forward and onto the floor. Beth turned her head quickly and saw Riley laying there his hat next to him. She darted a scowl look to Ed.

"I have found Riley, Malinda."

Malinda came around the corner as Riley was trying to stand up.

"Mr. Scott! You have got yourself all drunk and disorderly."

She walked over to him, and helped him up and then slapped the top of his head.

"That, Mr. Scott, is for being stupid."

Riley frowned. "Jesus Christ, woman..."

"Yes, the deity may have very well been a woman. Now let's get you home and cleaned up you stupid man," Malinda said as she pulled Riley to the door by the ear.

"You too, Ed, get your stuff and let's get you home," Beth slipped her riding gloves back on and headed for the exit.

"But...but I'm fine right here for tonight, Beth," Ed remarked. He knew what was waiting for him at home, a bloody scolding.

"Do as you are told, Mr. McCoy. I'll wait for you on the buggy," Beth stormed out.

"Goddamn it!" Ed looked around and made sure the office was locked up, and then went to meet his fate. He crawled into the buggy and sat next to Riley. The two scornful women sat at the helm and steered the buggy.

"She slapped the top of my head, pulled my ear off, and didn't let me pick up my hat, Ed," Riley said softly as Beth snapped the reins and the buggy slowly picked up speed.

"Lucky you, I missed dinner and Beth don't like that."

"I think women folk is crazy, Ed, I really do."

"Uhuh, some is, I think too."

The buggy slowed down and they pulled up to Malinda's house.

"Here is where you are getting off, Riley," Malinda said as Ed chuckled. She looked at him.

"What do you find to be so funny, Mr. McCoy."

At the same time, Riley was getting down and he looked at Ed and shook his head. Lucky for him, though, he was able to keep a straight face.

"It was nothin', Malinda, jus' some bad humour," Ed said meekly and somewhat embarrassed.

"The *getting off* is what made you laugh, Ed?" Beth looked over her shoulder and burned a hole through him with her eyes. "In that case, Ed, you can get off here too. I'll expect you home shortly. Have a nice walk."

"What? You want me to walk home, Beth. That right there isn't even funny. I can't walk that distance in this state. I'm drunk," Ed, pleaded.

"All the more reason for you to walk, Ed," Riley tossed in as he and Malinda headed up her walkway and to the front door of her house. Riley turned back grinning and waved. Malinda noticed this and she slapped the back of his head and dragged him in through the door.

Ed snickered now.

"So what is it going to be, Ed? Are you walking or am I?"

"Beth, you isn't serious, is you?" Ed asked again dreading the answer.

"You either step down off this buggy, Mr. McCoy, or I will," Beth was serious.

Ed shook his head, stumbled out onto the road, and started walking for home. Beth rode in the buggy alongside him, smirking the entire time. After about a mile, she stopped the buggy.

"Are you sober enough now, Mr. McCoy, to be civil?"

"I was soberly civil a half mile back. This right here is simple cruelty, Beth."

"Is it as cruel as not letting your wife know that you intended on drinking and missing dinner?" Beth snapped the reins and the buggy slowly started to move.

"Hold up a minute there, Beth. I can explain the whole thing," Ed said apologetically as he slowly ran up to her, holding his pants up as he went. He had lost his belt somewhere along the line. Beth slowed the horse and buggy down and waited for him to catch up.

Finally making the distance, Ed leaned up against the buggy to catch his breath.

"Here is how my day has been..." Ed told her the story.

"I guess then I can understand your need to get drunk. That is very good news. I know how you felt about that whole Crawford thing. Congratulations, Ed," Beth said with genuine sincerity and interest.

"You ain't mad at me no more?" Ed asked with hope. He was tired of walking.

Beth snapped the reins and once more, started- off.

"I didn't say I wasn't mad at you anymore, Mr. McCoy. I said I understood your reasons to get drunk. It still doesn't explain why you missed dinner," Beth and the buggy sped up, leaving Ed in the dark holding up his pants.

He hollered after her, "C'mon, Beth, I get the gist of this scolding. My feet are sore and my pants are fallen off. Goddamn it!" Ed continued to walk. He wasn't going to bother running anymore. He heard the horse and buggy stop around a bend and as he drew close, he could see the lit lanterns that gave the buggy light. He inhaled deeply and walked a bit faster. Beth was sitting in the buggy waiting for him.

"I have two things Mr. McCoy, that I want answers too. One is a question. The other is a promise. The question; whatever happened to your belt?"

Ed thought for a moment. He wasn't sure, but as he stood there forced to give an answer he seemed to recall that he might have used the toilet at the office.

"As I think about it, I think I might have left it in toilet room of the office. That's the only thing that makes sense. I do think I took a pee there."

"So you aren't sure, Ed?" Beth shook her head.

"No, no, I'm most certain that is where it is."

"That's better. Now the promise, promise me, Ed, that you will get out of this business in January."

Ed's mouth fell opened and he stepped back.

"What! You want me to retire. No bloody way, Beth. That ain't going to happen, not this January, no sir. Who would run McCoy's?"

Beth looked at him, shook her head, and snapped the reins. Ed walked the entire distance home after that. It wasn't so bad. He had time to think and the fresh air was certainly clearing his head. Hell, he didn't even feel drunk anymore. He stopped off at one place that he often stopped off at when the moon was high, like it was now. He looked up to it and at the shadows that were cast by the clouds as they floated by. It was peaceful and thought provoking. He averted his eyes to the wagon road and the black mass of shadows that the trees formed. After a few minutes of thought and rest, he continued with his walk.

Finally, the porch lanterns of their front porch came into view. He chuckled at Beth's audacity. It was one of the things that, he loved about her, and he wouldn't want her any other way. Beth was the backbone, of all his accomplishments, there was no denying that. She kept him on his toes and backed him every step of the way as he forged out a living. She may not have liked the career he had chosen, it being as dangerous as it was, and at times desperate, but every step of the journey she was always there with a canteen of water.

He stopped at the gate entrance and looked on. He admired the silhouette of their home, and he thought about all the hardships, disappointments, but most of all and the only thing that mattered was the happiness that the house emitted. He took his time as he walked down the road to the house. He noticed that there was bedding on one of the porch chairs. Shaking his head, he tried to open the front door, but it was locked and likely boarded inside. Chuckling, he blew out the porch lanterns and made himself comfortable. *He had been scolded.*

Chapter 22

Brady woke the next morning inside one of the holding cells at McCoy's. The door was even locked. He shook his head, he couldn't remember how he got there, but there he was. *This here is quite the twist,* Brady thought as he looked around inside the cell for the keys so he could unlock the damn door. Giving up a short time later, he lay back down on the bunk. He knew that eventually Ed or Riley would show up, and since he couldn't find the key, there was nothing more he could do. Looking up to the ceiling, he tried to put the pieces together, but he couldn't even grasp a memory on how he ended up locked in one of McCoy's very own holding cells.

Damn whiskey. That is how this happened. Should've stopped after the first bottle... Finally, he heard someone walking around in the office and he hollered out.

"Old man, Riley, is that you?"

"No, it's me the cat," Matt chuckled as he found his way to the holding cell area.

"There you are," Matt said as he looked at Brady.

"Hey, Matt any idea on how I ended up here?"

"No, idea, I woke up on a cot somewhere and then realised where I was. Where is the key so I can let you out of that cage?"

"It's usually in the top drawer of the counter on the right side."

"Okay, give me a minute I'll fetch it."

"Thanks, Matt."

A few moments later Matt returned.

"I found the key Brady. Now let's get you out of there." Matt unlocked the door.

Brady stood up and stumbled out.

"Thanks, Matt. Jesus I don't remember a damn thing about last night. How the hell did we end up here?" Brady questioned with confusion as the two of them made their way into the backroom kitchen. "I'll throw some wood into the stove and cook us some dark coffee. I could use about a pot myself."

"The stronger the better," Matt said as he sat down at the table.

"I wonder what happened to Ed and Riley. I don't remember them leaving. Then again, I don't remember much. We sure tied one on, eh. I'm good now for a year."

Brady added water and coffee grinds to the pot and set it to cook.

"There. That should be ready in a half hour or so. What do you recall of last night, Matt?" Brady asked as he sat down.

"Not much. I remember eating a steak, a couple of toasts that we made. After that, hell, it is a loss."

"We must've walked here 'cause, I don't remember riding to the Snakebite."

"I think we did walk. That part I can almost remember," Matt chuckled.

Brady looked up to the clock on the wall it was 8:00 a.m. "The old man and Riley should be coming around soon. Today is Friday, ain't it?"

"It is, Brady, yep Friday, day two of freedom, and I'm hung over," Matt rubbed his eyes.

"Some good strong coffee will straighten us up," Brady hoped. He was hung over like the dickens too.

"I hope the old man and Riley don't feel any better than us. Those two old codgers were slinging back the whiskey quicker than piss from a cow. If the old man never made it home, ma probably strung him up by the toes," Brady and Matt both chuckled.

They conversed for a few more minutes until the coffee was done. Brady poured them a cup.

"You want sugar and such, Matt?"

"Not at the moment. I want it black."

Brady handed him a cup and sat down with his own black coffee. He didn't want to add anything either. Black was best, under those circumstances. Two cups later, their heads were beginning to clear up. Brady asked what plans if any that Matt had now that he was free.

"I ain't made no firm plans. Might head out, go east maybe find some work on one of the ranches I often saw when I was running, I ain't running no more, though, Brady. Nope, I'm going to find a decent job or at least one that can keep me alive and fed. In two years, like, Lieutenant Cannon mentioned, I'll apply for Canadian citizenship. Of course, that depends if I'm still walking on earth or not."

"You'll be walking earth for a long time, Matt; long enough I'd say to enjoy being Canadian."

Brady poured them each another coffee.

"Life holds no promises, Brady. We often think it does. We start doing good and things look up, then thunder strikes. We can only live each day as though it is our last," Matt took a slurp from his coffee.

"You know, Matt, you was once in law and I know I asked this before, but you ever think about going back to it?"

"Nah, I ain't worthy of up keeping the law, not no more anyways. Broke too many and I have blood on my hands."

"That doesn't mean a thing though, nothing at all. I reckon every lawman has blood on his hands, from one thing or another. Besides crimes you have committed up here in Canada have all been excused. Hell, you even have a Patch of High Regard coming to you and it is well deserved too. You saved them folks in Vermillion. You even saved me, and

268

Riley, when that Pinkerton shot our horses. If you hadn't given us his horse, who knows what might have come of us up in them woods. We was a long walk from the Fort, and not on no trail either," Brady, pointed out.

Matt nodded. All that Brady said was true, but he wasn't sure he was up to becoming involved with law enforcement. He knew U.S.A. law not Canadian law, and he knew exactly where Brady was going with the question.

"All that boils down to though is a man doing what any man would or should do under the same circumstances. I ain't a hero. In fact, I'm quite the opposite."

"Nope, nope, you are a hero, Matt. The Mounted Police, the Police Commissioner, and I imagine the folks and citizens of Vermillion see you as a hero."

Brady paused for a moment as he slurped his coffee.

"The Patch of High Regard ain't offered to folks that ain't heroes," he added.

Neither Brady nor Matt knew that Ed had already taken care of all the legalities so that Matt could, if he wanted to, be put on McCoy's payroll. The only stipulation was he couldn't help with any investigations that he was a witness of. In other words, he couldn't help Travis with the investigation into Gabe Roy nor could he help Tanner McBride in investigating Emery Nelson's murder.

There were other cases though that he could work. One that had come to Ed's mind when he filled out all the documents was the five hundred in gold nuggets that McCoy's agreed to put into Whiskey Tooth George's hands. It was the perfect case for Matt. It would keep him incognito and away from the public eye for the time being.

It would be up to Matt, though, if he wanted to be on the payroll. If so, the papers were ready for him to sign. Ed took care of all that in the first week that Matt was their prisoner.

He had discussed it with Lieutenant Bob Cannon and Cannon had told him that it would be okay as long as he followed the stipulations, and if and only if, he was found innocent of the crimes, he had committed. He had been and so, he had a job with McCoy's if he wanted it.

It was around 10:00 a.m. when Ed finally showed up at the office. Unfortunately, Matt and Brady had already said their goodbyes and he had already ridden out of town. He was heading east, to one of the ranches he recalled passing. Ed was disappointed and so was Brady. There was nothing either one could do though. Matt was gone. He promised to keep in touch, and swore to be in court whenever it was that he was needed. He told Brady that once he found work, he'd let McCoy's know where. Brady couldn't stop him. There we no legalities that prevented Matt from travelling or looking for work.

"Too bad he's already left and that I never got to speak to him beforehand. I had papers ready for him to sign. He could've been on the McCoy's payroll by now."

Brady was somewhat surprised that Ed had already taken care of the legalities.

"When did you start that process old man?" he asked.

"Week one of his stay here. Cannon helped me out with it. Said it would be no problem if we hired Matt as long as the crimes he had been charged with here in Canada never came to fruition, which they didn't. There were stipulations, of course."

"Naturally, obviously there are cases he couldn't have worked due to the conflict of interest thing."

"You nailed it, Brady."

"Well, that is a damn shame, old man. I think Matt would have done well with us. He decided though he weren't ready for working law," Brady shrugged. "Who knows, maybe one day he'll walk through that door and ask for a job."

"We can always hope, I suppose. I'm glad things turned out for him and that he is free. I was most certain he'd have got exonerated, but I guess a stay of proceedings is pretty good too."

"I reckon anything is better than being hung."

"He crosses into the U.S.A. that might be what comes of him. I don't think though he's too inclined to step foot down south."

"I don't think so either. He said to me that he wanted to apply for his citizenship in two years. I hope he wasn't blowing smoke up my ass."

"I think Matt is a man of his word. If he wants to be a Canadian citizen then that is what he'll do."

As Ed and Brady continued to converse, Riley finally made his way to work. He was clean-shaved and his silver grey hair was combed. He smelled of cologne or perfume and his hat was missing.

"You better go roll 'round in the stable, Riley. You don't look yourself nor do you smell like you usually do."

"It's my new look, Brady. Once I gather my hat which I think is in the other room, I'll look the same."

Ed chuckled.

"Shit, you lost your hat and I lost my damn belt. What the hell did we get ourselves into last night?"

"Whiskey and a lot of it, I woke up in one of the cells. The door was locked and everything and no damn key. If it weren't for Matt I'd have been there 'til you showed up, old man, and I ain't got a clue how I ended up there. Matt passed out in the backroom luckily and unlocked the door once he realised where I was."

The three of them sat in silence for a few minutes as they thought back to their past night of whiskey drinking.

"My story is simple. I walked home and slept on the porch. Didn't even see your ma this morning, she didn't let me in. Told me to go to work and to not be late for dinner or to come home drunk," Ed shook his head. "And you, Riley. Whatever came of you?"

"I was given a sponge bath in *cold* water. Was shaved with *hot* and sent to a room where some unmentionables took place," Riley's face grew slightly flush, but since they were all telling their story, he told his.

"The moral of these tales, I reckon, is to not drink two bottles of whiskey in one drunk," Brady chuckled. "I know I ain't going near that shit for a while and that is my final tale on past events."

"So we all got drunk and probably stupid. Let's see if we can't come up with some work to do."

Ed stood up and walked into the toilet room and sure enough, he did find his belt. He threaded it through the loops of his pants, and smiled.

"I knew it. I knew I lost my belt here," he said as he made his way to his office.

Riley and Brady continued to sit.

"I take it Matt has already skedaddled?" Riley questioned.

"He left an hour or so before the old man showed up. He said he was goin' to head east."

"Shit, I'd have liked to have said goodbye to him. I wish him happy trails, anyway."

Finishing their coffees, they faced the day. Riley found his hat and Brady threw up. Afterwards Brady sat sickly at his desk up front and thumbed through some wanted posters. Getting bored with that, he headed outside, and cleaned the horse stable and sprayed the horses down with fly spray.

This, of course, didn't help his hangover, but it was something that needed doing and so he did it.

Riley cleaned the McCoy's office and straightened things up. He read through some newsprint and looked through the same stack of wanted posters that Brady had started to look through. Things were changing though for old Riley and he couldn't find the drive to be excited about bounty hunting. The past few months had been busy. He was, in a sense, burnt out.

Ed too was sitting at his desk thinking about what Beth had tried to get him to promise. He wasn't feeling the excitement anymore either, but knew he couldn't simply walk away from the business he worked so hard to keep afloat. He wasn't sure if Brady was in a good place in his life yet to take over for him. He still thought of Brady as a greenhorn. Sure, he was learning, but Ed wasn't certain that he was ready to take over the reins. And, he knew that as soon as he walked away from the business, Riley would too. That would leave only three men working for McCoy's, Travis Sweet, Tanner McBride, and Brady, hardly enough men to handle any workload.

They could down size he knew, but that had never been his desire. He wanted McCoy's to grow, to become one of the first private investigation offices in the region, with enough good men to take on any situation. Perhaps it was a dream, but it wasn't only his dream. Brady had the same one. If only Matt had stuck around, things then might have looked different.

For now, Ed decided they would carry on, as they were, five men strong, ready, able, and willing to take on any investigation that walked through the front door, or was wired to them. In a month or so, maybe he would reconsider and make that promise to Beth. He nodded his head as he thought about it. *Yep, we'll see how things go for a month or so. Maybe I'll make the announcement of my retirement at Christmas.* He leaned back in his chair and put his feet up on his desk, his eyes closed every now and again, as he drifted in and out of hung-over sleep.

Perhaps that is why he felt as he did. He was hung over and feeling blue. In fact, that was likely how all three of them were feeling. Copious amounts of whiskey always did that.

Their hangovers beat them up and spit them out and they closed up shop early. It had been a long and sickly day for the three of them. A good night's sleep was needed. Maybe in the morning they would feel better.

Days came and days went. For three weeks, Matt Crawford travelled great distances to find work, and Tyrell, under the name of Travis Sweet shadowed Gabe Roy. He had learned a few things about Gabe and had gathered more evidence into Gabe's shoddy business deals. Things were coming together for McCoy's in regard to that investigation. As for the investigation into Heath's death, there was nothing more known about that than what Gabe already assumed. That is how Travis was playing it for now.

The ranches and farms that Matt applied to for work weren't looking for help, leastwise not from anyone who had never worked cattle or farmed. It became clear to Matt as the weeks came and went, that he only had one option left and that was to return to law enforcement. He headed back to the Fort and on November 17, 1891, through early winter snowstorms and sleet, the Fort finally came into view. He slowed his horse to a stop as he pulled the collar of his felt jacket up and around his neck. A cold November wind seemed to have picked up. He looked on. The streets were silent and the Fort was like a ghost town.

The Missing Years- Part IV
A Tyrell Sloan western adventure

He made his way down the street to McCoy's office. He swung off his saddle and tethered the horse. Walking in, he was met with surprise and excitement as Brady, Ed, and Riley greeted him.

"I'll be damned! Hello, Matt!"

Matt nodded.

"Hello, Ed, Brady, Riley," he said as he approached the front counter.

"Wasn't expecting to see you, how have you been, Matt?"

"Pretty good, Ed, I'm alive at least. The Fort seems quiet. Not many folks are out and about."

"It's that time of year folks are staying home and keeping their fires going. It has been damn cold around here," Brady mentioned as he leaned up on the counter.

"It has been cold. I've travelled through most of it. I went east, then north, stopped off at every ranch or farm I came across. Folks in this area really don't want to hire less experienced hands. So, I decided I'd see if perhaps you folks is looking for help. I can work the stable keep your horses fed and whatnot."

Matt looked at Ed who had a big grin on his face.

"We don't need anyone to work the stables, Matt, but we could use a fellow with your credentials to work investigations and whatnot. Are you interested in something like that?"

Matt tilted his head and nodded.

"I most certainly would be interested, Ed."

The three of them, had big smiles on their faces.
"Excellent!" Brady replied.

"Damn right," Riley added, "having a fellow like you working with us, Matt, is something the three of us have wished for since you left. You missed Ed by an hour the day you left. Shit, he had everything ready for you to sign."

Matt had a look of both shock and surprise on his face. He hadn't expected Ed to have already gone through all the trouble, and for a brief moment, he felt like an ass for not sticking around and at least say bye to Ed and Riley, all those weeks ago when he left.

"It is true, Matt. I was going to offer you a position on that day. I've kept the documentation hoping one day you would return and, by God, here you are."

"I know Brady was trying to get me to say I wanted to work law again. Only thing was, back then, all I wanted was some space to clear my head. The weeks I've travelled looking for work, has made me conclude that, law is what I'm accustomed to, I don't know what all the legalities are to work under McCoy's, but whatever they are, I will abide."

"There really aren't any legalities Matt. You've been cleared and freed of the charges that were against you here in Canada. There are stipulations, though. Obviously, you can't work any case where a conflict of interest lies, but, I'm sure, you already knew that. I have taken care of getting an okay from Lieutenant Cannon and the Police Commissioner both of them told me that you would be free to work for us, if you were so inclined," Ed pointed out and made clear.

"I thank you for that. I'm ready and willing to start anytime."

"We'll have to swing by the Mounted Police station. Bash will have to get you to read an oath and you'll have to be fingerprinted. Then we can go over our contract. It is the same contract that is offered to the others. First things first though. Let's all go have a sit down."

Ed gestured to Matt, Brady, and Riley. Making their way into the backroom kitchen, the men sat down. The feeling in the room was that of relief and excitement. To have a man such as Matt Crawford, an ex-US Ranger working for

McCoy's was a big deal. There was no doubt about that. The things Matt could bring to the table to help with the growth of McCoy's were unsurpassable. His vast knowledge of law and training that the United State Ranger's were known for, from survival to shooting abilities, would only improve McCoy's Private Investigations and Security. There was no foreseeable downside, only improvement to what McCoy's was now.

"I have to tell you, Matt, I for one am thrilled to have this opportunity to have a fellow of your stature working with us," Ed said, as he looked Matt in the eye. He was sincere and honest.

Matt listened to what each had to say and he thanked them for their kind words.

"My turn to speak now, I guess," Matt began. "I've watched each of you over the period of time I was running. McCoy's Bounty Hunting Service were the only bounty hunters that ever came close to bringing me in, and so I have to say, I think this crew of professionals are exactly that, professionals. Each of you is equal to me.

And Riley, you and I were a time or three so damn close to one another that we could've poked each other with a stick. I knew if anybody was going to bring me in it would have been the men from McCoy's. The others, they never held a candle to you men. Most were easy to evade, fool, and otherwise simple to get away from, when you folks came into the picture, I had to keep my eyes and ears open at all times. Let me add this. I am honoured to work with and be among men like you. Thank you for the opportunity to redeem myself."

The room grew silent as the men soaked in what was all said around that table. It was Brady, who finally broke the silence.

"If I had tissues, I'd hand them out," he teased. "Now, let's get Matt signed up old man and get him on the payroll."

Brady stood up and shook Matt's hand. "Welcome aboard, Matt. I look forward to working with you," he said, as he exited and made his way back to his desk and to a stack of paperwork, he had been working on. Riley, too, shook Matt's hand and welcomed him, then went about doing whatever it was he had been doing before Matt showed up.

Ed and Matt headed over to the Mounted Police station, where Matt read back the oath Constable Rick Bash read to him. Signing the documents and giving up his thumb and trigger finger prints he became a full-fledged Private Investigator under Canadian law. Bash gave him the documents and badge that came with the induction. From there it was back to the McCoy's office and the signing of a few more documents. And on that day November 17, 1891, he was employed by McCoy's Private Investigations and Security.

He was given a key to the backdoor of McCoy's office and to start him off, Ed offered the cot and kitchen for him to use for as long as he needed, or until Tanner McBride returned, whichever came first. The upstairs apartment was and would always remain Travis's and so Ed never offered him the use of it. Matt, Ed could tell by the gravel in his voice, was grateful for all that had been offered.

"I don't know how to thank you. I really don't. I will tell you this though. I will never let McCoy's down. I will do my job as well as I possibly can. Thank you very much for everything."

Ed waved his hand through the air.

"No worries, Matt. I know you'll do your job. It is us, who should be thanking you for signing up with us. We really need men like you, for the direction we want McCoy's to go in. You're a blessed addition, if you ask me."

The two men grew silent for a moment, and then Ed smiled.

"The first case I want to throw at you Matt isn't anything special, but it is needed to get done, and I think you are quite suited for it."

"Whatever it is Ed, throw it at me."

"That five hundred dollars in gold nuggets that Brady got from that Vanfell fellow, when you two were making your way back here, needs to be handed over to Whiskey Tooth George. He's a helluva a codger to catch up to."

Matt chuckled.

"I know old Whiskey Tooth and I know where to find him too at this time of year."

Ed was surprised.

"How do you know ol' George? And how come you never mentioned that to Brady?" Ed asked.

"Couldn't see any point in mentioning it to Brady. It wasn't my place to say. Anyway, I ran across Whiskey Tooth a few times. I have even drunk some of that putrid whiskey that he brews in that still of his. I am quite familiar with Whiskey Tooth," Matt assured.

"Ain't that something? Well, there you go. You know where to find him and what he's all about, you are the perfect one to see he gets that gold then," Ed said and smiled.

"I'll pack up and head out right now," Matt began to stand up.

"Hold on. No need for you to do that yet. Rest up some and get familiar with the way we do things first. Maybe head out at the beginning of next week. That'll give you some time to rest up and get over the trail weariness I know you likely have. You've been on the trail for more than a month already, I can't justify sending you off today."

Matt nodded in agreement.

"Good point, Ed. I am a bit weary from all the miles I've put on. I could probably use a clean up too. Next week it'll be. You know Whiskey Tooth has a five hundred dollar bounty on his head, should I bring him in too?" Matt questioned.

Ed shook his head.

"Nope, no need for that. We only want to see that he gets the nuggets."

"That is how it'll be, then," Matt confirmed. And so it was settled, that on Monday, November 23, Matt would take on his first task to search for and deliver the gold to Whiskey Tooth George. The rest of the day went quickly after that, and as the tradition had always been with McCoy's; Ed bought everyone a steak at the Snakebite as a way to welcome Matt into their, ranks. They stayed away from the whiskey this time though.